the WELL-HIDDEN *Clue*

A WISHVILLE  MYSTERY

kari lee townsend

NATIONAL BESTSELLING AUTHOR

OLIVERHEBERBOOKS

To those who think they're forgotten, there is always someone looking and remembering...

A special thank you to the best beta readers ever...Marian West and Sue Nickles. Your input is invaluable.

What was Left Behind...

LONG BEFORE THE *Maple Hollow Library* stood on its tidy brick foundation, before book carts rattled across polished floors or Clara Winslow stamped a single due date, there were passages beneath Wishville that no human had ever named.

They were not mines.

They were not basements.

They were not recorded on any settler's map.

The first families who built Wishville simply raised their town over ground that had already been carved. Centuries earlier, when the wishing well was not yet a boundary but a bridge, the Dwellers walked freely between the glowing realm of Elarion and the forested ridges above. They shaped hidden tunnels beneath the town, quiet alternate routes leading toward the mountains, where a second portal shimmered deep within the stone.

Not the heart of Elarion, but its outer edges. The forgotten margins where wanderers once roamed and, in time, the rebels would build a secret refuge. Most tunnels collapsed with age. Others were sealed when the treaty divided the realms. A few survived only because humans never knew they were there.

The one beneath the library was among them.

For generations it lay concealed behind false walls and

forgotten blueprints, buried beneath shelves, renovations, and time. Even the Dwellers believed those old mountain paths were lost, becoming fading stories of hidden exits long abandoned.

But history has a way of surviving where no one looks. And in the autumn of 1984, during the library's first major restoration, a young teacher named Marjorie Winslow found a draft where no window could have breathed.

A loose brick.

A pocket of cold air.

A stair cut into earth far older than the town above it.

At first, she thought she'd discovered a forgotten storage crawlspace or an old foundation line. But the deeper she went, the less human the stonework became. Walls so smooth she couldn't tell how they were formed besides, perhaps, by magic. A tunnel sloping toward the mountains, toward something she had never seen listed on any map of Wishville.

Maggie told no one.

Instead, she documented everything: sketches, measurements, notes tucked into a worn notebook. She believed she had uncovered a lost chapter of Wishville's history, one she intended to understand fully before revealing it to the world. Except, she soon found out she wasn't the only one to have discovered the tunnels. When she finally tried to get people to listen to her about the tunnel activities, no one did.

Then, without warning, she vanished.

The town whispered theories for months, then years, until rumor faded into memory. Only her daughter, Clara—five years old at the time—was left with a mystery that hovered like a shadow around every library shelf she touched. For four decades, the tunnel slept again beneath the library, silent and unseen. Until the second renovation when Clara Winslow found what her mother left behind.

Then history opened its doors once more...

CHAPTER

One

FALL WISHFEST WAS in full bloom.

Pumpkin-orange banners fluttered from Main Street's lamp-posts, each one painted with a stylized well and a swirl of leaves. Up the hill on the festival clearing in the woods, booths were arranged in a cheerful horseshoe around the green, with the ancient wishing well sitting on the edge. Cider presses were chugging, kettle corn popping, and strings of tiny lanterns blinking like they were trying to outshine the sun. The air smelled like apples, cinnamon, and woodsmoke.

I stood near the green in our small, Vermont mountain town with my clipboard in hand, pretending this was all manageable. "Okay," I muttered. "Hay maze stable, first-aid tent stocked, well platform roped—"

"Lyra Wells," Tilda Nettlesblossom declared, jabbing a finger toward the main path, "tell me you are *not* approving that corn-stalk atrocity."

Tilly—resplendent in her purple coat and a knitted scarf shaped like a pumpkin vine that appeared to be slowly strangling her—stared accusingly at the crooked archway like it had personally offended her.

Beside her, Maribelle "Belle" Crimp balanced three steaming

ciders in one hand and drank from a fourth, somehow unspilled, her expression severe enough to suggest she was prepared to issue a formal condemnation.

Dottie "Dot" Quench clutched a stack of flyers large enough to wallpaper a Victorian parlor and began handing them out to anyone who made eye contact, whether they wanted one or not.

"It's festive," I said.

"It's a safety hazard," Belle replied, taking another slow, judgmental sip. "I've already seen one child eyeing it like a challenge."

"That child was me," Tilly said. "And I still have the scar to prove it."

Dot thrust a flyer at me. "We made a sign," she announced proudly. "No running, no climbing, no calling upon ancient spirits in the hay maze."

I pinched the bridge of my nose. "Take out the ancient spirits part."

Belle leaned in, lowering her voice. "Too late. I already heard someone ask if the cornstalks whisper back."

Tilly nodded solemnly. "They do at night."

"They do not," I said.

Tilly smiled. "That's exactly what the spirits would want you to think, Guardian."

I froze. "Festival Chair," I corrected quickly. "Chair. Not that other word."

"Mmm-hmm," Belle hummed, clearly unconvinced.

The Wellies had a talent for knowing things they absolutely shouldn't. I always suspected it made them deeply unpopular on poker nights.

Vex flicked his tail and regarded the archway with clear professional interest. *If it starts whispering, I would like to be notified immediately. For Quality control.* To everyone else he looked like a sleek black cat. To me...well, he wasn't *just* a cat. Like me, he was a half-blood. A half-cat, half-Whispen creature, with magical powers from the world beneath the well, Elarion.

But Wishville didn't need to know that.

"You're enjoying this," I murmured to him.

He flicked his ear, his voice floating through my mind. *Always.*

Chief Holden Thorn's voice warmed my spine before I even saw him. "Looks good out here." He stepped beside me, his six-foot-four frame looking sharp in his gray sport coat, button-down shirt and tie, over jeans and boots. His dark buzzed hair and sleek beard were perfectly trimmed, and his stormy gray eyes shined that soft way they did when he thought I wasn't looking.

Which I always was.

"The green's holding together," he continued. "Only one cider-related spill, and the teenagers haven't tried to skateboard off the fountain down the hill in town yet. Could be a record."

"That's because you confiscated their boards during Summer WishFest," I said.

"Preventative policing," he replied gravely. "And I stand by it." His fingers brushed mine with the kind of touch that said, 'I can hold your hand in public now, and no one will burst into flames.'

My heartbeat trotted happily.

"We're still on for tonight?" he asked.

"As long as you survive the lantern walk," I said.

He leaned in and kissed my cheek. Vex hopped onto a stone wall as if refusing to witness such emotional frailty. Holden walked off to check the barricades, and I stood there feeling like the sun had reached down and poked me in the chest.

"You are very attached to him," a deep voice said from behind me.

I turned. Six-foot-ten Dweller and Chief Enforcer of Elarion, Calderis, stood near the well with his arms folded and posture perfect in a way only an immortal could manage. His "Detective Cal Deris human clothes" were technically a flannel shirt and jeans, his silver hair now a pale blond pulled back in a manbun, and his aqua eyes a pale blue.

But he still looked like he'd been carved out of dramatic dusk.

"Good morning," I said, smiling. "Or is it afternoon?"

He stared at me stoically. "Holden is good for you. Humans should be with humans." There was no sting in his words. Still, something in his tone made my chest tighten.

"Half-human, half-Dweller," I corrected him.

We had grown up together in Elarion and had always had a magnetic pull between us, but I spent more time in Wishville these days as The Guardian of the Well. It had never been good timing for us.

Once Holden was brought to town to become the new police chief, my heart was torn. And when investigative journalist Lourdes Morales came to town, Calderis's head was turned. We had agreed to explore our options with the mortals we had grown fond of...for now. Our time would come in the future, since he was immortal and I aged very slowly. Still, it didn't make it easy to see him with LuLu any more than him seeing me with Holden.

As if he could read my thoughts, Calderis glanced across the green.

Following his gaze, I saw LuLu making her rounds, covering the festival for the paper. Her espresso dark hair was in a messy knot as she smiled at festivalgoers like warmth in human form, getting them to open up and talk about anything. He watched her exactly one second too long for it to be nothing.

"You can go help her, you know," I said lightly.

"She does not require assistance."

"That's not the point," I said. "Just stand next to her while she interviews people. Be noble. Protective. It's an Elarion thing."

His eyes narrowed. "Standing next to someone is not noble or protective, and definitely not an Elarion thing."

"Okay, so it's a Wishville 'work' thing, and well, you're here now," I said, nudging him gently.

He hesitated just long enough to show he cared what I thought, then he crossed the green to her. LuLu brightened when he approached, handing him an extra notebook. He took it, and she laughed at something he said. Something eased in his shoulders. Good. Maybe Dwellers needed a little normal once in a while too.

Tilly suddenly appeared in front of me like she'd teleported, which, to be clear, she absolutely could not do. Though I sometimes wondered.

"Guardian," she said again, too casually.

"Chair," I corrected, having had to correct them more and more lately.

Vex's tail lashed behind me as if emphasizing my thoughts.

"The well looks gorgeous," Belle said, stepping up with fresh ciders. "People are already lining up to toss in their tokens and make their wishes."

"Wishes," Dot echoed dreamily. "Imagine if this is the year the wish actually *works*."

"It always works for someone," I said.

"Yes, but *actually* works," Dot said, widening her eyes. "Like...magic."

My mother Serenna's pendant pulsed around my neck just once, a faint vibration against my skin, like a whispered word I couldn't quite make out. *Not now*, I told it silently. My father was human and had died three hundred years ago, while my Dweller mother, who had been the former Guardian, had gone missing one century ago. I had taken over her role and been trying to figure out what happened to her since. I discovered recently that she was still alive.

I just wasn't sure whose side she was on...defending Elarion or joining the rebels.

Dot didn't notice my strange behavior. None of them did. "Anyway!" she said cheerfully. "We'll keep an eye on the hay maze. You do your Guardian thing."

"Chair thing," I insisted.

They nodded like they agreed, which meant they absolutely did not.

After they wandered off, I made my way over to the ancient wishing well. From there, I could see all of WishFest—the crowds, the families, the kids tugging on their parents' hands, and the swirl of color and laughter and sugar. Mr. Finch, the handyman who helped at every WishFest, was securing a loose board on the platform where our most esteemed elderly resident, Ruth Bingham, would lead this season's festival toast.

Connie Hale stood near the edge of the green by Mayor Doug Delaney with her hands folded over her purse, watching WishFest with the quiet focus of someone who'd spent decades keeping the town's records straight. The retired town clerk still attended every public event, as if habit alone might summon order from chaos. And ever since the mayor's assistant left, Connie had been a big help.

To all of them, the well was history. Tradition. An ancient stone circle with a rope and a bucket no one used anymore. A place to drop a token and make a whispered wish, knowing it was symbolic and nothing more.

Only a handful knew the truth. That beneath this well was a portal to Elarion. And if this treaty of granting one wish per season to keep the peace between Dwellers and humans ever snapped, war could resume, and Wishville would feel it long before they understood it.

But right now, it was just a town celebrating Fall.

Holden waved from across the green. Calderis stood next to LuLu. Weylan, my Dweller eyes in the sky, manned his hot-air balloon rides. Sparks, my Dweller eyes on the ground, helped Finch with any mechanical issues. Kids chased each other with paper leaves. The air was cool, crisp, ordinary.

Normal.

I inhaled deeply, hoping things stayed that way. "Happy Fall WishFest!" I called out by the well, my voice rising over the music and chatter.

The crowd cheered.

For the moment, it was simply a festival. A good one. A peaceful one. And for now, that was enough.

WishFest had just reached peak bustle when my phone buzzed in my coat pocket. Clara Winslow took phone calls as seriously as she took shelving systems. She didn't believe in unnecessary ones, which meant something was wrong.

I stepped away from the well and ducked behind the cider tent for a little privacy. "Hey, Clara. Everything okay?"

There was a pause on the line. "Lyra?" her voice rang out, tight but controlled. "Can you come to the library?"

My stomach dipped. "Now?"

"I...yes." She cleared her throat. "It's not an emergency, but it *is* important. I just...well...I found something. Something strange."

Clara did *not* use the word *strange* lightly. She used it the way Holden used "suspicious activity": carefully, deliberately, and usually with paperwork.

"Are you safe?" I asked more urgently than I meant to.

"Yes. It's just...I really think you need to see it."

My eyes tracked the crowd as Holden approached the cider stand, laughing with one of the vendors. People were throwing tokens into the well. A kid was trying to convince his mother that buying a pumpkin was a matter of life-or-death importance.

Calderis handed LuLu a sample pastry from one of the vendors, and she nudged his arm like he'd said something unintentionally funny. Fenrin, the full-Whispen cat from Elarion, circled her legs protectively. Fenrin was sweet on Vex, and had sneakily gotten LuLu to adopt her when she decided to stay in Wishville and move in with me. Vex acted like he wasn't happy about it, but it was clear he was charmed.

WishFest was glowing, humming, and alive as the well did its job.

Meanwhile, Clara sounded like she'd seen a ghost rearranging her nonfiction section.

"I'll be there in five minutes," I said.

Her relief was palpable through the line. "Thank you."

When I hung up, Vex slunk out from under the cider table where he was hiding from Fenrin, his whiskers twitching. *Library,* he said in my head. *Your voice changed. You're worried.*

"Clara sounded off," I admitted. "She found something."

Of course she did, Vex said dryly. *Humans can't resist hidden compartments. It's how they cope with mortality.*

I stared at him. "What does that even mean?"

But he'd already hopped onto my shoulder, his tail flicking. *We go now.*

Holden spotted me crossing the clearing. He wove through the crowd to meet me halfway. "You heading out already?"

"Clara called," I said. "She needs me at the library. Something weird."

"Library weird?" he asked. "Or *your* kind of weird?"

After Holden had jumped into the well to save me when he thought I was drowning, he'd discovered Elarion. But after proving himself useful, Chief Elder and Calderis's father Vaerion, decided I didn't have to erase Holden's memory. The three of us were declared The Covenant Three, in charge of keeping the peace above and below the well.

"My kind of weird," I said, with the tone that meant possible-magic-but-let's-not-panic.

He nodded, his expression sharpening. "Do you want backup?"

"I think I've got it." I touched his arm, and he covered my hand with his. "Finish your rounds. I'll text if it's anything suspicious."

He gave me a look that was equal parts trust and protective instinct. "Okay. But do not go rogue on me, Wells. I have enough gray hairs."

"And I have Vex." I winked.

"Vex does not count."

"I heard that," Vex grumbled out loud from his perch around

my neck. He could speak out loud, but he only did so in front of those who knew what he really was.

"I can handle myself. I have my own abilities and far more strength than humans," I added.

Holden sighed at the sky like he needed celestial intervention to survive the two of us. Then he kissed my forehead quickly, glancing around to make sure no one saw him being soft on duty. He cleared his throat. "I'll see you soon."

Calderis caught my eye with one raised brow, a silent question, *Do you require assistance?*

I shook my head.

He dipped his chin in acknowledgment.

LuLu gave me a knowing wave. Nothing got by her, which sometimes landed her in trouble. Like when she'd followed us through the portal, got kidnapped, and Calderis had nearly died. His father had ordered her memory erased. I'd tried, but it didn't work on her.

We discovered LuLu had her grandmother's "shine," which she was still exploring how to use. But she promised not to reveal our truth because that would reveal her own, so she'd become an unofficial ally to our covenant and an even better friend to me.

I waved and then I was moving through the festival, past the booths, and down the sidewalk toward the maple trees that shaded the back road to the library.

Wishville's *Maple Hollow Library* sat like a storybook cottage dipped in Victorian seriousness. Brick walls. Arched windows. Wide stone steps. It was beautiful in autumn, framed by red and gold leaves drifting lazily onto the path.

Clara stood at the top of the steps, twisting her library badge lanyard like she was trying to snap it in half.

"Hey," I said, climbing up to her. "What's going on?"

She turned, looking pale but determined. "You just...you need to see. It's in the archives. I swear I wasn't looking for anything unusual. As you know, we're just finishing the second library restoration, so I was just putting things back in order. I was reorganizing the time capsule display for WishFest, and I found a space behind the wall."

I blinked. "Behind the wall?"

"Well, an old cabinet that was painted over during the first restoration, to be exact. The backing looked as if it were haphazardly slid back in place. I saw the tip of something peeking through, so I moved it aside to investigate." She swallowed. "I've lived in Wishville for over forty years and worked in this library for over twenty, Lyra. I know this building. There shouldn't *be* a space there."

My skin prickled.

Vex's tail puffed slightly. "Mmm," he purred. *Hidden things. I approve.*

Clara led us inside.

The library smelled like warm paper and autumn through the cracked window, with sunlight slanting across reading tables and dust motes drifting lazily into golden beams. Kids laughed somewhere in the children's section. Someone was photocopying something aggressively in back. But near the archives, everything felt still. Clara unlocked a door and guided us into a narrow room filled with old photographs, binders, and marked storage boxes.

"It's over here," she said, stopping beside a section of shelving she'd already dragged away from the wall. Her hands trembled slightly as she pointed to a square outline in the brick. "I was straightening the 80s time capsule display and something felt off," she said. "Like a breeze. There shouldn't be a breeze *in a wall*. So, I pushed a little, and..." She pressed lightly against the outline.

A small door swung inward with the softest whisper of motion. Vex's ears perked. I felt my pulse stutter. Inside was a hollow cavity about two feet deep. Nestled within, wrapped in dusty cloth, was a metal box with tarnished hinges.

"What is *that*?" I whispered.

Clara shook her head. "I don't know. But Lyra, look." She

donned a pair of gloves and reached carefully inside then lifted the box. Even through the cloth, I could see letters carved faintly into the lid.

M.W.

My throat tightened. "Maggie Winslow." I had been in Wishville for the past century and remembered when Maggie went missing, but over time even I had forgotten some of the details. Of course, no one from back then had memory of me since I'd had to erase their memories of me several times over the years.

Clara's face folded. "My mom. This was hers. And I don't know why she hid it."

My hands hovered over the box, careful and reverent. "Clara, this is incredible. Do you want to open it?"

She hesitated, her eyes shining with moisture, then she nodded. "Yes. I need to know."

I donned a pair of gloves, and we set the box on a nearby table. Clara unwrapped the cloth, her fingers shaking. The hinges groaned softly as she lifted the lid.

Inside lay:

- A notebook with frayed edges
- A folded map
- A tiny glass jar of soil
- A carved stone fragment the size of a plum, etched with lines too smooth and too deliberate to be human-made

The moment the stone caught the light, something in me recognized it. As if some old memory stirred in my bones.

Vex leaned close, his whiskers trembling. *That's not from Wishville.*

No, it wasn't. It was carved with unmistakable Dweller craftsmanship.

Clara's voice was a thin thread. "Do you know what it is?"

I met her eyes, my heart thumping a slow, deliberate rhythm.

"I think," I said quietly, "this is the first clue your mother left behind as to what might have happened to her." And I knew, as surely as I knew the taste of WishFest cider, that the peaceful festival behind us had just become the backdrop to something far deeper. Something forgotten. Something buried.

Something ready to surface.

CHAPTER

Two

IF CLARA HADN'T BEEN SHAKING, I might've taken my time. Instead, I moved carefully but fast, like the box might vanish if we blinked too long. We'd set it on the archive table under the brightest lamp. The rest of the room faded into stacks and shadows, while old yearbooks, town ledgers, and dusty binders lined up like witnesses who'd taken a vow of silence.

Outside, faintly, I could still hear WishFest's distant music, laughter, and the muffled call of a raffle announcement bleeding through the old brick walls. In here, the air felt thick with dust and something tighter. Anticipation, maybe, or grief with somewhere specific to land.

Clara stood beside me, with her arms wrapped around her middle like she was trying to hold everything in place. Her cardigan was buttoned crookedly. She normally would never let that happen. Her gaze was fixed on the box like it might bite.

"Do you want me to...?" I asked gently, my fingers hovering over the notebook inside. I hoped she would say *yes* because of what it might contain. If there were Dweller secrets, I needed to make sure they stayed hidden.

She swallowed hard. "I need to see it." A beat passed between us. "But maybe you turn the pages. My hands are shaking."

"You're human. That's allowed," I said casually, hiding my relief that she allowed me to help.

Vex hopped lightly onto the far end of the table, sitting with his paws tucked neatly beneath him like a carved obsidian cat statue. Only his eyes betrayed his interest: bright, attentive, and tracking every move. The well-shaped pendant on his collar glinted faintly when he shifted.

I picked up the notebook.

The cover was worn soft, the cardboard edges feathery, and the metal spiral slightly bent at one end. A strip of faded masking tape on the front bore Maggie's handwriting in blue ink: **MAPLE HOLLOW RENOVATION NOTES—FALL 1984**. My throat tightened. There was something about touching a person's notes that were private, messy, and unpolished. It felt more intimate than flipping through their photo album. This wasn't how Maggie had wanted to be remembered. This was how she'd wanted to *understand* the world.

I opened it.

Neat, slanted script marched across the first page. Maggie's handwriting had the same tidy precision as Clara's, only a little looser at the edges, as if the writer occasionally got too excited to stay within the lines.

> *October 2, 1984*
> *Documenting the library renovation for our town's history books. Initial survey of lower stacks and foundation walls seems standard. Construction crew insists the plans are "simple as a shoebox."*

Despite everything, Clara's mouth twitched. "She hated that phrase," Clara whispered. "Simple as a shoebox. She said buildings were never that simple. People certainly weren't."

I turned the page. More notes, neatly dated. Measurements. Tiny sketches of floor plans. An occasional underlined bold words like, **_draft?, hollow, not on blueprints_**. As I flipped halfway through, Vex leaned closer, sniffing the pages.

Old paper, dust, and obsession, his voice slid dryly into my thoughts. *Classic human scholar.*

"Be nice," I murmured under my breath.

"I am being nice," Clara said automatically, then blinked. "Wait. Were you talking to me or the cat?"

"Yes," I said, which seemed safest. Thankfully, she let it go.

Near the middle of the notebook, the tone shifted. The handwriting pressed darker into the page, as if the pen had been held tighter.

October 14, 1984—Found it.

Beneath the sentence, she'd drawn a small square, shaded lightly with arrows pointing at one side. A wall? No, a cabinet like the one she hid the box in. The caption read, **Breeze here. No window. No duct. No explanation.**

"Found what?" Clara asked.

I shrugged and turned the page.

There's nothing simple about this renovation. Something is off. There's a gap inside the wall of the east archive. I can't see it, but I feel a draft. All I see is a square cabinet. I opened it, but I don't see anything inside. I suspect there's an opening beneath it that I can't get to. There is no record of repairs beneath the library in any of the logs.

I frowned. An opening beneath the library sounded suspicious. I kept reading.

Henry says I'm imagining it.

The name sent a quick flicker of annoyance through me. Henry

McAlister, the town developer, had a long history of wanting to make things "cleaner" and "more modern," usually at the expense of history and common sense.

I am not imagining it. There's air moving where there shouldn't be. There must be an entrance somewhere. I'll come back later. Clara had a nightmare again. I can't leave her for long.

My chest ached.

Clara pressed a knuckle to her mouth. "She never told me any of this," she whispered. "I mean, I was five, but still..."

"You were five," I echoed gently. "You weren't supposed to carry this then."

There was another page with more sketches. The rectangle again, this time with a dotted line curving downward beneath it.

If there's a gap, there's a hollow. And if there's a hollow, there might be a passage. Old foundations don't just forget themselves. We built on something. What?

Clara's eyes shone. "She used to say that," she murmured. "'Foundations don't forget themselves.' I thought it was about relationships."

"It was probably about both," I said, and then turned another page. Here, the ink wavered slightly, like she'd been writing faster.

Nov. 1, 1984
I opened the cabinet again. There's a secret door with a shallow cavity beneath, and then more stone behind. I felt cold air from below. It must lead to something bigger. Deeper.

A quickly sketched spiral of stairs descended into blankness.

My skin prickled over the word *spiral*. "Stairs," I said quietly. "That lead to under the library."

Clara shook her head slowly. "No one's ever mentioned stairs. There's a boiler room, the foundations, storm drains, but not stairs."

Because no one's supposed to know, Vex murmured inside my mind. Out loud, he merely let out a soft chuff.

I set the notebook aside for a moment and reached for the folded map. The paper crackled with that stiff texture old documents get when they've been folded too long. Maggie had drawn her own version of the library with rectangles labeled with sections, arrows pointing toward exits, and tiny notes in the margins.

Along the bottom edge, she'd continued beyond the outer wall. A thin line dropped beneath the building, then angled outward. It zigzagged, dipping lower, with thin hash marks marking stairs. At the far end of the page, near where she'd quickly sketched a hump of something, Maggie had drawn a tiny X.

Beside it, in small, tight letters she wrote:

If I'm right, this goes all the way to the ridge. Old passage? No records. No mention in any town minutes. No maps. Why?

I exhaled slowly. "She thought it led to the mountains." I wanted to tell Clara everything, but I reminded myself that it would crush her if she knew the truth. I had been so focused on finding my own mother back then, I let both Maggie and Clara down by believing she ran away like the rest of the town. This time would be different. I refused to let them down again.

Clara stepped closer, clutching the edge of the table. "We never had tunnels," she said faintly. "We have stories. Old ones. About magical creatures and other realms, but everyone knows about those."

"That's right," I said carefully. "Folklore is a wonderful marketing strategy to draw tourists to our town. It's great for Wishville's economy."

Clara nodded.

The carved stone fragment glinted dully in the box. Until now, I'd been avoiding touching it. I knew Dweller craftsmanship when I saw it. The angles were too precise, the lines too fluid, the texture of the stone polished in a way human tools rarely achieved. But the pattern etched on its surface was different from Elarion's usual motifs. No swirling rivers or constellations. Just a series of clean, repeating grooves that reminded me more of boundary markers than art.

"You should look at the soil sample," Clara said quickly, as if she could sense my hesitation.

Right. One mystery at a time. The tiny glass jar had been stoppered with wax and labeled in that same neat script: **Tunnel floor. 10 ft down. Smells...unusual.** I popped the wax seal carefully and lifted the lid. The scent rose immediately, damp, cool, and mineral-heavy, but not moldy like basement concrete.

"This isn't from under a normal building," I said softly.

Clara wrapped her arms around herself, rubbing her palms over her sleeves. "I knew she was obsessed. After the renovation started, she was always staying late at the library. She said it was for research, and I believed her, because, well, she *loved* paperwork. But this—"

"She was onto something big," I said.

"She disappeared a week after the last date in that notebook." Clara's voice went quiet. "I used to think that if I was older back then, I could've made the police chief, Ron Maddox, keep looking. My father worked for the town. Facilities and infrastructure, roads, municipal buildings, maintenance. He knew every crawl-space and locked door in Wishville. He tried to help, but no one listened. He died a year later of a broken heart. I thank the Lord every day for Dorothy Rourke. She was my mother's best friend and fellow teacher. Since I didn't have any family left, she stepped in and raised me."

I thought of my own mother. Of how many missing person

cases in tiny towns back then got filed under *tragedy* when they should've been filed under *not enough questions asked*.

"You were five," I said again. "It was never your job to fix it."

She looked at me, her eyes shining. "Maybe it's my job now."

Vex's tail flicked. *That's your job*, he murmured privately. *Can't risk her discovering Elarion secrets.*

"*Our* job," I said, secretly agreeing with Vex. "You're not alone in this, Clara."

I finally picked up the stone fragment. It was cool to the touch, even through my gloves, almost unnaturally so, given the warmth of the room. As if it remembered a place where the sun never really reached.

As my fingers traced one of the carved grooves, a faint sensation rippled through me, like the echo of a note I couldn't hear but could feel along my bones. For a second I could almost see it in context, set into a wall, maybe, or part of a larger marker at the edge of a path.

"Lyra?" Clara asked, watching my face. "What is it?"

I forced myself to relax my grip and keep my expression neutral. "It's not like anything I've seen in town, but the tool work is old. Specialized." I met her gaze. "Your mom was right. This isn't just a utility tunnel or someone's hidden wine cellar. Whatever she found, it predated the library."

Clara exhaled shakily, some of the tension leaving her shoulders. "I keep thinking," she said quietly. "When she found the tunnel, why didn't she tell anyone sooner? Why hide this?"

"Maybe she wanted proof of something first," I said. "Maybe she thought she was onto some big discovery she would get credit for." Or maybe there was more going on than anyone knew. Maggie never came to me with any of this back then, and I hadn't seen anything to indicate Elarion had a hand in her disappearance, so I hadn't dug any deeper. I'd let her be someone else's *problem*. How could I have been so selfish?

We stood there for a moment, absorbing everything we'd

found. The library hummed softly around us, an old building with old bones and a new crack in its story.

"Can I...?" Clara gestured to the notebook like she was asking for something sacred.

"It's yours," I said. "It was your mother's. I'm just here to help you read it."

She held it gently in her gloved hands like it might crumble if she squeezed too hard.

"What do we do next?" she asked.

"We compare this map to the current blueprints," I said, thinking aloud, knowing what it felt like to lose a mother. I couldn't help but hold her hand and walk beside her in it so she would know I was here to stay, and she wasn't alone. "We'll see what lines up and what doesn't. And then..."

"And then?" Her voice was steady now, but braced.

I looked at the little square door in the wall, the hidden hollow behind it, and the decades-old clues on the table between us. "Then," I said, "we find your mother's stairs."

Vex's eyes gleamed, as if warning me about involving Clara too much before we knew what was down there.

I understood his warning, but I couldn't help myself. I couldn't stop thinking if I had paid more attention back then, maybe Clara would still have her mother. Outside, a festival cheered and laughed and tossed wishes into a well, blissfully unaware that under one of their quietest buildings, a different kind of history was waiting to be uncovered.

The moment we stepped out of the archive room, the library felt different. Like Clara's discovery had stirred the dust in old corners, revealing a truth it had held too long. The light through the tall arched windows slanted across the reading tables, warm and amber, but the quiet beneath it felt taut. I didn't realize how tense Clara and I both were until she startled violently at the sound of footsteps.

"It's just LuLu," I said, recognizing her walk before I even turned.

Lourdes Morales appeared around the corner with her messenger bag slung cross-body, camera clipped to the strap, and notepad sticking out like an eager dog. Her dark waves were windblown, her cheeks flushed, and her brown eyes were sharp and curious. The perpetual expression of someone who'd spent her whole life trying to see the truth under things people hoped she would ignore.

"Okay," she said breathlessly, "I saw you leave earlier like you'd seen a ghost, and Holden nearly choked on his kettle corn, distracted with worry, and Calderis looked like he was planning a tactical extraction, so..." She narrowed her eyes. "What happened?"

I blinked. Leave it to LuLu to notice every detail.

"Wishville is small," LuLu said. "News travels at speeds normally reserved for lightning and bad decisions."

Clara let out a thin laugh. It was the first sound of levity she'd made since we'd opened the box.

LuLu immediately softened. "Hey. You okay?"

Clara hesitated, then nodded, but only barely.

I pressed a hand lightly to her shoulder. "We found something," I told LuLu. "In the archive wall."

LuLu's eyes widened. "A body?"

"No," I said quickly. "Definitely not a body."

"Shame," she muttered. "Professionally, anyway."

Clara made a small sound somewhere between disbelief and apology. "It's something of my mother's. Something she hid."

LuLu froze. Then her voice gentled in a way few people ever got to hear from her. "I'm so sorry, Clara." She moved forward slowly, giving Clara space to retreat or accept comfort. "What did she leave?"

"Notes," Clara whispered. "A box. A map. Lyra thinks it's important. It has to be important. Why else would she hide it?"

LuLu glanced at me with questions simmering in her expression, but she didn't ask them, no matter how much she wanted to. That was one of my favorite things about her. She was relentless when she needed to be, but she was never cruel.

"Can I see?" she asked Clara.

Clara opened her mouth and hesitated, looked at the archive door, then looked at me.

"It's your call," I said. "I won't show anyone without your permission."

After a long slow inhale, Clara nodded. "LuLu can see."

We returned to the archive room, and LuLu shut the door behind us with a soft click. She moved around the table like she was approaching a sacred site. Carefully and reverently, with a journalist's laser focus. When she saw the initials on the box, her breath caught, as if seeing that human mark made it more personal.

"Maggie Winslow," she said quietly. "Oh, Clara..." Even though LuLu was relatively new to town, she'd done her homework in the newsroom, pouring over current and cold cases, looking for the next big story.

Clara pressed her lips together and nodded.

LuLu set her bag down, pulled out a pair of gloves, and leaned over the map first, scanning it quickly. "This is...what even is this? These lines look like tunnels, but the scale is all wrong. There's nothing under the library except the foundation and a storm drain."

"Foundations don't forget themselves," Clara murmured, repeating her mother's old phrase.

LuLu's brows lifted. "She used to say that to you?"

"Yes. I thought it was metaphorical."

LuLu traced a finger down the drawn staircase, her expression sharpening with recognition. "But these go down." She squinted, studying it closer, then pointed at the far end. "Why is there an X marked near the ridge? There are no mines up there."

"We don't know," I said. "Not yet."

LuLu studied the soil jar next. "This smells like minerals from a cave..." She cleared her throat. "From a place I once visited."

Clara snapped her head toward her. "What place?"

LuLu blinked, then shook her head. "I don't know. Maybe I dreamed about the place. Let's just say it wasn't around here."

Clara arched an eyebrow high but didn't say a word.

Vex's ear flicked sharply. *Her gift wakes again,* he murmured in my mind.

I kept my outward expression calm. "LuLu, your instincts are getting sharper. It's okay."

She stiffened. "It doesn't feel okay. It feels like déjà vu having a panic attack in my brain."

Clara offered a small smile. "I've heard about people with a sixth sense. At least you're consistent. Even your psychic awakening is dramatic."

LuLu snorted, but her eyes were grateful. Humor was her shield and her grounding cord. Then her attention snapped to the carved stone fragment. "What is that?" she asked.

Clara answered first. "Mom labeled it from ten feet down, I think. But she didn't identify it."

LuLu picked it up cautiously, rolling it in her gloved palms. "It feels old." Then she flinched. "Sorry. Weird, I know. Ignore me as I think out loud." Her fingers tightened unconsciously around the grooves. "It's not from here, either," she added softly. Her voice shivered just a little.

"Do you feel sick?" I asked quickly. "Dizzy? Pulled?"

"No. It's nothing like that." She shook her head. "It's just...familiar? Like I've seen the pattern somewhere, but I haven't. There's nothing like that in town or any archives. I would remember something like this." She put it gently back in the box, almost reluctant to release it. "Okay," she said, straightening. "What's the plan?"

LuLu always expected to be included, period, end of story.

I bit back a smile. "We will compare Maggie's map to the current blueprints and look for mismatches. If there's a hollow space behind the wall, we need to see where the entrance is."

"And after that?" Clara asked quietly.

"After that," I said softly, "we figure out how deep this goes."

LuLu pulled her camera from her bag. "Do you mind?" she asked Clara. "Documenting this could help us track changes in the brickwork and the wall structure. I won't publish anything. This isn't a story unless you want it to be."

"I appreciate that." Clara thought for a minute, then nodded. "Do it."

LuLu photographed everything: the box, the objects, the map, Maggie's handwriting, even the hollow in the wall cabinet. Then she slipped her camera back into the bag. "Holden's going to want to know. And Calderis." Her tone dipped lower for that name.

I nodded. "One thing at a time. Clara and I need to get our facts straight. Cross-check the blueprints first."

"Actually..." Clara hesitated, chewing her lip. "We don't have the original 1984 renovation files. A lot of the early library documents went missing in the early 90s."

LuLu's expression sharpened instantly. "Missing," she repeated. "Convenient."

"Suspicious," Vex muttered aloud, then blinked.

Clara jumped. "Did the cat just—"

I coughed loudly. "Isn't it funny how his meows sound like words sometimes?" I glared at Vex.

He gave another gargle-like meow for effect and then walked away.

"We need to find out who had access to those blueprints," LuLu said, steering the conversation back on track. "Who supervised the renovation? Who signed off on the repairs? Who might have been down in the walls with your mom?"

Clara hugged her elbows. "I only remember one name from

the old stories. Mr. Teagan. He was the foreman at the quarry back then. He consulted on foundational integrity when the library was remodeled."

LuLu snapped her fingers. "Gerald Teagan? He's still alive. His daughter runs the hardware store."

I made a note on my phone. "We start with him then."

Clara nodded, some of the fear melting into focus. "I want to do this. I need to know what happened to my mother."

I could relate.

LuLu stepped close and squeezed her hand. "We'll find out. Together."

The sudden chiming of the library door startled all three of us. A patron called a faint "Hello?" from the front.

Clara blinked. "Oh, right. The library." She gave us a flustered smile. "My actual job. Patrons, books, reality." She hurried out.

LuLu watched her go, then she turned to me with that sharp, relentless mind of hers spinning gears behind her eyes. "This isn't just a hidden box. This is the start of something huge. It's bigger than a renovation. It's a mystery."

"I know it matters to Clara," I said carefully.

"And to you," she added softly.

I didn't deny it. There was no way I could. LuLu knew me well enough by now to see how guilty I felt.

LuLu drew in a slow breath. "Lyra, whatever this is, I'm in. My abilities or instincts or whatever—they're waking up whether I like it or not. And this feels connected somehow. So, I'm helping, and you're not stopping me."

I gave her a small, grateful smile. "I wasn't planning to."

Her shoulders relaxed a little, then she grabbed her bag. "I'll meet you back at the house tonight after WishFest winds down. We'll cross-reference everything over a glass of wine."

"Sounds good to me. Tonight it is," I said. My date with Holden would have to wait.

Vex flicked his tail. "This will end with someone falling into a hole," he predicted out loud.

"Helpful," I muttered.

LuLu grinned faintly. "I like him." Of course she did.

We stepped out of the archive room and into the main library, where everything looked normal with books, patrons, and autumn sunlight drifting between old shelves. But between those ordinary shelves, inside one hidden wall, under decades of dust...something had waited to be found.

And now the waiting was over.

CHAPTER
Three

BY THE TIME I made it back to the town square, Fall WishFest had slipped from "busy" into "borderline unhinged." Music thumped from the main stage, kids ran wild with caramel-smeared faces, and the smell of cinnamon bread tangled with woodsmoke.

Magnolia McHoggin was at her *Blooms of Glory* shop holding a wilted chrysanthemum and dabbing her eyes with a lace handkerchief. "Too beautiful for this cruel world," she sniffed.

Across the way, Bartholomew "Bart" Gildersnipe wiped down his brisket cart out front of his butcher shop, shaking his head. "Magnolia, it's a plant."

"Have some respect," she wailed. "Her name is Gloria the Third."

I wove through the crowd, my mind still half in the library replaying images of Maggie Winslow's map, the hidden box, and the stone fragment Clara couldn't bear to touch. WishFest demanded cheer, but my brain was still in the shadows under the stacks.

I didn't get three steps before the Wellies descended.

Tilly, Belle, and Dot approached in a jingling, sparkling wall of over-accessorized chaos—shawls fluttering, bangles clacking, scarves shedding fringe like festive debris. Somewhere in the noise, a bell chimed that I was fairly certain had not been approved by the Festival Committee.

"Guardian," Tilly said, seizing my arm with alarming strength. "We need a ruling."

"Festival Chair," I corrected for the umpteenth time, prying her fingers loose before my circulation was cut off. "What's the crisis?"

Dot thrust a teacup under my nose, the liquid sloshing dangerously. "My leaves predict disaster."

Belle leaned in with her eyes narrowed as she pointed across the square. "Trip Danderly is on the fountain ledge giving a safety lecture about *bad wishing*. I do not have enough pigeons to save him."

Sure enough, Trip stood atop the fountain in the center of the square like a man campaigning for Mayor of Chaos, his arms spread wide and scarf flapping dramatically. "No wishing for your ex back during Fall WishFest!" he announced. "That's a Winter RegretFest wish!"

The crowd cheered.

Someone handed him a cider.

"I think he's fine," I said. "As long as he doesn't fall in."

Tilly squinted hard, flipping open a small, aggressively tabbed notebook. "My spleen journal says he will."

Belle sniffed. "Your journal also told you I'd marry a man with a yacht. I'm not married, and Carl's canoe barely seats two. That's why he didn't get a second date."

"Because of the canoe?" Dot asked.

"No," Belle said firmly. "Because he kept calling it a *yacht*."

I put a steadying hand on Belle's shoulder. "If Trip goes in, I'll fish him out."

The three of them exchanged a look that was long, knowing, and deeply theatrical.

"You're troubled, Lyra," Tilly said gravely.

"I'm fine," I said. "Just multitasking."

"Mmm." Tilly patted my cheek like I was a particularly over-wrought houseplant. "We'll be nearby if fate needs supervision."

"And if the fountain claims another victim," Belle added.

"Or if my leaves start screaming," Dot said.

They swept away in a clatter of charms, scarves, and purposeful urgency, leaving behind the faint scent of clove and impending meddling.

Vex padded at my heels, his tail flicking. *They know something is wrong. Their old-woman senses tingle.*

"I'm pretty sure they just like drama," I muttered.

Same thing, he replied calmly.

Fenrin spotted him at that moment, her eyes lighting up with predatory delight, and Vex leaped into a nearby tree with the grace of someone who had absolutely planned this.

Below us, Trip raised his arms again. "Also, no wishing for revenge!" he called. "That's an all-seasons mistake!"

The crowd cheered louder.

I sighed. WishFest was going beautifully.

I saw Holden across the square talking to Ruth Bingham, Mayor Doug Delaney, and Connie Hale. Doug looked vaguely winded, his navy tie crooked.

"Lyra," Doug called. "WishFest is a triumph. The town is, well, behaving this time. Bless you."

"That seems premature," I muttered, praying it would remain true this season.

Holden gave me a look that went straight through the surface layer of my smile as he reached my side. "How's Clara?" he asked.

My throat tightened. "Holding on. We found something in the archive wall."

"Related to her mother?"

"Yes. A box Maggie hid." I swallowed. "We're going through everything tonight."

Holden's jaw flexed. "And you didn't call me?"

"You're on duty. Sorry about having to reschedule our date," I said. "This might still be nothing more than a weird draft and a forgotten renovation."

He studied me. "And if it's not?"

"Then I'll tell you."

He brushed his thumb along my knuckles, grounding me. "Just don't do anything crazy without backup."

"No spelunking," I promised. *Today, anyway.*

Weylan flew overhead in his hot air balloon full of festivalgoers, while Sparks and Finch worked on fixing a couple of streetlamps that were out. Nearby, Maisie Flint lectured a pack of teenagers about "ethical charm-purchasing practices," Willa Hartman passed out soup shooters, and Trip Danderly slipped off the fountain.

Dot was going to collect payment from the universe at this rate. Before I could check on him, LuLu appeared with her camera bouncing against her hip. Calderis walked beside her carrying a huge crate of extension cords like it weighed nothing.

"There she is," LuLu called. "Our fearless festival tyrant."

"Chair," I corrected, but she ignored me same as the Wellies did.

LuLu snapped a few atmospheric shots. "Boss wants 'heartwarming WishFest content.' If anyone spontaneously proposes in front of a cider tent, tell me."

Calderis nodded politely, then glanced over her shoulder at her camera screen. "Your photography is improving."

"It's literally part of my job." LuLu shrugged. "Also, Cal, you look like you're about to arrest someone."

He blinked. "I am simply standing."

She sighed. "Sorry. Long day, and it's only the afternoon."

I approached them. "Everything okay? You look strained."

LuLu raised a brow. "My head has been buzzing since the library. In a 'my psychic abilities are doing jazz hands' way."

"We'll talk tonight," I said. "About all of it."

She nodded, but her gaze softened. "Clara's lucky to have you."

Calderis glanced at me with that unreadable, too-seeing expression of his. "You carry news."

"Questions," I said. "Not news yet."

He inclined his head. "I will remain nearby." Translation: brooding perimeter guardian mode activated.

My pendant gave a faint, warm pulse—one brief tap of energy.

The town clerk, Amanda Carter, boomed over the speakers, "The wishing well is ready to receive. Bring your tokens!" People drifted toward the hill that led to the festival clearing and the well.

Holden squeezed my hand once before heading to coordinate with his officers.

LuLu lifted her camera. "I'll get B-roll, then meet you at home. And get some wine. I think we're gonna need it."

"Already have some chilled and ready."

Calderis followed LuLu, his gaze sweeping the crowd like a silent sentinel every step of the way, with Fenrin darting in between his long strides.

Vex hopped onto my shoulder as we climbed the path to the festival grounds. *Ready to perform, Guardian?* he asked.

I looked out at my town with its lanterns, laughter, and chaos, and said, "Yeah. I'm ready." Ready for the wishes, Maggie's clues, and whatever waited beneath the library.

By the time WishFest wound down and the last lanterns were dimming, my legs felt like they'd done three marathons, and my brain felt like it had watched all of them while juggling paperwork. The treaty felt solid with no magical spikes, no cracks, and no drama. For once, the danger wasn't coming from Elarion.

It was coming from a library wall.

The walk home cleared my head a little. The air had that crisp edge it only got in October, cool enough that I could see my breath as I made my way up the last hill. My father's old house waited under the trees, barely visible from the road unless you knew where to look.

Inside, it smelled like cedar, worn books, and the faint stubborn ghost of pipe tobacco even though it had been centuries and I didn't smoke. I sometimes wondered if my father was haunting me. I toed off my boots and followed the murmur of voices into the living room. Clara sat on the sofa with her hands wrapped around a glass of red wine and Maggie's box on the coffee table in front of her. LuLu was on the floor, cross-legged, with her laptop open and printouts fanned around her. She had a glass of white wine in her hand and a pensive look on her face.

Vex had claimed one armchair, his jet-black fur sleek and expression self-satisfied. Fenrin, her ginger fur shiny and bright amber eyes full of mischief, occupied the other. They looked like a matched set someone had ordered from a catalog titled "Questionable Familiar Energy."

"Hey," I said. "You two started the party without me."

LuLu didn't look up from the screen. "We needed something to do while you were out there being adored by the townsfolk."

Clara managed a small smile. "You looked very official on that platform."

"*Official* is just tired with better posture," I said, dropping onto the sofa beside her. I poured myself a glass of red and asked, "What've you got?"

LuLu grabbed a stack of pages. "Current library blueprints, courtesy of Amanda Carter and her glitter squirrel empire."

"Bless Amanda," I said, thinking it paid off being friends with the town clerk.

"Forever," LuLu agreed, then sobered. "I overlaid the modern plans with Clara's mom's map." She slid the documents toward me. The top sheet showed the library's clean lines. Beneath it sat Maggie's hand-drawn version with stairs drawn in hash marks and a tunnel line leading away. "We lined up the archives first. Here's the wall where you found the box." She tapped the square cabinet section. "According to the official plan, that's solid brick with no cavities, no access, Nothing."

"But there *is* a cavity," I said. "A hidden one in a cabinet."

"Exactly." LuLu pointed to another page where she'd traced Maggie's stair markings in red. "She drew steps down from somewhere outside the library into tunnels beneath, but the blueprints don't show anything like that."

Clara's voice was quiet but steady. "So, the blueprint is either wrong or lying because my mother wasn't a liar."

"Paper doesn't lie," I said. "People do."

Clara's fingers tightened on her mug. "I've been walking around the library grounds for twenty years. If there really are stairs that lead under the building, how many times have I almost found them without knowing?"

"Stairs stay hidden until they're ready," LuLu said gently. "Like secrets. Or my high school yearbook photos."

Despite herself, Clara chuckled.

I leaned closer, studying the pages. The discrepancy was obvious now that I knew to look for it. There was a section of wall and foundation that didn't match up the way the rest of the building did.

"This patch of wall was reinforced after the renovation," LuLu went on. "There's a note about added support. But no separate work order in the digital files to show a cabinet, no contractor name, nothing."

"Which means the paperwork never made it to the scanned archive," I said. "Or someone didn't want it there."

Clara frowned. "We did a big digitization push when the town went online. Some things were missed, but not usually structural alterations. Those were priority."

"Unless someone 'misplaced' them on purpose," LuLu said. "Henry McAlister does love his disappearing documents."

Clara's mouth thinned. "He interned for the planning board during that renovation. He loved the phrase 'clean slate.'"

"Good thing he's not running things anymore," I said. These

days he had his own land development real estate company. "But in 1984, he could've helped vanish inconvenient records."

LuLu nodded. "He probably didn't have the authority to order modifications, but he could make sure the paper trail was fuzzy."

Vex flicked his tail. *Humans erase what they fear*, he remarked. *Or what they're ashamed of. Or both.*

Fenrin made a soft chirping sound and batted at one of the printouts, her paw landing squarely on a shaded area at the bottom of the foundation diagram.

LuLu peered at it. "You see that too, huh?"

I leaned over. "What am I looking at?"

"This little section." LuLu circled it with a pen. "The foundation shading is different here. Lighter lines, like they were added later. If you overlay the two..." She grabbed another sheet: a topo map of town and the forest rising into the foothills. A red line traced Maggie's sketched tunnel from under the library toward the mountains. "Okay, here's the part that makes my brain itch." She lined up the library on both maps, then tapped the red line. "Following the angle and distance Maggie drew, this tunnel, if it's real, would end up around here." Her finger landed on a small shaded patch at the base of the mountains marked: **Old Quarry—Closed**.

"Teagan's quarry," Clara whispered.

I felt a deep, bone-level recognition. That path under town, slanting toward the mountains. Toward stone that had once brushed against Dweller borders. My pendant grew faintly warm beneath my shirt, like it had turned its head toward something interesting.

"According to the town records, Gerald Teagan consulted on the library foundation," LuLu said. "Being a quarry foreman, if there were old passages under town, he would know."

"And he might have had a reason to keep them quiet," I added. "If Maggie found something that could stop the quarry from expanding..."

Clara stared at the line of red ink like it might reach out and drag her into the past. "She protested the expansion," she said. "I remember hearing my father talk about that. She argued at town meetings. Said we didn't need to desecrate historical grounds." Her hand tightened on the notebook. "No one listened, not even the Historical Society."

I remembered those arguments and agreed with her at the time, but not everyone did. "Someone might have listened," I said quietly. "Someone might have acted before she could prove it."

The room settled into a thoughtful hush. The heater clicked. The clock ticked. Outside, a car passed on the road, its tires whispering over fallen leaves.

LuLu shoved her hair back and blew out a breath. "So, we have missing blueprints, an extra line of foundation shading, a secret hollow in the archive wall, stairs that officially don't exist, a tunnel that probably points at a defunct quarry, and a possible murder."

Clara covered her mouth over a soft sob.

"Or not," LuLu quickly corrected.

"She might still be alive, Clara," I said. "Maggie must have known she was in danger. Her box is like a personal time capsule. She wanted someone, maybe even Clara, to find this if she went missing."

Clara's eyes shimmered with tears. "She didn't trust anyone else, not even my father for some reason. Or she did, and it got her..." She swallowed hard. "Either way, she left it for me, and I missed it for forty years."

I turned toward her fully. "You didn't miss it. Someone sealed it inside a wall. You can't blame yourself for not having x-ray vision as a child." And I should have seen the signs that something was wrong instead of accepting her disappearance so easily.

"If this is anyone's fault," LuLu added, "it's whoever decided to hide stairs and hope no one ever noticed.'"

Vex flicked an ear. *Always suspect the ones who hate stairs.*

Fenrin hopped onto the back of the couch behind Clara, pressing her forehead gently against the top of Clara's head. Clara reached up and stroked her fur with a trembling hand. "So, what now?" she asked. "We can't exactly start hammering at the archives."

"Not yet," I said. "We should do this in order. First, we talk to Gerald. LuLu, can you set that up? You're the investigative journalist. Ask for an interview about 'the history of Wishville's building boom' or something."

LuLu's mouth tipped into a smirk. "You have no idea how easily old men talk when you mention the words 'legacy feature' in the newspaper."

"Terrifying," I said. "Useful, but terrifying."

"I'll call his daughter, Renee, at the hardware store in the morning," she said. "He still comes in some days. If I play it right, he'll have maps out on the table before I even hit record."

"Meanwhile," I said, "Clara, keep the box close. Don't leave it in the archive overnight. If anyone ever knew about this, they might not be thrilled to hear it's been found."

Clara looked down at the box, at her mother's initials and the worn edges. She drew it into her lap, her hands cupping it like it was something living. The only piece of her mother she had left. "I'll lock it in my office safe," she said. "If anyone tries to take it, they'll have to get through me first."

There it was again, that steel under the librarian cardigan. It made something proud and fierce uncurl in my chest.

"Good," I said. "We're not losing this."

LuLu shut her laptop with a soft click. "I should go to bed before I start pinning these pages to your family room walls like a conspiracy board."

"That's what the white board in the formal living room is for," I said with a wink. "I bought one after my first case."

She hesitated, then shook her head. "If I stay up, I'll keep you up all night talking. Besides," she added, standing and slinging her bag over her shoulder, "you've had a long day. You should rest. Or text Holden until your battery dies. You owe him a date." She winked.

Heat crept up my neck. "I hate how well you know me already."

She pointed at me. "You love how well I know you. That's what best friends are for." Then she bent and hugged Clara tight. "Tomorrow, we question the quarry man at the hardware store. I'll give you an update."

"Tomorrow," Clara echoed.

LuLu headed for her bedroom. Fenrin hopped down to follow her, then glanced back at Vex. He watched her go for a moment before jumping from the chair and trotting after them.

She'll get lost without supervision, he said. *She never remembers where you put the snack drawer.*

The door closed behind them, leaving the house quieter.

Clara stood with the box still in her arms. "I should go home. If I stay, I'll start organizing your books by emotional damage level."

"They'd like the attention," I said. "But yeah. Big day tomorrow."

At the door, she paused. "Thank you, Lyra, for taking this seriously and not telling me I'm chasing ghosts."

"You're not chasing ghosts," I said. "You're chasing the truth."

She nodded, her eyes bright with hope, then stepped out into the cool night.

When I was alone, I leaned back against the couch and let out a long breath. My mother had once told me some doors should stay closed, for the safety of both worlds. But Maggie Winslow had pried one open anyway, and now her daughter, LuLu, and I were about to follow.

I pushed off the couch, turned out the lights, and headed toward my room, my mind already racing ahead to old quarries and lost tunnels...

And a man named Gerald Teagan who might hold the first real answer.

CHAPTER

Four

IF THE LIBRARY smelled like history and old secrets, *Teagan Hardware Supply* smelled like cut lumber, oil, and fifty years of people trying to fix things themselves before finally calling a professional.

The bell above the door jingled as LuLu and I stepped inside. Morning light slanted through tall paned windows, catching on coiled ropes, boxes of screws, and rows of paint cans stacked like obedient soldiers.

The hardware store had been in business longer than most marriages in Wishville. It was the kind of place where you could buy nails by the pound or get unsolicited life advice with your purchase of duct tape.

Renee Teagan, Gerald's daughter, stood behind the counter with her red hair in a messy braid and flannel shirt rolled to her elbows. She looked up from her inventory and grinned. "Lyra! LuLu! If you're here to buy paint, please don't tell me it's for WishFest props. I've seen the state of your storage sheds."

"It's not paint," I said quickly.

LuLu leaned on the counter. "We were hoping to catch your dad. I called earlier. You mentioned he stops in most mornings."

Renee's expression softened. "Yeah. He'll be in any minute. He likes to 'supervise the screw wall,' which is what he calls staring at it until inspiration strikes." She paused. "You two aren't doing a human-interest story about him, are you? Because the last time someone wrote about Dad, he tried to autograph the newspaper machine. He thinks he's a bigger deal than he is." She winked.

"No, worries," LuLu said smoothly. "We just have some questions about the old library renovation."

Renee blinked. "The 1984 one?"

"That's the one."

Her brows lifted a little. "You girls dig up some dusty drama?"

"Possibly," LuLu said. "But nothing scandalous."

It was too soon to promise that, but Renee didn't need the details.

The bell jingled again behind us. Gerald stepped in, leaning slightly on a walking stick carved with whorls that looked like quarry markings. He wore heavy work boots and a canvas coat, and his eyebrows could have been charcoal smudges, they were so dark, thick, and expressive.

"Morning, Renee," he boomed.

"Morning, Dad." She gestured toward us. "The Sleuth Sisters are here to ask about the old library project."

"We are not sisters," LuLu and I said simultaneously.

Gerald chuckled. "Close enough. What can I do for you ladies?" He shuffled to the counter, his hands braced on its edge. I noticed his nails were still stained with dust. Old habits die hard for quarry men.

LuLu gave him a friendly smile. "We're hoping you can tell us what you remember about the 1984 renovation. Specifically, the foundation work."

Gerald's gaze sharpened. He studied us like he was trying to see what we weren't saying. "What about the foundation?" he asked.

"There's a hollow spot in the archive wall," I responded. "We found something in it that dates back to the renovation. A hidden space."

His eyebrows rose. "Hidden space? Well, that's interesting."

"Do you remember sealing anything?" LuLu pressed gently. "Stairs, possibly? Or an access point?"

Gerald let out a low whistle and rubbed his jaw. "Now that's a question I haven't heard in a long time."

"What do you mean?" I asked.

Gerald glanced at Renee.

She lifted her hands. "Hey, don't look at me. I was just a kid."

He sighed, leaning more heavily on the counter. "Back in '84, the library was settling funny. There were cracks along the eastern corner. The town hired me to take a look. I'd done quarry reinforcements for ten years by then."

"And?" LuLu asked.

"And Maggie Winslow was there," he said, looking at me.

My breath caught, and I couldn't speak.

"Oh, I remember Maggie like it was yesterday. Smart as a whip. Always asking about things like ground composition, drainage, and load-bearing tolerance." He chuckled. "Half my crew had crushes on her. Course, she was married."

LuLu nudged me gently with her elbow. "Continue," she said.

Gerald tapped the counter thoughtfully. "We opened a section of wall below the archives to stabilize the crack. Maggie was poking around, taking notes. Then she found something."

"What kind of something?" I asked.

"A draft," he said. "Cold as a cave. Coming from beneath a cabinet in the wall like it led nowhere good."

My heart thumped. "Did you see what caused it?"

"No," he admitted. "We chipped away below the cabinet, but the space had been filled in long ago. Not by us or anyone I ever worked with." That last part was too close to the truth for comfort.

LuLu leaned in. "Who *did* fill it in, then?"

Gerald shook his head. "Can't say. But you know how people get in Wishville. They start whispering about old folklore, tunnels, spirits. Maggie didn't buy into any of it, but she was disturbed. Said the space was older than the foundation."

Renee made a face. "Older than the building? How old?"

"Hard to say." Gerald folded his arms. "Maggie wrote a proposal for further exploration, but the planning board shut it down."

LuLu frowned. "Do you know why?"

Gerald hesitated. A Muscle-In-The-Jaw kind of hesitation. "Because Henry McAlister and the planning board said there were no budget funds for 'wild goose chases.' Weird thing is...Maggie stopped arguing pretty quick. Kept to herself after that." He frowned. "I think she started exploring on her own. The more she explored, the more secretive she got. She even tried to get the quarry expansion project shut down, but Pike was having none of that. He was more about making money than preserving history."

I believed Gerald. "Did she ever tell you anything more?"

"She came by the quarry one evening, asked me what types of stone formed the ridge tunnels. I told her dolomite, marble, pockets of chert." He straightened a little. "She asked if a person could walk them."

My heart did a strange, sharp flip.

"And could they?" LuLu asked.

Gerald's eyes drifted toward the mountains outside the window. "If they knew the way."

Silence settled among us.

LuLu broke it first. "Mr. Teagan, did anything happen before she disappeared? Anything strange?"

Gerald's expression shifted, his pain and regret etched deep. "I found an envelope sealed tight with her own name on it in the library during the renovation the day she went missing."

"You never gave it to the police?" LuLu asked.

"It wasn't mine to give. I respect someone's personal property. She addressed it to herself for a reason. Rumor was she left of her own free will. Skipped town." He shrugged. "I figured if she wanted her husband to have it, she would have given it to him. He died a year later. Little Clara was too young, so I held onto it, figuring I would give it to Maggie when she returned...only she never did."

I sat forward. "Do you still have it?"

He nodded slowly. "I never opened it. Didn't feel right. Still don't. I figured if she never showed up, I would give it to Clara at some point. But I kind of forgot about it." He eyed me. "Maybe now it's time."

My pulse thundered. "We're working with Clara to reopen her mother's cold case. I'll give her the letter. Where is it?"

"In the glove box of my current truck and every truck I've owned over the last forty years," he said. "That's what I do with all my important papers. There's so much in there, I forgot about it until now. A man's glovebox is like a woman's purse. No one touches it, so no one else ever saw it, either. I'll get it."

He pushed away from the counter, but Renee stepped forward. "Dad, you shouldn't be walking back and forth like that today. I'll grab it."

He nodded gratefully and handed her the keys. As she disappeared out the side door, Gerald lowered his voice. "Lyra," he said, leaning closer, "Maggie and I grew close during the renovation. She confided in me sometimes. She believed the town sits on old bones. Geological or maybe spiritual. She wasn't sure." He paused. "But she was sure something strange was beneath Wishville. That was why she didn't want the quarry site excavated. She wanted to be the one to break the story of the century."

A cold ripple went down my spine with the weight of unfinished truths. Renee returned, holding a sealed envelope, yellowed and soft at the edges. My breath hitched, and I swallowed hard.

"Thank you," I whispered to Gerald as Renee handed the envelope to me.

"Be careful," he said. "Poor Clara. I have a bad feeling Maggie never ran away after all."

LuLu cleared her throat. "We should go, before I open that thing myself."

Gerald rested a hand on the counter. "If you need me again, you know where to find me."

I nodded, my throat tight. "We will."

As LuLu and I stepped out into the autumn sunlight, she exhaled shakily. "Well," she said, "that was a lot."

I clutched the envelope to my chest. "Yeah. And I fear it's only the beginning."

By the time the last car rolled past my house and Wishville finally quieted for the night, Holden showed up just before midnight, his jacket zipped against the cold and flashlight in one hand. "Ready?" he asked softly.

"No. But you don't turn down a summons from the Chief Elder." Using my Moonveil power, we were free to dress in our ceremonial robes to enter Elarion and no one would see us. I handed Holden his garments and we changed before we left my house.

My robes were crafted from root-woven silk, a fabric grown rather than stitched, dyed in deep midnight blue that shifted to soft silver when it caught the light. The material felt alive—cool at first touch, then warming to my body like it recognized me as its keeper.

Thin bioluminescent threads traced flowing patterns along the sleeves and hem, echoing the shape of the wishing well above: spirals, gentle arcs, and a single vertical line representing the boundary between realms. The robe fastened at my collarbone with a crescent-shaped clasp of polished moonstone, the stone's glow resonating faintly with my pendant. The garment didn't sparkle or shimmer...it breathed. Quietly. With the old power of Elarion.

Holden's garments were simpler, out of respect for tradition.

As a human, he couldn't wear the robes of rank or lineage, but he was granted a tailored traveler's mantle of lightweight, charcoal-grey, and reinforced with Dweller-woven fibers that adjusted to the temperature and terrain.

It draped over his shoulders like a cross between a cloak and a long vest, marked only by a thin silver border representing sanctioned passage into Elarion. The mantle didn't glow, but it caught the ambient light. Beneath it he wore dark clothing with practical clean lines, nothing showy. Humans weren't allowed in Elarion without exception, so Holden was meant to blend and not command attention. His attire reflected quiet strength and respect.

Vex trotted ahead of us through the town square and then up the moonlit hill toward the festival clearing. The portal lay inside the ancient wishing well. Weylan, our hot air balloon operator, and Sparks, our mechanic, were actually Dwellers whom Calderis allowed to live in Wishville as my eyes in the sky and ears on the ground.

Other than them, only a reclusive hermit Dweller outcast named Alden knew it existed, but he stayed in the Whisperwoods unless we needed his help to track something in exchange for everyone leaving him alone. He preferred to communicate with our park ranger, Tiana Ellison, because he trusted her more than us after his banishment. Only Holden, Calderis, and I were allowed to use the portal. And then there was LuLu, of course. Vaerion still believed LuLu's memory had been erased, so she had agreed to stay up top.

Holden kept close beside me, his hand brushing mine, grounding me each time. "You sure Calderis wants us meeting him *there*?" he whispered.

"He said the boundary stirred this morning. If anyone felt it besides me, it's him."

"And Vaerion?" Holden asked.

I shrugged. "If the tunnels Maggie found connect in any way to the outer caverns, he needs to know before the wrong Dwellers find out."

Holden nodded grimly. "Then let's go."

Vex hopped onto the stone ledge. *Brace yourselves*, he warned, as I said the words in ancient Dweller tongue that would open the gate deep in the well and allow us to transport to another world. We held hands and stepped over the ledge. The air shimmered faintly, like heat ripples, then the gate parted just enough for us to pass through. No flash or sound, just the world gently folding aside until we landed on moss in Elarion.

We stepped into a silver-blue glow, lit by bioluminescent vines trailing from the ceiling like starlight spilled into threads. Pools of shimmering water reflected mineral arches that looked grown instead of carved. Soft mist drifted through the air, carrying the faint scent of riverstone and moonleaf.

Elarion was a realm built of light and breath and memory.

Holden stared, wide-eyed. It wasn't his first visit, but still not something a human ever got used to. "It's like walking inside the northern lights," he whispered.

"Yeah," I said softly. "It is."

Calderis stepped out from between two pillars of rootstone, the gentle luminescence catching on the lines of his face. He wore the traditional garb of an Enforcer, a uniform that looked carved rather than sewn. His long coat, woven from obsidian-thread rootfiber, fell in sharp fluid lines, black as the deep caverns and etched with faint silver sigils along the sleeves and spine. These markings weren't decorative; they denoted training, lineage, and the vows he'd taken.

Under the coat, his fitted tunic and trousers were dark charcoal with the sheen of polished stone. His boots were reinforced with the same mineral-infused leather used in ceremonial armor. Nothing about his clothing glittered or shouted. Instead, it projected a quiet, formidable authority like a shadow with a heartbeat, perfectly at home in Elarion's light.

"You came," he said.

"Of course we did," Holden replied. "You said the boundary stirred."

Calderis nodded. "Vaerion waits."

Holden tensed. "Great."

Calderis turned to me. "Are you ready?"

"No," I said honestly. "But take me anyway."

We walked together along a bridge of pale stone, smooth as bone and threaded with faintly glowing veins. Water rushed far below, fed by underground rivers whose currents lit up like blue fireflies in motion. Dwellers passed us quietly, some nodding respectfully, while others glanced away. Humans still made many of them uneasy. Holden, in particular, with his badge-like bearing and protective presence was a lot. They accepted him in Elarion only because Vaerion had decreed him part of The Covenant Three.

The Council Chamber stood at the heart of Elarion, where the light ran deepest. We stepped through the crystal doors into the hollow hall, like the inside of a bell carved from moonstone. It rose from the cavern floor like a natural crown, spiraled crystal columns arching upward and interlocking above us. Thin channels of silver light ran through the stone like veins. The Chamber's walls weren't decorated, they *were* the decoration, each twist and layer formed over centuries of mineral and magic.

Inside, the chamber widened into an immense circle. Seats grown from the stone itself curved in a ring along the outer wall. Each Elder's seat bore a natural pattern unique to their lineage: amber flecks, pale fractures, and shimmering rootstone trails. The floor held a single symbol embedded in soft light, a stylized well with four points around it, the ancient marker of harmony between realms.

And in the center, the Guardian's platform waited.

I had stood on that platform before. Each time felt like standing inside a held breath. Vaerion sat opposite the entrance, tall and still as carved obsidian, dressed in deep midnight hues that mirrored the crystal shadows behind him. His presence always felt like the room adjusting to accommodate gravity.

"Lyra Wells," he said, his voice full of authority. "You bring news."

Holden stayed close behind me, his hand hovering just near mine. Calderis took his place beside his father, his shoulders squared and tense. Their relationship had been strained ever since he decided to become an Enforcer instead of following in his father's footsteps as an Elder.

I stepped onto the center platform. "Chief Elder," I began. "Something human-side has been uncovered. Something that may connect to the old tunnels in the outer caverns."

Vaerion's gaze sharpened. "Explain."

"During the 1984 library renovation, Maggie Winslow found a hidden cavity inside the archive wall, with hollow tunnels beneath. Inside the cupboard, she placed a box for her daughter, Clara. We found it yesterday."

I told him everything: the hollow wall, the hidden stairs, Maggie's map, Teagan's memories, the letter, and the tunnel angled toward the mountain ridge. Vaerion listened without blinking. Their silence was a tool rather than a void.

When I finished, he lifted one hand slightly. "The tunnels beyond the ridge," he said slowly, "were once open routes between Elarion and the outer caverns. They were sealed generations ago."

"Not all of them," Calderis murmured.

Vaerion's gaze slid toward him. "One should know better than to speak assumptions, my son."

Calderis straightened. "I don't speak assumptions. I speak evidence. I walked the outer boundary this morning. There were fresh disturbances. Someone traveled those passages."

Holden stiffened. "Could it be human?"

"The passages, maybe," Vaerion said, "but human bodies do not tolerate the pressure of the unshielded caverns. If Maggie Winslow charted the tunnels, then it is unlikely she found the caverns and survived."

My stomach churned. "She did go missing, never to be found.

People assumed she ran away. Do you think she's somewhere down here?"

Vaerion studied me, and I could feel the weight of centuries behind his eyes. "There are numerous caverns and rebels afoot. Anything is possible."

Cold prickled down my back. "Alive or dead, her daughter Clara deserves to know the truth."

"Maggie's box and letter might be the first key," Calderis added quietly.

Holden stepped forward, breaking the unspoken rule of keeping his distance in the chamber. "So, what does that mean for Lyra now? For the town? Someone sealed that space and the secret stairs are still hidden to us all. If someone is moving in those tunnels—"

"—then both realms are in danger," Vaerion finished, his voice commanding and firm.

The room went still, the bioluminescence dimming a fraction.

"You summoned me here to warn me?" I asked softly.

"No," Vaerion said. "I summoned you because you are the bridge between realms, and because your mother's path may soon become your own if you're not careful."

Was that a warning...or a threat? "I gave an oath when I accepted my role as Guardian." My heart twisted painfully since my mother had also gone missing while in this role. I hadn't told the Council that my mother was still alive because I wasn't sure what that meant yet. "What is the Council's position?" I asked.

From the shadows, one Elder finally spoke, a woman with shimmering pale hair and amber-flecked eyes. "We agree," she said. "Someone must return to the outer caverns. Someone who can walk both worlds."

She meant me.

Holden stepped in front of me without thinking. "Absolutely not—"

Vaerion lifted one hand, and Holden fell reluctantly silent.

"Lyra Wells," Vaerion said, "if the tunnels beneath Wishville connect to the ridge caverns and someone is using them, then both realms remain vulnerable. The treaty relies on humans and Dwellers not crossing paths, with authorized exceptions, of course." He paused. "A Guardian cannot turn away from such a threat. The tunnels must be explored, the caverns searched, and the new breaches sealed once more."

My pendant throbbed once, and I immediately thought of my mother. Was she sending me a message or possibly a warning? I frowned.

Holden's voice was raw. "She's not doing this alone."

Vaerion regarded him for a moment, then inclined his head. "She will not."

Calderis stepped forward beside me. "I will accompany her. You are human. It is too dangerous for you if we find a cavern. Lyra is half human; therefore, her risk is less. I am the logical choice of escort."

Holden bristled, but we all knew it was the only choice.

Vaerion's gaze returned to me. "For tonight, you return to the human world. Do not disturb the tunnels yet. Learn more on the human side. We will investigate Dweller activity. When the time comes, Calderis will let you know."

The chamber dimmed slightly, a sign the Council was finished.

Calderis touched my arm gently. Holden moved to my other side. Surrounded by both of them, with the Council's decree echoing in my bones, I felt the weight of Maggie's path settle completely onto my shoulders.

Alive or dead, it was time we found out the truth.

CHAPTER
Five

BY THE TIME morning light crept through my bedroom curtains, I'd gotten maybe—*maybe*—two hours of sleep. Elarion dreams never really let go; they hummed beneath my skin long after I left the realm.

Holden hadn't slept either. He'd stayed until almost dawn, sitting with me on the couch, talking in quiet circles about dangerous tunnels, rebels, old maps, and Elders with strong opinions. When he finally left for his shift, he kissed the top of my head and said, 'Text me the second you get to the library.'

So, I did. **Heading there now.**

He sent back: **No surprises.**

I make no promises, I thought.

Vex stretched dramatically across the kitchen counter as I slipped on my hiking boots and grabbed my pack to head outside.

You're going back to the library, he observed. *Where the box is. And where trouble usually likes to nap until someone pokes it.*

"Trouble needs to get a hobby," I muttered.

Fenrin wound around my legs, her tail brushing my calves. She always got clingy when she sensed danger. It didn't matter if LuLu or I ordered her to stay home. She would simply shapeshift into another animal and follow whomever she was worried about anyway.

I scratched behind her ear. "I'll be back soon," I said. "Guard the house. No following me. I mean it."

She pounced off, looking over her shoulders as if echoing my earlier thoughts, *I make no promises.*

The ride into town on my bike felt sharper and colder. Missing leaves clattered along Main Street like scattered clues. Wishville was starting to wake. Willa Hartman flipped chairs off tables at *The Wishbone Café*, Maisie Flint swept her porch with militant ferocity, Mayor Doug Delaney jogged out of *Town Hall* with Connie Hale by his side, clutching a binder like it might explode.

Deceptively normal.

I locked my bike outside the *Maple Hollow Library* and stepped inside. The comforting scents of dust, ink, and sunlight on old carpets hit me like a hug I didn't have time to enjoy. Clara stood at the research table, surrounded by open reference books, notepads, and a thermos the size of a toddler. She looked up when she heard me, and relief softened her whole face.

"Lyra. Thank goodness." Her voice wavered. "I've been practically vibrating since I got here."

"That's my line," I said, walking over.

She gestured toward her office. "The box is locked up safe. I checked on it twice, just in case the floor developed a trap door overnight."

"Wishville has limits," I said. "Mostly."

She took a deep breath. "Okay, update me."

So I did, leaving out the parts about portals or Elarion or ancient council chambers. I just told her about the pieces she *could* hear safely.

"We talked to Gerald Teagan," I said, pulling the envelope from my coat. "He remembered your mom. He remembered the tunnel. And he gave me this."

Clara's breath caught as she read the handwriting. *Her mother's handwriting*. "Oh," she whispered. "It never gets old seeing her handwriting. It must be important if she wrote it down and addressed it to herself, like she wanted to make sure to document it so it wouldn't be forgotten."

I swallowed. "I haven't opened it yet. It's yours, Clara."

But she pushed it back toward me with trembling fingers. "No," she said. "If she wanted me to read it, she would've addressed it to me. It has her name on it only. I don't think she wanted anyone to see this, but we need to open it if we're going to find out the truth."

"Okay," I whispered, sliding a finger under the seal.

But before I opened it, the library door banged open. Both of us jumped. LuLu burst in, her wavy hair wild and scarf askew, looking like she'd run the entire length of Maple Hollow Road.

"Emergency!" she gasped, slamming her notebook onto the table. "And by emergency, I mean maybe not *life-threatening* but definitely *plot-thickening*."

Clara blinked. "What happened?"

"I went back to the hardware store to get more info from Renee," LuLu said. "And guess who showed up while I was there?"

Clara and I exchanged glances.

"Henry McAlister?" I guessed.

"Worse," LuLu said. "Henry's *cousin*."

Clara's eyes widened. "Colin?"

LuLu nodded grimly. "Yep. Colin 'I Collect Town Secrets Like Trading Cards' McAlister. And you know what he asked Renee?"

"What?" I asked, already bracing myself.

"Whether anyone came by yesterday asking about the 1984 library renovation."

My stomach dipped. "He asked *that*?"

"Oh yeah," LuLu said, flipping open her notebook, "and when Renee said *yes*, he demanded to know who. She mentioned us. He left without buying anything and headed straight here."

Clara stepped back. "Why would Colin care about something from that long ago?"

"For the same reason Henry cared," LuLu said. "The McAlisters know more about this town's dirty laundry than anyone. If Maggie found something important, something someone wanted hidden? They probably knew about it."

I exhaled slowly. "Okay. So, Henry's involved. Question is, what does he know, and how much is Colin trying to cover up?"

LuLu snapped her notebook shut. "We need to open that envelope."

Clara nodded, her throat bobbing. "Do it quickly so I'm in the loop and then get out of here before he arrives. I'll handle him."

My pulse fluttered as I peeled the envelope open, the old paper crackling in my hands. Inside was a single folded sheet of notebook paper, yellowed at the edges. Clara and LuLu leaned close. I unfolded it.

Maggie's handwriting spilled across the page—steady, sure, urgent.

> *If anyone is reading this, something has happened that I didn't stop in time. There is a passage under the library that leads east towards the ridge. I mapped only a portion before I met resistance. From someone who did not want it found.*

My skin prickled, but I kept reading.

> *If Clara is with her father, tell her I love her. And tell her I was close—so close—to proving I was right about the tunnels predating the town. But deeper in, there is an older path. I heard voices there. Voices! What kind of people live underground?*

Clara clutched my arm.

LuLu mouthed, *Holy—*

I continued.

Do not go down there alone. It's dangerous. Do not trust the planning board. And if you follow the tunnels, they branch off in many directions. There is one hidden path that leads all the way to a remote section of the mountain. If you reach it, do not go inside. Someone or something is in there. Inside the mountain! I'm too afraid to go in, but maybe someday.

By the time I reached the end, my hands were shaking.

I have to go. Someone is coming!
—Maggie Winslow

Silence swallowed the room.

LuLu sat back hard enough to rattle the table. "Well. That's not ominous at all."

Clara's hand flew to her mouth. "Everyone said my mother was crazy," she whispered. "Something was going on down there. She knew someone was following her. Did they find her and kidnap her? Could she possibly still be alive after all these years? Or did they kill her? I can't take the not-knowing. It's just awful."

I stared at the letter. Clara had no idea the person who was following her might not be human at all. Maggie hadn't just found a tunnel. She had found someone *inside* it. Someone who wanted her to stay, dead or alive. Someone who, forty years later, might still be walking the mountain caverns.

"We can't let you come with us," I said quietly, looking Clara in the eyes.

LuLu nodded. "Agreed."

Clara bristled. "Excuse me?"

"Clara," I said firmly, "your mother practically wrote 'danger ahead' in capital letters. Whomever she met in those tunnels hasn't been caught. That means they might still be out there." *And might not be human.*

Clara's eyes trembled. "I don't want to stay behind again. I've waited forty years for an answer."

"And you'll get one," I promised. "But first, we need to follow the tunnel. And that means going in prepared."

"But neither of you are detectives." Clara crossed her arms defiantly.

"No, but my boyfriend is the chief of police."

LuLu leaned in. "And I'm an investigative journalist who happens to be pretty tight with Detective Cal Deris."

Clara sighed. "Do you think they'll officially reopen my mother's case?"

"I think the box and the letter might be enough. I'll know more when I show everything to Holden and Cal."

Clara hesitated, as if torn between fear and fire. Finally, she nodded. "Fine. But I need updates. Constant updates."

"You'll get them," LuLu said.

I nodded, thinking, at least as many as we could safely give. Just then, my phone buzzed in my pocket. Holden. My stomach clenched when I read the text.

We need to talk. Some people are asking questions about you, LuLu, and Clara.

LuLu peered over my shoulder. "Oh," she said. "That's bad."

Clara read the text and swayed slightly. "What does that mean?"

I folded Maggie's letter hastily, knowing we had to get out of there. "It means," I said, steadying my voice, "that someone else just realized we're getting close."

And they're getting nervous.

The Wishville Police Station was all beige walls, humming fluorescents, and furniture that looked like it had been chosen specifically to make its patrons uncomfortable. Here we were after midnight, after WishFest, and after the kind of discoveries that didn't politely wait for office hours.

Holden stood at the main table with his jacket off, sleeves rolled up, and a legal pad already filling with notes in his neat, no-nonsense handwriting. Calderis leaned against the far wall, his arms crossed, and his human glamour perfectly intact but his attention sharpened in that unmistakable way that meant he was tracking more than one world at once. LuLu had claimed a chair, her notebook open and pen already tapping like it was impatient with the pace of reality.

And me? I stood there holding Maggie Winslow's box. Even under the station lights, it felt heavier than it had any right to be. "Sorry this was the only time we could meet," I said. "It's been a long day, juggling WishFest duties and cold cases."

"It's okay. I get it," Holden said, his voice calm but edged with purpose. "Let's start from the top. Lyra, tell us everything from the archive wall onward."

So, I did. I walked them through the hidden cavity, the box, Maggie's notebook, the map, the stone fragment, and Gerald Teagan's confession that the town had known something was wrong back in 1984—and chosen not to dig. When I finished, the room stayed quiet.

Holden blew out a slow breath. "That lines up with what I found tonight."

LuLu's head snapped up. "Found *how*?"

"Colin McAlister paid me a visit," Holden said flatly.

That earned him three identical looks of interest.

"Not subtle," I guessed. He must have gone straight to Holden instead of stopping by the library.

"Not even a little." Holden flipped the page on his legal pad. "He framed it as concern. Asked whether we were reopening any 'old business' tied to town infrastructure. Suggested Wishville didn't need rumors resurfacing."

"Which means he's worried," LuLu said. "People don't warn you away from nothing."

Calderis's gaze sharpened. "Did he mention the library?"

"No," Holden said. "Which tells me he's smart enough to avoid specifics."

"And arrogant enough to think you'd take the hint," I added.

Holden nodded once. "Exactly."

I set Maggie's box down on the table, the soft thud sounding far louder than it should have. "Then let's stop dancing around it. Maggie Winslow didn't run away. She was investigating ancient uncharted tunnels, and something was going on that someone clearly didn't want exposed. And now we have physical evidence."

He studied the box for a long moment. "Maggie's case was filed as a voluntary disappearance," he said quietly. "There were no signs of a struggle and no body found, so there was no pressure to pursue anything further. Back then, that was enough for the department to close ranks and move on."

LuLu's jaw tightened. "Convenient."

"Negligent," Holden corrected. Then he met my eyes. "But that changes now."

My chest loosened just a fraction.

"I'll reopen the case officially," he continued. "Missing person reclassified as suspicious disappearance pending investigation. The box, the map, and Teagan's statement give us cause."

Clara, I thought, *you were right to push.*

Calderis straightened slightly. "If the tunnels Maggie traced correspond to the outer routes, I will investigate quietly. Not all records of those paths are public knowledge, even in Elarion."

"Risk assessment," Holden said. "Not assumptions."

Calderis inclined his head. "Always."

LuLu flipped to a fresh page. "I can start cross-referencing town council minutes, zoning changes, and planning board records from the '80s forward. Patterns matter, especially when paperwork goes missing."

"Off the books," Holden said. "For now."

She grinned. "I wouldn't dream of publishing anything."

I opened Maggie's box and laid the contents out carefully: the notebook, the map, the soil sample, and the carved stone fragment.

Calderis's gaze lingered on the stone, his expression tightening just slightly. "That marker is not Elarion-made," he said. "It's boundary craft. Used on older paths meant to guide rather than invite."

"Guide who?" Holden asked.

Calderis paused. "Those who already knew where they were going. Secret passages."

A chill slipped down my spine. "The question is, were rebel Dwellers using the ancient tunnels forty years ago, or were humans down there back then? And if so, why? Could they still be using them today?"

Holden tapped his pen once. "Then here's how we divide this." He turned the legal pad so we could all see. "I handle the human side. Anyone who had authority or motive to suppress what Maggie found."

LuLu nodded. "I'll assist quietly. Anyone who might have had direct conflict with Maggie."

Calderis shifted his weight. "I will look into Dweller histories connected to outer passages. If someone from Elarion or beyond interfered by reopening them, I will know."

"And I'll coordinate," I said. "Between both sides, like Vaerion wanted. Clara stays protected, the box stays secured, and no one moves without checking in."

Holden's gaze softened just slightly. "You sure you're ready for this?"

I thought of Maggie's handwriting, of Clara holding the notebook like it was something alive, and of my own desire to figure out what happened to my own missing mother. "It doesn't matter if I am or not," I said honestly. "But I'm not turning away from my duty."

Calderis met my eyes. "Nor should you."

LuLu snapped her notebook shut. "So, we're agreed. We dig carefully."

"Figuratively." Holden nodded. "And we don't let Wishville bury this again."

I looked down at Maggie's box, and at the life she'd tried to preserve in notes and sketches and quiet warnings. "For forty years," I said softly, "this town pretended that Maggie was crazy and nothing was wrong." I closed the lid gently. "That ends now."

CHAPTER

Six

BY THE THIRD morning of Fall WishFest, Wishville had slipped into a familiar rhythm. Lanterns were still strung from the night before, chalkboard menus were still smudged with yesterday's specials, and locals moved a little slower, like they were already nostalgic for something that hadn't ended yet.

For everyone else, it was day three of cider and crafts.

For us, it was the first official morning of the investigation.

Which meant Wishville was about to stop being charming and start being honest.

The Twisted Loaf was already packed when I arrived. Betsy Plum's bakery always smelled like butter, sugar, and cinnamon. Wide-plank floors were dusted with flour, mismatched mugs hung from hooks, and the front window fogged with warmth even on crisp mornings like this one. A handwritten sign by the register read:

WELCOME WISHFEST-SLEEP-DEPRIVED LOCALS.
YES, WE HAVE EXTRA COFFEE.

The front bell jingled constantly as festival volunteers filtered in and out. They wore aprons over sweaters, with clipboards tucked under their arms, and their voices already raised with the day's logistics.

"Betsy, we're out of gluten-free scones again!" an employee said.

"That's because even people who refuse to eat gluten-free will try anything when cider gets involved," Betsy called back cheerfully without looking up from her icing.

The Wellies had already claimed their usual table near the front window, the one with maximum visibility and absolutely no privacy. Tilly was in the middle of shrugging out of her purple coat like she was shedding an identity. Belle stirred cream into her coffee with the calm, unwavering focus of a surgeon mid-procedure. And Dot was meticulously rearranging sugar packets into neat rows while muttering darkly about "supply chains," "festival waste," and something that sounded suspiciously like "accountability."

Dot spotted us first. "Well," she announced, her voice carrying cleanly across three tables and at least one pastry case, "if it isn't the entire town's power structure here before ten a.m."

Two heads turned. A muffin froze mid-bite.

Tilly leaned over the table, her eyes bright. "Is this official business or unofficial panic?"

"Both," I said, sliding into the bakery heat like I could burn the dread straight out of my skin.

Belle's gaze drifted to Calderis as he stepped in behind me, tall and imposing and clearly unsure what to do with his hands. She assessed him in a single, thorough glance, then nodded once. "You look like you don't trust baked goods," she said.

"I am undecided," Calderis replied gravely.

Belle took a slow sip of her coffee, satisfied. "Wise. This place smells friendly, but that's how they get you."

Dot shoved a sugar packet back into alignment. "If he's here, something's wrong."

"Or very right," Tilly added cheerfully. "Sometimes destiny comes with pastries."

Calderis blinked. "Does it?"

"Rarely," Belle said. "But when it does, it's usually sticky."

I sighed and leaned back, bracing myself. "Can we order before you start diagnosing my soul?"

Tilly patted my arm. "Too late. You're tense."

Dot squinted at me. "You're carrying secrets."

Belle tilted her head. "And you didn't bring them croissants. *Not* wise."

I closed my eyes briefly. "This is why I drink coffee."

Calderis studied the pastry case like it might explode. "Which is safest?"

Belle pointed. "None of them, but that one will hurt you the least."

He arched a brow and moved toward the counter, choosing a different one.

Dot gasped, slapping a hand over her mouth.

Belle shrugged. "Don't say I didn't warn you."

Tilly clasped her hands together. "Oh, I like him. He lives life on the edge."

Holden had claimed a corner booth, his jacket draped over the back of the bench and two empty mugs already pushed aside. I sat next to him. Calderis sat across from him, his posture perfectly straight and hands folded as he studied the croissant he'd chosen like it might reveal secrets if approached correctly. LuLu slid in beside Calderis a moment later, balancing a tray overloaded with pastries and her notebook already open.

"This," she announced, setting everything down, "is our Preliminary Suspect Universe."

I sighed into my coffee. "Why does it not surprise me that you named it."

"Of course I named it," she said brightly. "I also color-coded it. You're welcome."

Holden leaned forward. "All right. Let's hear it."

LuLu flipped her notebook around. "Human side first. Here are the obvious players." She ticked them off with practiced ease.

"Henry McAlister, planning board intern during the 1984 library renovation, and later a full-blown development menace. Motive: suppressing anything that could expose hidden land features. He was against the quarry expansion."

"Colin McAlister," Holden added. "Modern pressure arm. He knows just enough to be dangerous."

"Gerald Teagan," LuLu continued. "The foreman of the quarry expansion and the library renovation back then. He's not a suspect, but definitely a witness. He knew Maggie was onto something."

"And the planning board at large," Holden added. "Collective apathy is still culpability. Ron Maddox was the police chief in 1984. He filed a suspiciously thin final report after Maggie disappeared and then retired shortly after. Possibly to protect himself or someone else. Also, Evelyn Hart is still the town's archivist and keeper of old town blueprints. She controlled access to all historical building plans during the 1984 renovation. She could have known Maggie was requesting documents and piecing something together. She could fear Maggie's finding would expose something she falsified decades earlier."

"I did some digging as well," I said. "Maggie threatened to report Randall Pike, the Historical Society President back then, for mismanaging Historical Society funds. He was for the quarry expansion and making money. He believed she was ruining his career. And then there's Howard Kline, the former library groundskeeper. Maggie reported him for mishandling rare books in the basement collection. Howard almost lost his job because of her complaints. And finally, Maggie's academic rival, Professor Bernice Galloway. Maggie was a history teacher and Bernice a history professor. She was jealous of Maggie and always competing to discover the next great historical find."

LuLu nodded. "So, what now?"

Holden rubbed his jaw. "Today, we observe."

Calderis finally spoke. "I walked the perimeter of the old quarry before dawn."

We all looked at him.

"And?" I asked.

"The ground remembers disturbance," he said calmly. "There are sealed paths there. Old ones. Human tools reinforced them, but they were not originally human-made, which confirms our suspicions."

My pendant warmed faintly against my chest, letting me know I was on to something. "So, Maggie was right," I murmured.

"She often was," a gentle voice said from behind us.

We turned.

Dorothy Rourke stood at the counter like she'd always belonged there, a pink bakery box tucked neatly under one arm, her cardigan buttoned to perfection, and her snow-white hair pulled back in a low clip that suggested both order and stubbornness. Her smile was warm and unassuming.

"Oh," she said mildly. "Am I interrupting?"

Before anyone could answer, Clara appeared as if summoned by the sound of her name, her eyes lighting up. "Dorothy!"

Dorothy's smile deepened. "Of course I ran into you here," she said fondly. "Betsy makes the only cinnamon rolls worth leaving the house for before nine. Everything else can wait."

Across the bakery, Dot's head snapped up. "Dorothy!" she called, already halfway out of her chair. "Over here!"

Dorothy laughed, genuinely delighted, and lifted a finger in Clara's direction. "One moment, sweetheart. I've been spotted."

She detoured immediately, making a beeline for the Wellies' table like it was a scheduled stop on her morning route. She kissed Dot on the cheek, then Tilly, then Belle in quick succession, like they had a standing appointment.

"You three still running the town from bakery tables?" she teased.

"Someone has to," Belle said serenely. "These youngsters keep mishandling everything."

Dorothy nodded gravely. "That tracks."

Tilly leaned in. "We've already issued three unofficial opinions and one warning about baked goods."

"Good," Dorothy said. "I was worried you'd gone soft."

Dot patted Dorothy's hand. "You're late."

"I had errands," Dorothy replied. "And opinions."

Satisfied, the Wellies released her back into the wild.

Dorothy finally returned to Clara, her expression softening in a way that had nothing to do with age and everything to do with love. "And there's my girl," she said, kissing Clara's cheek and pulling her into a tight one-arm hug. "How's my favorite librarian holding up?"

"As well as possible," Clara admitted, her voice honest but steady.

Dorothy nodded, as if that was exactly the answer she'd expected. Without asking, she set the pink bakery box squarely on our table, nudging aside a notebook in the process. "You can't solve anything on an empty stomach," she said briskly. "That's how mistakes happen, and poor decisions, and unnecessary heroics."

Holden blinked. "We weren't—"

Dorothy gave him a look.

He stopped talking.

She glanced around the table, taking in the notebooks, the half-drunk coffee, the tension humming beneath the surface, and the way Holden's posture sharpened instead of relaxed, like a man bracing for impact. "Well," she said gently, folding her hands over the box. "This feels important."

Behind her, Belle was already reaching for a napkin. "I told you she'd know."

Tilly nodded. "She always does."

Dot sighed happily. "Cinnamon rolls *and* emotional clarity. What a morning."

Dorothy's smile remained warm...but her eyes missed nothing.

"It is," Clara said, knowing what we were up to because we'd kept her informed, as promised. "But you don't have to worry. They're just talking through old records."

Dorothy's gaze settled on Maggie's box tucked beneath the table. Her smile never wavered. "I'm glad," she said softly. "Your mother hated loose ends."

Something tightened in my chest, a mother's love I gravely missed. I was so glad Clara had Dorothy. She radiated warmth that wrapped around you without asking permission.

"I raised her to finish what she starts," Dorothy continued, squeezing Clara's hand. "Even if it takes forty years."

Holden stood politely. "Ms. Rourke, it's good to finally meet you. I'm Chief Thorn."

"Oh, I know who you are," Dorothy said with a twinkle. "Maggie would've liked you. She trusted people who listened."

"Detective Cal Deris." Calderis inclined his head. "You cared for Clara?"

"I did," Dorothy said simply. "After her father passed, she needed someone steady. I was the closest thing she had left to family. Children don't need heroes. They need consistency."

LuLu blinked rapidly as if fighting back tears.

Dorothy opened the bakery box and held out a pastry to Calderis. "You look like you forget to eat enough. Big serious man like you needs some tender loving care, I'm thinking."

LuLu coughed, her eyes now twinkling.

He hesitated, then accepted it solemnly. "Thank you."

"You're welcome, dear."

I had watched Dorothy Rourke grow into a lovely seventy-year-old, retired, deeply kind woman like my Wellies. The woman who had packed Clara's lunches, taught her how to drive, and showed up to every library fundraiser with baked goods and quiet pride. It made me miss my mother and relate to Clara with a father who was gone and mother who was missing.

The Wellies were my Dorothys.

"I won't hover," Dorothy said after a moment, "but Clara, I'm around if you need anything. You know that, right?"

"I know," Clara said, her voice thick. "Thank you for everything."

Dorothy smiled at her like a mother would. "Lyra, you take care of her," she looked at me knowingly, "and yourself, dear."

"I will," I promised.

She left a few minutes later, the bell over the door chiming softly behind her. The table felt emptier...until the Wellies descended upon us before leaving.

Dot said with absolute certainty, "Dorothy Rourke is a blessing."

Tilly nodded solemnly. "That woman's a saint."

Belle sipped her to-go coffee. "And a major asset to this town. You don't keep that many committees functioning without divine intervention or a very firm calendar."

LuLu glanced between them. "She's lovely."

"She raised Clara," I said. "When no one else stepped up."

Dot sniffed. "That tracks."

Calderis inclined his head. "That bond is strong."

"And uncomplicated," Holden added, his gaze flicking to me. "Which is rare."

I paused, my mug halfway to my mouth. For a split second, I wasn't sure we were still talking about Dorothy.

Holden had been patient...mostly. But patience had limits, and I'd canceled more dinners than I'd kept lately. The investigation had to come first. It always did. Justice for Maggie mattered more than missed reservations.

Our romance would still be there afterward...I hoped.

I wrapped both hands around my mug, letting the heat ground me, and deliberately changed the subject. "Okay. What's next?"

Holden straightened, his expression shifting from casual to focused. "We start watching. Quietly."

Tilly leaned forward immediately. "Define quietly."

"Without clipboards," Holden said, adding, "or civilians."

Dot frowned. "That's restrictive."

"That means no investigating on your own by confronting suspects in public," he said.

Belle sighed. "You're taking all the fun out of this."

Vex flicked his tail beneath the table. *They will ignore him*, he observed calmly.

"I know," I murmured for his ears only.

The investigation had officially begun. And Wishville—true to form—was about to remember everything it preferred to forget.

By midafternoon, the sky had settled into that pale Vermont blue that made everything look deceptively calm. Leaves skittered across sidewalks. Shop windows glowed. The festival banners still fluttered like nothing beneath them had ever re-opened.

Town Hall sat at the edge of Main Street, a square brick building with white trim and an attitude of quiet authority. The steps were crowded with festival volunteers arguing over logistics like the fate of the world depended on hay bale placement and lantern spacing.

"Chief Thorn!" a woman called as we approached, a clipboard tucked under her arm. "We still on for the lantern release tonight?"

Holden didn't break stride. "As planned."

"Good," she said, relieved. Holden met me on the front steps. His sunglasses were pushed up on top of his head, and his expression was set in what I'd come to recognize as official patience, which told me he expected resistance. "You ready?" he asked.

"Born ready," I said.

He snorted softly and held the door for me.

Inside, the building hummed with low-level activity. Clerks moved between offices, the clack of keyboards in the background, and the soft murmur of voices behind closed doors. We signed in, flashed our credentials where necessary, and were waved toward the records office in the back.

The records vault was less dramatic than it sounded. There were rows of metal filing cabinets, rolling shelves, and a single long table sat beneath a flickering fluorescent light. A clerk named Suzie, sixtyish and sharp-eyed, sat chewing gum like it was a personal vendetta.

She handed Holden a clipboard. "You've got an hour. And I'm not pulling anything that's sealed."

"We won't need sealed," Holden said mildly.

I shot him a look.

He smiled thinly. "We'll start with what's missing."

Suzie narrowed her eyes, then shrugged. "Whatever floats your boat." She left us alone.

I dropped my bag onto the table. "You really think there'll be gaps?"

"I'd be shocked if there weren't," Holden said, already sliding open a drawer. "Small towns don't erase history. They just misplace it."

We worked quietly at first, looking through renovation permits, inspection logs, and planning board approvals. I took notes while Holden cross-checked dates against Maggie's notebook.

"That's strange," I murmured.

"What?"

"This inspection report," I said, tapping the page. "It references a structural anomaly near the library foundation, but there's no follow-up. No remediation order."

Holden frowned. "There should've been."

"There was," I said, flipping to Maggie's notes. "She logged a secondary inspection two weeks later."

"And it's not here," he finished.

"Someone pulled it."

Holden's jaw tightened. "Or never filed it."

The fluorescent light buzzed overhead. "That wasn't apathy," I said quietly. "That was intent."

Holden nodded. "Which narrows our list."

We were mid-shelf when footsteps echoed down the corridor, unhurried and confident.

"Chief Thorn," a familiar voice drawled. "Imagine my surprise."

Holden didn't look up. "Colin."

Colin McAlister stepped into the vault like he owned it, wearing a tailored jacket, polished shoes, and a smile sharpened just enough to count as a warning. His gaze landed on me. "Lyra Wells," he said pleasantly. "Enjoying your civic duties?"

"I enjoy accuracy," I replied. "This seems like the place for it."

His smile didn't falter. "Town Hall records can be...misleading."

"So I'm learning." Holden closed a drawer with deliberate care. "What brings you here?"

"Concern," Colin said smoothly. "There's talk you're reopening old matters. Things that were resolved decades ago."

"*Resolved* isn't the word I'd use," Holden replied.

Colin sighed. "Wishville thrives on stability. Digging into the past risks—"

"—discovering the truth," I finished.

His eyes met mine, assessing. "Truth is subjective."

"Evidence isn't," Holden said.

A beat passed, then Colin smiled wider. "Just thought I'd remind you both that WishFest brings a lot of attention to town. Investors. Tourists. The last thing we need is panic over rumors."

"As *Chair* of WishFest, I don't need reminding, Mr. McAlister."

Holden stepped closer. "Then it's a good thing we're dealing in facts."

Colin held his gaze, then inclined his head. "Of course." He turned to leave, pausing just long enough to add, "Careful what you uncover. Some foundations weren't meant to be disturbed." The door closed behind him, and the room felt colder.

"Well," I said. "That was friendly."

Holden let out a slow breath. "That was a threat."

"Or fear," I countered. "He doesn't know what we have."

"Not yet," Holden agreed. "But he knows we're close."

My phone buzzed. A text from LuLu.

Saw Colin heading into Town Hall. Thought you'd want to know. Also, someone just paid cash to pull old quarry maps from the public kiosk.

I showed Holden.

He swore under his breath. "All right. Time check."

"Twenty minutes left of our hour," I said.

"Then we copy everything we can."

We worked fast after that, photographing documents, flagging dates, and noting inconsistencies. When our time was up, Suzie reappeared and eyed our stack of notes.

"Find what you were looking for?" she asked.

"Enough," Holden said.

Outside, the afternoon had shifted. Clouds were rolling in, and the wind was picking up. WishFest music drifted faintly down from the clearing up the hill, tinny, cheerful, and completely unaware.

Calderis waited by the stone steps, his arms folded and gaze fixed on the tree line beyond the parking lot.

"Did you feel something?" I asked. Dwellers could feel vibrations from far away.

He nodded. "Someone moved today. Near the quarry."

"Human?" Holden asked.

"Unclear," Calderis replied. "But the stone was disturbed recently."

"Which lines up with—" I started to say.

"Whoever pulled those maps," Holden finished.

I looked back at *Town Hall*. The brick, the flags, and the quiet certainty of a building that assumed it would always stand. "We're narrowing the case," I said. "They're starting to feel it."

Calderis met my eyes. "Pressure reveals fractures."

"And fractures reveal what's buried," Holden finished.

The truth rarely came from where you expected, but it always came. And Wishville was running out of places to hide it.

CHAPTER
Seven

BY EVENING, the wind had shifted. It came off the lake sharper than it had that morning, threading cold through the gaps in my jacket and carrying the damp, mineral scent of water and fallen leaves.

I took the long way to *Mistfall Overlook*, following the narrow dirt path that hugged the edge of the lake instead of cutting back through Main Street. Festival noise drifted faintly through the trees. Laughter, a fiddle, and the distant thunk of a cider press sounded far away.

As I walked, voices drifted up the path behind me. Dot's unmistakable cadence carried over the water. "—I'm just saying, if the lanterns tilt again, someone's going in the lake."

"That's tradition," Tilly said. "Like taxes."

Belle replied, dry as ever, "If anyone falls in, it'll be a man. They don't respect gravity."

Their laughter faded as they must have turned back toward town, returning to the lantern committee like it was a sacred calling.

Wishville never really stopped watching itself. Holden's voice replayed in my head as I walked. Missing inspection reports. Altered quarry maps. McAlister watching you watch him. It wasn't proof of anything yet, but there was enough to make the ground feel unsteady beneath my boots.

Mistfall Overlook wasn't much to look at if you didn't know it. A low stone barrier, a worn wooden bench, and a slope of rock and roots that dropped down to the lake. But the view opened wide, with dark water stretching out under the dimming sky, and mist curling along the surface like breath.

I stopped at the edge and rested my hands on the stone, letting the quiet settle.

"I'm guessing you always come here when things get complicated. I do the same."

I turned, my heart jumping despite myself.

Dorothy Rourke stood a few yards back on the path, her coat buttoned to her chin and scarf wrapped neatly around her neck. Her snow-white hair caught the low light, and her smile was gentle.

"Dorothy," I said on a whoosh of air. "I didn't hear you."

She laughed softly. "That's because I walk quietly. Old habit from my teaching days. Clara used to call me her 'shadow mom.'" She stepped beside me, careful on the uneven ground, and looked out over the lake. For a moment, neither of us spoke. The water lapped softly against the rocks below, rhythmic and patient.

"This place helped me think," she said finally. "After Maggie went missing. It still does, I suppose."

"It's good for that," I replied. "Thinking."

"And remembering," she added. "Even when you don't want to."

The mist thickened as the light faded, the shoreline blurring at the edges. I had the strange sense that if I looked away too long, the lake might swallow the view entirely.

"How is Clara holding up?" Dorothy asked. "She doesn't want me to worry about her, but I do. She's not my own, but she might as well have been. Mothers never stop worrying about their babies.

"She's strong," I said. "But this is reopening things she thought she'd made peace with."

Dorothy nodded slowly. "Time doesn't make peace. It just teaches you how to live beside the ache." She folded her hands together, her fingers interlacing and unlacing again, like she was working through a thought she'd carried a long time. "Maggie never learned how to do that," she continued. "Live beside things, I mean. She wanted answers and never stopped searching for the truth."

I glanced at her. "You knew her well."

"I loved her like a sister," Dorothy said simply. "She had a family. A purpose. Everything I wanted for her. I was proud of her, even when she scared me."

"Scared you how?" I asked.

She smiled a little rueful. "Curiosity can be dangerous, especially when one becomes obsessed with something. She wasn't around much at the end. Her husband, Larry, wasn't happy about it."

Interesting. It made me wonder if anyone had ever looked into the grieving widower. The wind stirred, lifting the mist in pale ribbons across the water. "Did she ever tell you about her work?" I asked.

Dorothy shook her head. "No. We were both teachers and talked about everything, including her marriage troubles, but she kept her research work to herself."

I thought of Maggie's notebook. Her careful handwriting. The way her notes grew more urgent near the end.

Dorothy paused in thought, then said, "Bernice Galloway was determined to discover what Maggie was up to at any cost."

"The professor at the University of Vermont in Burlington?" Her academic rival, who was already on our radar.

Dorothy nodded. "Former professor at UVM. She now works at Wishville Community College. We all went to high school together. Larry, Maggie, Bernice, and me. Maggie and Bernice have always been in competition with each other. It got worse in later years when Maggie became a better historian as a high school history teacher than Bernice, who couldn't cut it at the university. The pressure from Bernice got to be too much in the end. I can't blame Maggie for running away. I just don't see how she could leave Larrry and little Clara behind." She shook her head sadly.

"That's why we reopened this case. There were too many suspicious things that were never looked into around the time Maggie disappeared. If something bad did happen to her, she didn't deserve that," I said.

Dorothy's hand brushed my arm, warm and steady. "No. She deserved to grow old and complain about town council meetings like the rest of us."

I smiled despite myself.

Footsteps crunched farther up the path. Holden emerged from the trees, his jacket zipped and his presence unmistakably solid against the shifting dark. He slowed when he saw us, reading the moment before stepping closer.

"Evening," he said, nodding to Dorothy.

"Chief Thorn," she replied warmly. "Still keeping everyone safe?"

"Doing my best," he said.

Her gaze moved between us, perceptive without prying. "I won't intrude," she said. "I just wanted to check on Lyra and remind her to eat something that isn't festival food."

"I appreciate that," I said, and meant it.

Dorothy smiled, then turned back toward the path. "Good night, both of you. And Lyra...thank you for watching over Clara. Maggie would've trusted you." She disappeared into the trees, her footsteps fading so completely it was like she'd never been there at all.

Holden watched the path for a long moment before speaking. "Dot will be telling everyone by morning that Dorothy checked on you," he said.

"She checks on everyone," I replied.

He nodded. "Exactly."

Calderis joined us without a sound, appearing at my other side like he'd always been there. Sparks and Weylan emerged shortly after him.

"The quarry is quiet," Calderis said.

"I checked with Alden," Sparks said, electricity snapping between his fingertips. "The woods are still."

"The sky is calm," Weylan added. "Clear with low wind on my last ride."

"Calm skies, still woods, and quiet quarries should be a good thing," I said, "yet I can't shake the feeling that a storm is about to break loose."

"That's not comforting," Holden muttered.

"No," Calderis agreed. "It is not."

The lanterns across the lake flickered as the wind suddenly picked up, their reflections shattering and reforming on the water's surface. Day three of WishFest was ending. And somewhere beneath Wishville, beneath forty years of silence, something stirred.

The call came just as I was unlacing my boots. Holden's name lit up my phone, followed immediately by that familiar, unwelcome prickle at the base of my spine, warning me that something had shifted.

"We've got movement," he said without preamble. "And you're going to want to see this."

Ten minutes later, I was back out in the night, my jacket zipped and hair still damp from the lake mist. WishFest lights glowed through the trees like nothing was wrong. The Historical Society had their meetings in the old *Farleigh House,* a 19th century house donated decades ago by the family. There were two public rooms downstairs, with offices upstairs, along with basement and attic archives.

There were monthly meetings in the front parlor, with closed-door committee sessions upstairs. The Town Hall was where official, legal, and current documents were held. The library was a research access point and bridge between the Town Hall and the Historical Society. While the Historical Society served as an off-site storage for original documents, maps, and plans of intent.

Tonight, the back annex of the *Farleigh House* sat dark except for one lit window. A temporary sign taped to the door read, **ARCHIVES—AUTHORIZED ACCESS ONLY**, which might as well have said someone didn't want to be interrupted.

Holden met me at the steps. Calderis stood a little apart with his gaze fixed on the treeline beyond the parking lot. LuLu's car idled nearby, her headlights off.

"What happened?" I asked.

"A records clerk flagged a late-night access request," Holden said. "Original handwritten ledgers, early funding records, planning sketches, marginal notes, etc. The kind no one touches unless they're nervous."

LuLu shut off her car and climbed out. "My mother always says nothing good happens late at night."

"Follow me." Holden led the way.

Inside, the annex smelled like dust, moth balls, and mildew in the long narrow hall. An old lightbulb flickered from the low ceiling with exposed beams, and the uneven floorboards creaked when you walked on them. The man inside the records room froze when we stepped in. He was tall, in his late sixties, with thinning gray hair and a jacket that still smelled faintly of aftershave and authority. I recognized him immediately.

"Randall Pike," Holden said coolly. "Former Historical Society President."

Pike's jaw tightened. "Chief Thorn. This is highly inappropriate."

"What's inappropriate," Holden replied, "is accessing restricted files after hours."

Pike gestured sharply to the open cabinet behind him. "Those files belong to the town. I was verifying information, as is my right."

I stepped closer, my heart pounding with recognition snapping into place. "You managed the funds back in 1984," I said.

"And?" Pike snapped.

"And Maggie Winslow reported you for fund mismanagement. You used your social influence and access to historical spaces for your own personal interests," I continued. "Ones that disappeared from the official records in the Town Hall."

His eyes shot to the rows of boxes piled on the shelves, then quickly away. "She was misinformed. Nothing ever came of her accusations."

LuLu snorted. "Sir, if Wishville had a dollar for every unproven accusation, we'd all be retired. Doesn't mean they weren't true."

Holden held up a photocopied map. "You pulled the original quarry survey. The one with the hand-marked boundary notes. Why?"

"That map was incorrect," Pike said defensively. "It caused unnecessary concern."

"So, you corrected it?" I asked.

"I simplified it."

Calderis spoke then, his voice calm and precise. "You removed markers that predated the town."

Pike stiffened. "I removed irrelevant information."

"No," Calderis said. "You erased access points."

Silence dropped hard into the room.

"You knew," I said quietly. "You knew there were tunnels, and you didn't want them found. Why?"

Pike's face flushed. "Those tunnels threatened the town development. Funding. Safety."

"Maggie didn't threaten safety," I said. "She threatened secrecy. She was trying to prove the ancient tunnels were created long before Wishville was established as an official town."

Holden stepped forward. "We reopened her case. And now we have motive."

Pike laughed sharply. "You're reaching. A missing history teacher from forty years ago doesn't get solved by chasing ghosts."

I looked at the papers in his shaking hands. "Then why are you here tonight?"

That did it. Pike's shoulders stiffened with frustration as he went on a rant. "Because if those tunnels resurface, everything we worked for comes apart."

"And Maggie?" I asked, hoping he would continue talking before he realized what he was giving away.

His mouth tightened and he ground out, "She wouldn't stop digging into matters that weren't her business. She had to be stopped!"

"At any cost?" I pressed.

"Yes," he roared, and then blinked and his lips parted as if he'd just realized what he'd said out loud.

That was enough. Holden read him his rights, charging him with killing Maggie Winslow, which he backpedaled and tried to deny. As Pike was escorted out, his gaze locked on mine, resentful. "She didn't belong down there," he muttered as he passed me. "Some people don't know when to stop." The door closed behind him as Holden called his officers and led him outside to his cruiser.

Meanwhile, LuLu photographed everything in sight. Calderis moved toward the cabinet, his eyes narrowing as he traced the empty spaces where files should have been.

"He removed more than maps," Calderis said quietly. "Something else was taken."

My pulse quickened as I focused on the space he was talking about. "That's where the Inspection logs are kept. If I had to guess, I'm betting the ones from the same week Maggie vanished are gone." The pieces slid together fast and sharp. "So, we have a man who suppressed evidence, erased tunnels, and tried to control the narrative."

LuLu nodded. "Classic cover-up behavior."

"And a motive that fits," Holden added as he reappeared inside. "Protecting development interests."

I felt the click of a case tightening. It felt too neat. Too obvious. Like a story that wanted very badly to be believed. For a moment, no one spoke. Then we stepped outside and realized Wishville had already started rewriting the narrative in real time.

A small crowd had gathered at the edge of the parking lot, not close enough to interfere with the investigation, but close enough to feel involved. Phones were out. Heads leaned together. Someone whispered dramatically while very clearly recording.

"That's Randall Pike."

"My uncle worked with him. He was more about making a buck than preserving history."

"Knew something was wrong back then."

Across the lot, the Wellies had positioned themselves with strategic precision. Arms folded, feet planted wide, and expressions solemn. Unfortunately, they could not hold the solemn part for more than six seconds.

Dot squinted so hard at Randall Pike she nearly tipped over, then corrected herself by grabbing Tilly's sleeve. Tilly, distracted, lost her balance and knocked directly into Belle, who sloshed half her cider onto her own boots and hissed like she'd been personally betrayed.

"Careful," Belle muttered. "These are my *thinking shoes*."

Dot finally caught my eye and lifted her chin sharply, like a general signaling a covert operation. *We see there's more here*, the look said. *Also, my foot is asleep.*

Tilly leaned toward Belle, stage-whispering far too loudly. "Well. That's going to absolutely destroy the lantern release vibe."

Belle sighed, brushing cider off her coat. "At least if everyone cries, they'll think it's seasonal."

Dot added, "I already hate the third act."

A man near them glanced over, unsettled. Dot stared back until he looked away and pretended to text.

"This is it, isn't it?" LuLu said softly beside me. "He's our guy."

Holden hesitated just a fraction too long. "He's *a* guy."

Calderis hadn't moved. His gaze had gone distant, unfocused, like he was listening beneath the noise. "There is something missing from this story."

Unease crept up my spine. I crossed my arms. "What?"

"Fear," Calderis said quietly. "This man is angry. Defensive. But he does not carry the weight of a killer afraid of being caught."

The words settled cold and heavy in my chest.

Behind us, Tilly gasped softly and clutched her chest. "Oh no."

Belle glanced at her, startled. "Your heart?"

"No," Tilly said grimly. "Vibes."

Belle rolled her eyes.

Dot nodded, then immediately tripped over absolutely nothing and windmilled her arms before regaining her balance. "I don't like him."

"You never like anyone," Belle said.

"I liked the librarian," Dot shot back. "And she *earned* it."

Calderis continued, oblivious to the chaos behind him. "There is defiance here. Not panic."

"Agreed," Holden said, straightening. "We will follow this lead further, push harder."

"And if that doesn't work?" I asked.

LuLu's voice was steady. "Then we find out who else is hiding."

Tilly leaned in again, whispering fiercely, "I vote for the man with the smug coat."

Belle frowned. "Everyone has a smug coat now. It's fashion."

Dot jabbed a finger vaguely toward the crowd. "My tea leaves say someone here is *far too calm.*"

"Dot," Belle said, "you just knocked over a traffic cone."

"That cone was suspicious."

I looked back at the annex and thought about the empty spaces where truth should've been, and where answers had been removed or never left behind at all.

Randall Pike made sense, and that scared me. Because the truth rarely chose the neatest answer. Somewhere in Wishville, someone slept just fine, knowing Maggie Winslow never came home. The investigation wasn't over by a long shot. It was accelerating.

Behind me, Tilly dropped her scarf, Belle stepped on it, and Dot hissed, "Abort. Abort."

And the real danger wasn't the wrong answer. It was how convincing it could be.

CHAPTER
Eight

THE NEXT MORNING, by the time I left *The Twisted Loaf,* my stomach felt like it had been filled with warm croissant dough and quiet dread. Randall Pike was already out on bail. We decided to split up.

Holden was off chasing down more evidence on Pike, Evelyn Hart, and Ron Maddox. LuLu was digging into Colin and Henry McAlister like a terrier with a grudge. Calderis was poring over leads in Elarion. And I had drawn the two names that didn't come with shiny political connections, but did come with the potential to snap in unexpected directions: Howard Kline and Professor Bernice Galloway.

Vex rode on my shoulder as I stepped out into the crisp Fall WishFest morning, his tail flicking against my neck like a punctuation mark. The bakery door chimed behind me, releasing one last breath of cinnamon and comfort before it shut again.

You're doing the two most emotionally unstable suspects, Vex observed.

"Thank you for your support," I muttered, tightening my jacket.

You're welcome. I'm here to offer truths you don't want and commentary you don't need.

I mounted my bike, The Starling, and pedaled down Main Street, letting the cold air slap my cheeks into focus. Wishville was awake in that gentle autumn way, with porch brooms scraping, shopkeepers flipping signs, and the smell of coffee and woodsmoke threading between buildings like gossip. The Starling's charms chimed with each pedal, entirely too cheerful for my mood.

I kept thinking about Maggie's words, *I heard voices there. Voices!*, and the way her letter had ended, sharp and panicked, like she'd dropped the pen and run. Humans didn't know Dwellers existed. Which meant voices in a tunnel could only turn into misguided assumptions in the town narrative if the wrong person got hold of that letter.

Smugglers. Cultists. Quarry squatters. A serial killer with a lantern fetish. Anything but the truth. My pendant warmed faintly against my chest, like it was listening to my thoughts and disapproving of my stress management techniques.

"Stop that," I whispered.

Vex's ears twitched. *Talking to jewelry again?*

"Talking to my anxiety," I corrected. "It just happens to be wearable."

Howard Kline lived on the edge of town, in a weathered white bungalow tucked behind sugar maples already dropping their leaves like they'd decided to quit early. His yard was meticulous with the hedges trimmed, the porch swept, and the wind chimes aligned just so. The kind of precision that came from someone who'd once worked among fragile things and learned exactly what happened when you mishandled them.

I chained my bike to the railing and climbed the steps, forcing my face into something that read *friendly WishFest Chair* and not *Magical Guardian investigating the disappearance of your former coworker*.

Vex hopped down and sat by my boot like an ominous accessory.

I knocked.

Three locks clicked in quick succession.

The door opened just wide enough for one wary brown eye and a slice of cheek to show. "Yes?"

"Mr. Kline?" I said. "I'm Lyra Wells."

His gaze flicked over my jacket, pack, and hiking boots then dropped to Vex. "I don't do interviews," he said flatly.

"I'm not with the paper," I said quickly. "This isn't about headlines. It's about old library history. The 1984 renovation."

His mouth tightened at the year like I'd cursed at him. "You should talk to Pike."

"I did, but he's not talking," I said lightly, "and I doubt he will again unless there's a donation check involved."

That earned me a sharper look. Then his eyes slid toward the street, as if he expected someone to be watching. Finally, with a sigh that sounded like defeat, he opened the door wider. "Five minutes. And the cat stays off my furniture."

Vex thrust his nose in the air and walked in as if he were royalty.

Kline's living room smelled like wood polish and floor wax. Books lined the walls in double rows with cracked spines and careful bookmarks. A pair of white cotton gloves lay folded on the coffee table, waiting.

I perched on the edge of an armchair, careful not to disturb anything. It was obvious he took great pride in keeping his place immaculate. Vex settled on the rug and began washing a paw with pointed innocence.

Kline didn't sit. He hovered with his arms crossed and body angled like he could bolt at any moment. "You said 1984," he repeated. "Why now?"

I chose the truth that wouldn't start a war. "Clara Winslow has been organizing archival material related to her mother."

His face shifted just a hair, but then went neutral fast. "Maggie," he said quietly.

"You knew her?" I asked.

He nodded. "She brought her classes in for research. Before

she started her own project and then decided she was the library's personal crusader."

"She reported you for mishandling rare books."

His eyes flashed. "I would never mishandle anything. I was the groundskeeper. I fixed pipes, replaced panes, and hauled boxes. Those books were falling apart long before I touched a shelf."

"Then why did she report you?"

He stared at the carpet like it might confess. "Because she needed a villain." His jaw clenched. "Or because someone else needed one, and she was a convenient scapegoat."

My spine straightened. "Someone else?"

"Don't twist my words."

"I'm not," I said softly. "I'm trying to understand what happened to the library and to Maggie."

Silence stretched between us, then he huffed out a breath.

"She wasn't wrong about everything. She was...intense about history, but she cared. She acted like the building was alive."

"And the basement?" I asked. "Did she spend time down there?"

"She was always asking for keys, and access to places she didn't belong, and for blueprints." His mouth tightened. "Said there were cold drafts where there shouldn't be. Walls that didn't match the plans."

My skin prickled. Those were Maggie's exact words. "Did she ever find anything?"

He hesitated. "She found something, all right. I don't know what. But after she did, she acted like she was being followed."

Chills ran down my spine. "Did she say who she thought it was?"

"No. She didn't trust anyone. Not me or Pike or the planning board. Especially not Evelyn Hart."

"Why Evelyn?"

He laughed, humorlessly. "Because Evelyn controlled the records. If a page disappeared, it disappeared through her hands.

Maggie knew that." He rubbed his jaw. "She told me once that if anything happened to her, it wouldn't be an accident. I thought she was just being paranoid."

"And then she vanished."

He nodded slowly. "Chief Ron Maddox turned it into a 'runaway mother' story in under a week." The pieces slid into place: police minimization, archival control, money, motive. "She wasn't alone that last week," he added.

I went still. "What do you mean?"

"Larry Winslow."

"Maggie's husband," I said carefully. "I thought they were estranged?"

"They were, but he was begging her to take him back. Always hovering," Kline said. "Always helping. Bringing coffee and snacks, waiting around for her. Like Maggie couldn't be trusted to take care of herself."

"That could just be him caring."

"Or controlling. Caring doesn't look like surveillance."

Vex paused mid-lick, his pupils narrowing. I knew he was cataloging everything as my second set of ears.

"Wishville thrives on over-involvement, even from family members," I said lightly. "We have committees for our committees."

Kline didn't smile. A shadow crossed his face. "Larry loved her, but he was tired. Lonely and desperate, if you ask me. The library consumed her. Whatever she was up to consumed her." He swallowed. "When she disappeared, Larry died not long after. Broken heart, they say. Dorothy Rourke was like family to them, so she took poor little Clara in." He crossed the room and pulled a thin folder from a shelf, holding it like it burned. "This is why you came."

Inside were crooked photocopies of library incident reports from the early '80s. Personal copies. One with Maggie's name. One with Kline's. And a maintenance log noting *unusual draft in the east archive wall* in his handwriting.

"Why keep these?" I asked.

"Because when Maggie disappeared, the town swept all her findings under the rug. I wanted to cover my butt in case there was any truth to it. I didn't need any more false accusations about me."

"Do you know what Maggie found?"

"No, but she asked me if I believed in strange things that can't be explained. I figured she was talking about UFOs and aliens, but then she said things beneath towns. Old things. Things people build over because it's easier than understanding." He shrugged. "I just figured her obsession was making her a little crazy."

I shivered.

Kline's gaze narrowed, suspicion flashing in his eyes.

I smiled quickly. "Cold building." I rubbed my arms. "More drafts."

He didn't argue, but he didn't look convinced, either. "If that's everything, I have things to do, Ms. Wells."

"Thanks again for your time." Vex and I stepped back onto the porch and Kline closed the door firmly behind us. My phone buzzed.

LuLu: **Henry's on the move. Colin's spooked. Stay tuned**.

Then another.

Holden: **Pike isn't answering. Evelyn Hart bolted when I walked in. Ron Maddox's old report is missing pages. Be careful.**

My stomach tightened.

Vex hopped onto my shoulder. *You're seeing the professor next.*

"Yes."

She'll be awful.

"Yes."

And you'll do it anyway because you have hero issues.

I pedaled toward the community college extension, Bernice Galloway's territory. "Yes," I said through clenched teeth. "Because someone killed Maggie Winslow, and I'm tired of Wishville pretending foundations forget themselves."

Vex purred with approval.

And as The Starling carried me forward, my pendant warmed again, more insistently this time, as if the past were leaning close to whisper, *You're getting warmer, Lyra. And so is the danger.*

Bernice Galloway's office sat at the far end of the *Wishville Community College* extension building as if it had personally applied for distance from humanity. The hallway leading to it was a museum of beige: beige tile, beige walls, beige bulletin boards stapled with flyers that promised *Mindful Movement for Midlife,* and *Intro to Excel,* and *Local History Night,* as if a spreadsheet could soothe a town's collective denial. Somewhere overhead, fluorescent lights hummed with the enthusiasm of a burned-out office printer.

Vex rode on my shoulder as I walked, his weight warm and steady. He'd been purring ever since Kline's house, like he was pleased we'd made the universe slightly more uncomfortable for someone who deserved it.

That woman's going to hate you for interfering, he said.

"Half the town hates me when I ask them where they were on a certain day," I muttered.

This is different. This is...competitive hatred. You have centuries of history on her, and she'll smell it.

"That can't be helped, and I certainly won't let it intimidate me." I stopped outside Bernice's door and took a breath.

A brass nameplate, polished to a threatening shine, read:

PROFESSOR BERNICE GALLOWAY
HISTORY & CULTURAL STUDIES
VISITING SCHOLAR—WISHVILLE PROGRAM

The word *visiting* was a lie. I'd learned that she had been here long enough that the building should have started charging her rent. If another university had wanted her, she would have left long ago, but community college was apparently all she could handle. And it infuriated her.

I knocked.

"Come in." Her voice had the crispness of starchy paper being bent.

I stepped inside.

The office was immaculate in the same way Kline's house had been immaculate...and controlled. Every pencil was aligned. Every book was squared. A framed certificate hung in the most visible spot, angled to catch the light, as if academic validation needed to be displayed like a saint's relic.

Bernice sat behind her desk with perfect posture, a gray cardigan draped over her shoulders like armor. Her gray hair was swept into a bun so tight it looked painful. She didn't smile when she saw me. She did, however, look down at Vex. "Animals aren't permitted."

"He's not an animal," I said before I could stop myself.

Bernice lifted one eyebrow. "Oh?"

I felt my cheeks warm. "He's...my emotional support cat."

"Then where's his service harness?"

"He's...particular about what he wears."

Vex flicked his tail against my neck in a way that felt like laughter.

Bernice sighed, as if she were too tired to argue the point. "Fine. Make it quick. I have a lecture to revise."

I sat in the chair across from her desk. It was the sort of chair that made you sit upright whether you wanted to or not, designed for a confession. "I'm Lyra Wells," I began.

"I know who you are," she said. "Wishville's festival darling. The one who smiles for tourists and talks about 'community' as if it's a historical concept."

"That's one description," I said, keeping my voice even.

Her gaze shifted to my pendant, lingering a fraction too long. "That's an interesting piece. Where'd you get it?"

"Old family heirloom." I slipped the necklace beneath my shirt.

Her eyes drifted back to my face. "What do you want?"

I chose my words carefully, not wanting to draw attention to the tunnels to anyone who might not know about them. Humans didn't know Dwellers existed, which meant I couldn't ask what I wanted to ask...whether she'd ever heard of a sealed entrance, or ancient tunnels beneath the earth, or hidden caverns in the mountains, or voices in stone. So, I went with the only safe question. "Information on Maggie Winslow the scholar," I said.

Bernice's expression didn't change, but the air in the room did, growing cooler and sharper. "She was a teacher," Bernice said. "Not a *true* scholar."

"A *history* teacher. She was also a researcher," I said. "And you were her academic rival."

A faint, humorless smile tugged at Bernice's mouth. "Is that what people are saying now? Rival? How dramatic."

"You published in the same areas," I pressed. "Local history. Foundational documents. Early settlement records. The kind of discoveries that make careers."

Bernice leaned back in her chair as if I'd amused her. "Careers are built on rigor, Ms. Wells. Not enthusiasm."

Vex's claws flexed gently through my sweater. A warning or encouragement. It was hard to tell with him.

"I'm not here to argue Maggie's credentials or yours," I said. "I'm here because she disappeared the week she believed she'd found something significant under the library. Something connected to the 1984 renovation."

Bernice's eyes narrowed. "*Under* the library."

"Yes," I said, watching her closely. "I'm trying to understand what Maggie was chasing. And if anyone had reason to stop her."

Bernice's gaze slid to the bookshelf behind her desk. One shelf in particular, where a row of journals sat in perfect order, their spines matching as if they'd been curated for appearances.

Then she looked back at me. "And you think I stopped her?"

"I think you might have wanted to," I said carefully.

That finally did it. Bernice's smile vanished. "You're a young woman," she said, her voice tight, "playing detective because your life is built on whimsy and lanterns. But some of us live in the world of evidence."

I held her gaze. "Evidence like missing pages? Altered blueprints? A police report that doesn't add up?"

Bernice's nostrils flared. "Chief Maddox was incompetent. Everyone knows that."

"You knew him," I said.

"Everyone knew him," she snapped. Then she caught herself and smoothed her expression. "In a town this small, you can't buy bread without hearing a life story."

I leaned forward. "Did Maggie ever bring you anything? Notes, documents, or maybe a theory? Did she ever tell you what she thought she found?"

Bernice tapped a pen against her desk once. Twice. A metronome of restraint. "She came to me," she admitted at last, each word clipped. "Once."

My pulse kicked.

"She never usually shared anything with me, wanting all the credit for herself, but she was hitting dead ends and needed help," Bernice continued, like it irritated her to remember. "She believed she'd discovered a discrepancy in the architectural history. Something about the library's east wall. She thought it didn't match the plans."

"And?" I asked, trying to keep my voice steady.

"And I told her to be careful, because towns don't like being told they're built on mistakes."

"That's not an answer," I said.

"It's the only answer you'll get," she snapped, then smoothed her hair back. "She accused the planning board of hiding something. She accused Evelyn Hart of limiting access to documents. She said Randall Pike was 'too interested' in what she was finding."

My stomach tightened. "Did she have proof?"

"She had suspicion," Bernice said with disdain. "Maggie's favorite hobby."

Vex's tail lashed once, sharply.

I ignored him. "Did she mention tunnels?" I asked, keeping my tone casual, like it was just a word. Clearly I wasn't getting anywhere by *not* mentioning the tunnels.

Bernice's pen froze mid-tap. A fraction of a second, that was all, but it was enough. "No," she said too quickly. "The library is not a mine, Ms. Wells."

I let the silence stretch.

Bernice's gaze sharpened. "What are you really asking?"

I could have lied. I could have danced around it with festival words and pleasant smiles. Instead, I said, "I'm asking if you ever went looking yourself."

Her eyes snapped to mine, cold and assessing. "I didn't crawl around basements, if that's what you mean. I have standards."

"Did anyone else?" I asked, not sure I believed her.

Bernice's lips tightened. She looked at me like I'd tracked mud onto her floor. "Maggie was not liked by everyone," she said slowly. "She was invasive and asked questions that made people uncomfortable."

"And you?" I asked.

Bernice's gaze dropped to her desk, then lifted again. "She embarrassed me." The admission landed in the room like a dropped book.

"How?" I asked.

Bernice's jaw clenched. "She found a document I had been searching for. A minor thing. A letter, a reference, a footnote that mattered in a small, scholarly way. She brought it to a local history night and presented it like it was a gift to the town."

"She didn't credit you."

"She didn't know I'd been looking," Bernice grudgingly admitted. "But she didn't care. She liked being the one who made discoveries that would be recorded in the history books. Her job didn't even require it. Mine did. When I didn't publish enough papers, the university let me go. Now look where I am, and it was all because of her."

Vex purred against my neck like a cat enjoying a mouse's confession.

"So, you were jealous," I said.

Bernice's eyes flashed with annoyance. "Don't reduce me."

"I'm not," I said quietly. "I'm trying to understand your motive."

Bernice leaned forward, her voice lowering. "If I wanted to destroy Maggie Winslow, Ms. Wells, I could have done it with words. Her reputation was everything to her. I could have sent letters to the right boards and committees. I wouldn't have destroyed her with whatever melodrama you've decided happened underground."

My pendant warmed again, glowing faintly, insistent this time like a warning...but a warning about what? I clutched it instinctively.

Bernice's gaze flicked toward it once more. "What is that exactly?" she asked sharply.

"It was my mother's."

Something unreadable crossed her face. "You're going down the same path Maggie did," Bernice said, in a way that made my skin crawl. "Digging at foundations, poking your nose in places it doesn't belong, asking the wrong questions."

"Were they wrong questions or just inconvenient?"

Her eyes hardened again. "This town does not forgive women who make noise."

Her tone sounded more like she was talking about herself rather than Maggie. Possibly about what she'd learned, what she'd survived, what she'd chosen to become to keep standing in rooms like this.

I stood. "Thank you for your time."

Bernice didn't stand. She watched me like she was watching history repeat itself. As I reached the door, she said very softly, "If you find something under that library, Ms. Wells...don't assume people will want it documented in the history books. Some would just as soon it stay buried."

My hand paused on the knob.

Vex's fur prickled under my fingers.

I turned back. "Did Maggie say something like that to you?"

Bernice's smile returned, thin as a blade. "Maggie said a lot of things."

I left before I could say something that would ignite her into full battle mode. The hallway's beige air felt like freedom. Outside, the wind had picked up, tossing leaves down the sidewalk like confetti for a parade no one wanted. I mounted The Starling, my hands shaking slightly as I gripped the handlebars.

That was fun, Vex said.

"She knows more than she's admitting," I murmured.

She's not the murderer, Vex said, too certain.

I glanced at him. "How do you know?"

His tail flicked. "Because she would have published a paper about it first."

A laugh escaped, quick and sharp from between my lips. But the laugh didn't last, because my pendant warmed again, pulsing against my skin like a heartbeat that wasn't mine. A message without words. My mother was trying to tell me...

Someone is listening.

And as I pedaled away, I couldn't shake Bernice's parting warning and wondering what else Maddie Winslow had said to her.

CHAPTER
Nine

CALDERIS DIDN'T KNOCK. I was in the back room of the festival supply warehouse, pretending to organize inventory while actually staring at the same frayed rope for the tenth time, when the air shifted. I could sense him before I saw him.

"You're needed," he said from behind me.

"I was already needed," I said, setting the rope down and dreading what news he was about to drop.

His reflection caught in the glass-front cabinet. Tall, still, wrapped in the quiet authority that made rooms feel smaller. His pale hair was pulled back at the nape of his neck, his coat dusted faintly with stone residue that hadn't been there this morning. Which meant he hadn't come straight from Elarion.

"Say it," I said.

"The rebels have been active," Calderis replied. "There are signs that the sealed paths beneath the quarry and the eastern ridge have been reopened and are in use."

My stomach tightened. "Recently?"

"Recently enough to matter."

I turned to face him. "Do you think they connect to the tunnels Maggie found?"

His jaw tightened. "Yes," he said. "I have Weylan and Sparks keeping a lookout. If they show up in Wishville, we'll know it."

"I'll text Ranger Ellison and have her get word to Alden to keep an eye on the woods." I pulled out my phone and shot off a text.

Tiana didn't know that Dwellers existed. All she needed to know was to report back with any suspicious activity from strangers. Alden, however, was a Dweller outcast hermit. He would be able to spot a rebel right away. He liked to stay as far away from them as possible, and made it clear that he preferred to deal with the ranger.

Vex appeared from nowhere, hopping onto the worktable and swishing his tail. Fenrin was suddenly at his side, studying us closely.

Calderis glanced at him. "She doesn't need your support."

"She always needs my support," Vex said, speaking out loud to both of us. "I love it when secrets get legs."

I crossed my arms and tried not to roll my eyes. "Who do you think is using the tunnels?"

Calderis didn't answer immediately. He stepped closer, lowering his voice. "Vaelis. Thyssara. Korrin. Elowen. Maelis. Rhae." The names landed like stones dropped into deep water. Some I knew by reputation. Some only by whispered tension in Elarion's corridors.

None of them were small players.

"And Ithrel?" I asked.

"A watcher," Calderis said dismissively. "Loud, obvious, and uninvolved."

Convenient, Vex meowed, back to whispering his thoughts through our minds.

Calderis ignored him. "The rebels have been active for a long time, but they did not kill Maggie Winslow."

I let out a breath I hadn't realized I'd been holding. "You're sure?"

"Yes." His gaze held mine. "But they are responsible for

opening the passages that allowed a human to venture deeper than she should have been able to go."

The word *allowed* settled cold in my chest. "So, the tunnels. They lead to the mountain caverns?"

"Some," he corrected. "Not all and not safely."

"Do you think Maggie encountered any Dwellers or went into any caverns? Your father said she wouldn't have survived if she did."

Silence stretched between us, thick with what he wasn't saying.

"I'm not sure, honestly," he finally answered. "There is one way to find out."

"You want to go in," I said.

Calderis inclined his head. "It's time. As my father said, you already know we must."

Vex hopped onto my shoulder. *Please tell me we're not doing the 'first time in the ancient murder tunnels' thing without snacks.*

Fenrin meowed in agreement.

"We are not bringing snacks," Calderis said, having heard Vex's thoughts as well. "And there is no *we*. Neither of you are going."

That's how people die. Vex huffed. *You won't stand a chance without me.* He glanced at a hissing Fenrin and rolled his eyes. *Us.*

Calderis gave Vex a hard look. "My word is final, and I expect you to obey it."

I grabbed my jacket and flashlight without another word.

Vex and Fenrin disappeared, and I followed Calderis through the woods.

The entrance he led me to wasn't anywhere humans would think to look. It wasn't the library basement or the quarry or the obvious cracks in the ridge that drew hikers and thrill-seekers. This was older and subtler. A narrow seam hidden behind a thicket of spruce and rock, where roots twisted like fingers guarding a secret. The air smelled different there, damp stone and something faintly metallic, like old rain trapped underground.

"You feel it," Calderis said. "The energy."

"I always do," I replied.

He pressed his palm to the rock face and murmured a phrase in the old cadence. It wasn't a spell exactly, but more like a request. Stone shifted with a sound like a sigh, and a narrow opening revealed itself, just wide enough for a person to slip through sideways. How had I never known this entrance existed? As Guardian, I didn't like being kept in the dark.

Vex appeared from out of nowhere again, alone this time. I should have known he wouldn't listen to us. His fur bristled over the stone entrance. *That's unsettling.*

Calderis gave Vex a hard glare. "You may remain here. That's an order."

Vex laughed, sharply and humorlessly. *That's not happening. I am responsible for her safety.*

"And I'm responsible for the well and making sure WishFest grants a wish to keep the peace and the treaty in place," I said. "Which means if something's wrong down there, I need to see it. Besides, I do have a certain set of skills, not to mention, I have the Chief Enforcer with me. I'll be fine."

Vex's whiskers twitched in displeasure, then he stepped aside. *I'll be the lookout.*

Calderis nodded, then turned to me. "Stay close."

"I always do."

We stepped through the entrance, and the tunnel swallowed us whole.

The temperature dropped immediately, the air cool and heavy against my skin. Calderis moved with practiced ease, his steps sure even where the floor dipped and twisted. My flashlight cast long, distorted shadows across the walls.

This wasn't a mine. This wasn't human work. The stone curved too smoothly in places, spiraled in others, and the walls were etched with patterns that looked almost intentional. Like the earth had been guided rather than cut. Like the stone that was in Maggie's box.

"Vaelis," I murmured, suddenly realizing why the stone had looked familiar.

"Yes," Calderis said. "His work is unmistakable."

We moved deeper, past a junction where newer reinforcement beams had been wedged into older stone. I sighed. Human attempts to stabilize something they didn't understand. The clash made my teeth ache.

"Humans shouldn't have touched this," I said.

"They rarely listen," Calderis replied.

The tunnel narrowed, then widened abruptly into a chamber that stole my breath.

The ceiling arched high overhead, with roots coiling through cracks like snakes. The floor bore marks like footprints, scuffs, and disturbed dust.

Recent.

Human.

My heart pounded. "Someone's been here."

"Yes," Calderis said quietly.

We followed the trail to the far side of the chamber, where the stone wall bore faint scratches that looked old. Not tool marks. Fingernails. And holes where the mineral rich soil had been dug up.

I swallowed hard. "Maggie was here," I whispered, horrified over what she might have gone through.

Calderis knelt, studying the markings. "She was searching, not fleeing."

I breathed a sigh of relief. "Because she thought she was close to a discovery of the century."

"Yes. And she was...just not of her world."

My flashlight beam caught on something half-buried near the wall. I crouched and brushed away dust with trembling fingers. It was a button, plain and wooden, worn smooth with age. My chest tightened. "This was from her coat."

Calderis's expression darkened. "Then this is where she lost her way."

"Or where someone made sure she did." I stood slowly, the chamber suddenly feeling too small. "The rebels reopened this section. Why? What were they using the tunnels for? They might not have killed her, but they created the path for someone else to, if she is in fact dead."

"Correct."

"Her journal said someone followed her. Whoever that was didn't need magic, just access."

Calderis's gaze sharpened. "You believe she was murdered?"

"I believe someone *could* have killed her," I said, "but I pray that I'm wrong."

We moved on, deeper still, until the tunnel shifted again. Older stone gave way to something stranger. The walls curved inward, spiraling subtly, like the beginning of a coil.

My pendant burned hot.

"Stop," Calderis said, at the same moment I did. The air here felt wrong. Pressurized. Heavy with memory. "This is close. Too close."

"To what?" I asked, though I already knew.

"The sealed places," he replied. "The ones we swore would remain untouched."

"The Veiled Vault?" I asked.

He shook his head. "There are other places even more dangerous."

A faint vibration thrummed through the stone beneath my boots, like a distant heartbeat. "We shouldn't be here," I said.

"No," Calderis agreed. "But someone else has been, and we need to know who for sure...and why."

We backed away carefully, retracing our steps until the air lightened and the stone felt less watchful. Only when we emerged back into the trees did I realize my hands were shaking.

Calderis sealed the entrance with a press of his palm. The rock slid back into place, seamless once more.

"That was only the outer layer," he said, looking grim. "The rebels have endangered both realms by opening the passages. They must be stopped and the tunnels resealed."

"Yes," I said. "Dead or alive, we need to find Maggie."

We stood there in silence, the forest rustling around us like it knew something we didn't.

My phone buzzed in my pocket, human life insisting on being part of this. I didn't check it. Instead, I said, "Someone followed Maggie down there. I'm certain of it."

Calderis studied me. "You are thinking of a particular human."

"Her husband maybe," I said. "Or someone who had illegal activities going on down there and didn't want her to put a stop to them. Either way, I won't rest until we find out which one. Maggie deserves that and so does Clara."

Night settled over Wishville. The lanterns along Main Street glowed low and amber, festival crowds thinning to locals and late diners, and the air sharp with fallen leaves and woodsmoke. From the surface, everything looked peaceful. Contained.

Beneath it, the truth waited.

Calderis met me again at the well just after dusk, when the last tourists had drifted back to their inns and the town turned dark. He stood at the edge of the stone ring with his hands folded behind his back and his expression unreadable in the half-light. He wore his Elarion armor tonight, not battle-ready but formal. The kind meant for judgment and record, not violence.

"You're tense," I said, stepping beside him.

"We were in the tunnels today," he replied. "That tends to linger."

"On me, maybe," I said. "On you, it's basically a personality trait."

One corner of his mouth twitched in almost a smile.

Vex hopped down from the well wall and circled once before

sitting, his tail wrapped neatly around his paws. *I assume we're going somewhere secret, politically sensitive, and emotionally uncomfortable.*

"Yes," Calderis said, not trying to stop him from accompanying us this time.

Excellent.

I suddenly wished Holden was with us, but there were some places too dangerous for humans to venture. I rested my palms on the stone lip of the well and focused, reciting the familiar incantation. The water below shimmered, darkening, then thinning until the surface split like silk under a blade and the grate vanished.

We descended. Elarion rose to meet us in layered light and shadow, the air humming with magic that felt older than memory and sharper than truth. Bioluminescent moss traced the walls in slow pulses of blue and green, and crystalline growths caught the light like frozen stars. But Calderis didn't lead me toward the Council chambers, the lower markets, or the training halls.

Instead, he turned east.

"I've never been this way," I said. "My mother forbade me."

"These districts are not meant to be public," he replied. "It's a forbidden area."

We passed beneath a high arch of living stone and into a quarter of Elarion that felt restrained. The glow dimmed here, its colors cooler, and the architecture more severe. Buildings rose directly from the cavern floor, carved in precise angles, their surfaces etched with sigils of record and restraint.

"*The Veinward,*" Calderis said. "Where top secret Dweller histories are kept...and sometimes hidden."

Vex's ears flattened. *I've heard this place is dangerous.*

"It is," Calderis agreed.

Our first stop was a narrow hall carved deep into the cavern wall, its entrance marked by a single symbol—a spiral broken at the top. Inside, the air was thick with memory. Crystalline panels lined the walls, each one faintly glowing, holding echoes of past actions. Impressions and emotional residue.

"This is where Thyssara works," Calderis said.

As if summoned by her name, a figure emerged from between the panels. Tall, composed, with silver-veined markings tracing the line of her throat and disappearing beneath her layered robes.

"Chief Enforcer," Thyssara said coolly. Her gaze slid to me. "And the Guardian."

"Archivist," Calderis replied. "You've been busy."

Thyssara inclined her head. "History never rests."

I stepped closer to one of the panels. It thrummed faintly, vibrating against my senses. "These look recent."

"Yes," Thyssara said. "Humans leave very loud echoes when they trespass."

My stomach tightened. "You knew Maggie was there."

"I knew a human was approaching a truth she could not possibly understand," Thyssara said calmly. "I also knew she was not my responsibility."

Calderis's voice sharpened. "You did not intervene."

"No," Thyssara agreed. "Because intervention creates ripples, and ripples draw attention."

"To Elarion," I said.

"And to worse," she replied, her gaze sweeping briefly toward the deeper caverns.

"What did she find?" I asked.

Thyssara studied me for a long moment. "She found absence. Places that didn't exist on any records." Human records, she meant. "Places removed from Dweller maps."

"Who ordered the removals?" Calderis asked, a muscle in his jaw flexing.

Thyssara's lips curved in a faint, humorless smile. "That is not a question you ask unless you are prepared for the answer."

Vex snorted but kept his thoughts to himself for once.

I was surprised when Calderis didn't press her for an answer, unless she was right and he already knew but wasn't prepared to act on the information.

We left *The Veinward* heavier than we'd entered. From there,

Calderis led me downward, into a cavern I'd never seen. A wide basin where stone terraces curved inward like an amphitheater. At its center lay a pool of black glass, perfectly still.

"*The Echo Basin,*" Calderis said. "Vaelis has been seen here."

The air vibrated faintly, like it remembered sound even when none existed. I knelt at the edge of the pool, peering into its dark surface. For a moment, nothing happened. Then the glass rippled and images surfaced. Suggestive with stone shifting, hands pressed to walls, and passages opening where none had been before. And a human silhouette, small and determined, with a lantern held high.

"Maggie," I whispered.

"She walked these paths," Calderis said softly. "Closer than she should have been allowed."

"Did Vaelis see her?" I asked.

Calderis studied the visions and frowned. "Yes. He was the one who left the portal open for her."

The answer landed like a blow. "He let her in and let her continue?"

"Many Dwellers don't agree with the treaty. He believed knowledge belonged to those brave enough to seek it."

I stood abruptly. "That belief might have gotten her killed."

"Maybe," Calderis agreed, "but not by him."

We didn't find Vaelis there. Only the evidence of his work, the scars of reopened stone, and the arrogance of someone who believed he didn't have to play by Elarion rules.

Next came the *Cavern of Breath,* a narrow, vertical space where warm air rose in slow currents, carrying whispered sounds from far below. Rhae's territory. We found him perched on a ledge, slim and restless, his eyes darting as if the cavern itself might overhear his thoughts.

"I carried messages," Rhae said quickly before Calderis could questioned him. "That's all. I didn't read them."

"You knew where they led," Calderis replied.

Rhae's gaze landed on me. "I knew they weren't meant for

humans." He looked at Calderis. "Dwellers, either." Which meant the messages were being passed by the rebels. The tunnels were how they had gotten around without the Elders knowing.

"Did any humans go missing?" I asked.

He hesitated just long enough. "One," he admitted.

My chest tightened.

Our final stop lay far from the others, a forgotten quarter where Elarion's glow thinned to pale opal. The structures here were half-ruined, overgrown with luminous vines, as if the city itself had decided to let them fade.

"The Hollow Steps," Calderis said quietly. "Elowen's refuge." We found her tending a basin of glowing water, her hands gentle and expression weary.

"I healed injuries," Elowen said when questioned. "Scrapes. Stone-burns. Fear."

"And Maggie?" My voice caught despite my effort. "Did you heal her?"

Elowen shook her head. "No. She never reached us."

Which meant Maggie had been intercepted before she ever crossed fully into Dweller space. I was relieved she hadn't suffered in some unpressurized cavern, but that still didn't mean she had escaped alive and run away.

As we left *the Hollow Steps,* the weight of the evening pressed in on me. Names, places, and truths brushing close but never quite aligning.

"They're hiding something," I said. "All of them."

"Yes," Calderis replied, "but not murder. Rebels maybe, or a hideout. Whatever it is, they fear someone's wrath more than Vaerion's."

We returned to the portal in silence. The well shimmered, waiting. Before we stepped through, Calderis paused. "Lyra," he said. "Whatever happened to Maggie was born of proximity, not politics or rebellion."

"I know," I said softly.

Because the tunnels had shown me that. Because the clues

were no longer pointing outward toward power or ideology, but inward toward something else. We stepped through the portal and returned to Wishville in silence.

The night felt too quiet. Too ordinary. The lanterns flickered. Somewhere, music drifted from a late-night bar. Above, life went on. Below, the truth waited. And as my pendant cooled against my skin, I knew one thing with chilling certainty...

The Dweller suspects had opened doors, but the humans had done the rest.

CHAPTER

Ten

BY THE MORNING of Day Five, attending Fall WishFest felt like waking up with a headache, the cause of which you can't quite place. Two days left. If I made it through them unscathed, it would be a miracle.

The hill clearing was still dressed for celebration, the lanterns sagging slightly in the daylight, ribbons damp with dew, and hay bales arranged in their familiar circles, but the magic had thinned overnight. What had glowed under firelight now felt exposed. Like a stage after the audience left, when the actors were gone but the set remained, waiting to be dismantled.

I stood at the base of the path with a travel mug cooling in my hands, watching volunteers move through their routines a little too carefully. Someone swept leaves that didn't need sweeping. Someone else rearranged pumpkins that were already straight. Booth owners spoke in low voices as they checked inventory they'd already checked twice. No one lingered near the well. Since the arrest and the reopening of the case, Wishville had gone quiet, with people thinking about the same thing but pretending they weren't.

What happened to Maggie Winslow?

Vex perched on my shoulder, his tail wrapped tight against my neck instead of flicking lazily like usual. Fenrin was absent, mad at him for leaving her behind at the stone portal.

This is a morning for judgment, he murmured.

"Fantastic," I muttered. "Nothing like civic judgment with a side of cider."

The morning crowd was mostly locals. Ruth was holding court near the benches, reminiscing about the old days with other retirees and gesturing so emphatically with her mittened hands that it looked like she might conduct traffic. Finch jogged past me twice in under a minute, fixing things that didn't appear broken and then fixing them again just in case.

Henry and Colin stood with their heads pressed together, talking to Evelyn in urgent, hushed tones. I distinctly heard Ron's name mentioned more than once, followed by a collective wince.

Parents with kids too young for school buzzed through the square, strollers bumping gently over packed snow as vendors began opening their stands. And threaded through it all, soft but constant, I heard Maggie's name.

"—they reopened it."

"—after forty years."

"—during WishFest, honestly."

"—poor Clara."

Her name passed between people like a fragile heirloom no one wanted to drop.

Right on cue, the Wellies appeared.

They clanked up the path in coordinated scarves and synchronized concern, their bangles knocking together and boots crunching in slightly off-tempo unison. Each of them clutched a hot tea like it was the only thing holding their bodies upright.

"Festival Chair," Tilly announced brightly, nearly colliding with a signpost before righting herself.

"Finally," I said, smiling. "Reinforcements."

"To everyone else," Dot said solemnly, adjusting her scarf until it nearly swallowed her chin, "still Guardian to us."

Belle nodded. "We took a poll."

"A poll for what?" I asked cautiously.

"I forget," Tilly said, blinking. "But we won."

I sighed. "What's wrong now?"

Dot leaned in so close I could smell her peppermint tea. "The rumors have the town picking sides on whose story they choose to believe. Team Connie or Team Dorothy."

That brought memories to my mind. Back then, Connie and Larry had been as close as overlapping footprints in fresh dirt...where one stepped, the other followed. "That didn't take long." I shook my head.

"Of course not," Belle said. "People get bored without someone to root for. Morning brings clarity," she added gravely. "And judgment."

Tilly clutched her chest dramatically. "Also baked goods. People are stress-eating. I saw someone buy four scones and call it 'self-care.'"

I scanned the path and spotted Connie Hale standing just off to the side, pretending very badly to inspect lantern cords that hadn't changed since yesterday. Her posture was stiff, shoulders squared, and purse clutched tight like it might make a break for freedom.

"Go supervise something," I told the Wellies.

They exchanged looks.

"We *are* supervising," Belle said. "You."

"Shoo."

They retreated with maximum volume and minimum dignity. Tilly nearly tripped over her own scarf, Dot paused to glare suspiciously at a trash bin "just in case." And Belle whispered loudly about energy shifts and narrative imbalance.

Tilly hissed, "I don't like her purse energy."

Dot nodded. "It's defensive."

Belle added, "Everything's defensive today."

I watched them go, exhaled slowly, and turned back to the crowd that was undoubtedly reshaping the story and choosing what felt easiest to believe. WishFest had barely started. And the town was already deciding whom it wanted to forgive.

Connie noticed me then, and gave a smile that didn't quite reach her eyes.

I walked over. "Good morning."

She nodded. "I suppose it is." That was the most optimism she could manage.

We stood side by side, watching people mill about. Someone tested a microphone near the stage, then shut it off abruptly, as if even amplified sound felt inappropriate today.

"Everyone knows the police reopened Maggie's case," Connie said quietly.

"I see that."

Her mouth tightened. "I never thought they would officially. Not after so much time has passed. Why open old wounds?"

"Because there's new evidence, and Clara deserves the truth."

Connie's shoulders slumped. "I wanted to talk to you before people start rewriting history. I worked closely with Larry for years, before Maggie disappeared and after." She paused. "He was devastated."

"I don't doubt that."

"He was confused. Angry. Humiliated." Her gaze stayed fixed on the path. "And yes...difficult. But people forget how disorienting it is when the person you live with becomes someone you can't reach."

I tightened my grip on the mug.

"There were rumors," Connie continued. "About their marriage. About Maggie pulling away, staying late at the library, and keeping things to herself." She swallowed. "I believed them."

"You believed Maggie was hiding something," I said.

"Yes," Connie replied. "She was awfully secretive about what she was doing at the library. Larry asked me more than once if I thought she was keeping secrets. I told him yes. That Maggie had always been private, even as a girl. That she shared only when she *chose* to."

"And that put you on his side."

"It made me understand him," Connie said firmly. "He felt shut out of his own marriage. I had felt shut out as her friend. People talk about emotional intelligence now, but back then? Men didn't have language for that kind of thing. They just had resentment and loneliness."

A couple paused near the well ahead of us, whispered, then moved on without making a wish. That wasn't good. We needed wishes to keep interest in the festival up so the treaty would remain intact, but people were too distracted.

"I defended Larry," Connie said quietly. "When questions started and people whispered." She drew a steadying breath. "I told myself Maggie would've told someone if anything serious was happening or she was in danger."

Vex shifted, his claws pressing lightly into my shoulder. *A common human error, assuming silence means insignificance.*

"Do you still believe that?" I asked.

Connie didn't answer right away. The breeze rattled the lanterns overhead, a soft hollow sound that reminded me too much of breath moving through stone. "I don't know," she said finally. "That's the problem."

I turned toward her. "What changed?"

She gestured vaguely around at the people. "This. The reopening of her case. The timing. Clara." Her voice softened. "She's steadier than I expected, not defensive or flailing, almost like she's been waiting for this."

I nodded. That felt true. I didn't stop looking for my mother, and especially not after getting word that she was still alive.

"Maggie was careful," Connie continued. "I mistook that for secrecy. Withdrawal." She shook her head. "There's a difference."

"Yes," I said gently. "There is."

Connie closed her eyes briefly. "If Maggie was trying to expose something and right not to trust the town, then I helped keep the wrong things quiet. I don't think Larry hurt her," she added quickly. "I need you to hear that." Her voice wavered just slightly.

"But I also know I wasn't looking for answers. I was looking for explanations that made my life easier. I won't rewrite what I believed back then," she added. "But I won't stand in the way of the truth now. Clara deserves that."

"She does," I said.

Connie nodded and walked away.

The Wellies drifted back in, quieter this time like a flock of suspicious sparrows pretending not to observe anything at all.

Dot leaned in and stage-whispered, "Accountability before nine a.m. is statistically improbable."

I shot her a look.

She shrugged, utterly unrepentant, and pretended to examine her tea as if it contained answers.

Tilly frowned around the clearing, tugging absently at the end of her scarf until it slipped loose and trailed behind her like a forgotten thought. "It feels unfinished."

"Unresolved," Dot corrected, tapping her cup twice for emphasis.

"Unthinkable," Belle added, crossing her arms and squinting at the crowd like she might scold the truth into revealing itself.

They nodded in grim, synchronized agreement. Three judges, one verdict, zero closure.

I had the distinct, unsettling feeling that they were right. I glanced toward the well. Maggie Winslow had no idea the tunnels she found led to a whole other world. And now, the town was waking up to the possibility that it had listened to the wrong people and ignored the wrong woman.

Vex leaned close. *Sides are easy*, he murmured. *Truth is not.*

I stepped forward with the rest of them, into a day that felt less like a festival and more like a reckoning.

By lunchtime, Wishville had decided what kind of day it was going to be.

The Wishbone Café was packed in that deceptively cozy way with every table full, voices overlapping, and the clink of silverware and coffee cups filling the air like static. The windows were fogged just enough to blur Main Street, turning passing pedestrians into smudged silhouettes. Normally, it felt like a refuge.

Today, it felt like gossip central.

LuLu and I had claimed a small table near the windows, our menus untouched between us. My soup had gone lukewarm. LuLu's sandwich sat uneaten, her foot bouncing beneath the table like it was trying to escape.

"They're saying it out loud now," she muttered, lowering her voice anyway. "No one's whispering or hedging anymore, they're just saying it."

I didn't need to ask who *they* were. "Accusations travel faster than facts, especially when they feel tidy."

LuLu snorted. "Oh, this feels very tidy. People always suspect the spouse first. 'Husband snaps, tragedy strikes, town moves on.' It's like people have been waiting forty years to dust that off."

I glanced around the café. People leaned close together near the counter. Two shop owners pretended to argue about pie while clearly discussing something else. Even Willa Hartman behind the register had that tight, careful look people get when they're bracing for bad news.

Vex lay curled beside me on the bench, his eyes half-closed and ears flicking. No one questioned him being with me anywhere I went, buying into our emotion support companion story. These days, it wasn't a lie.

Lies have a sound, he murmured. *Humans hear it even when they don't want to.*

The bell over the door jingled, and my stomach tightened before I even turned. Clara walked in with Dorothy Rourke. Clara looked composed at first glance, her hair neatly pulled back and cardigan buttoned correctly. Her library tote was slung over her shoulder, but I could see the tension in her shoulders and the way her gaze skimmed the room too quickly. Dorothy's hand rested lightly at the small of her back, guiding her forward with practiced ease.

"Here we go," LuLu murmured.

They spotted us at the same time. Clara hesitated, but Dorothy didn't.

"Well," Dorothy said pleasantly, steering Clara toward us, "isn't this nice? Running into friends." She leaned down. "May we?"

"Of course," I said, already shifting to make room.

LuLu gave Clara a cautious smile. "Hey."

Clara nodded stiffly. "Hi."

They sat. Dorothy settled with deliberate grace, folding her napkin into her lap like she'd done this a thousand times, which, given her long history in Wishville, she probably had. Clara sat rigid beside her with her hands clasped together on the table.

The silence stretched.

I opened my mouth, about to fill her in on my talk with Connie, but Clara beat me to it.

"I heard," she said flatly with her eyes on the tabletop, "that you think my father believed my mother was in the wrong. That he blamed her for their marriage problems. That he *cheated* on her."

"I never said—" I started to defend myself.

"I know, and that's the point. You promised to keep me informed."

"Clara, I just talked to Connie this morning."

Her voice wobbled despite her best efforts. "I heard it from three different people who heard it from someone else who said Connie was 'finally admitting the truth.' People think Connie was a home wrecker."

LuLu cursed under her breath.

"That's not what was said," I said carefully. "At all."

Dorothy tilted her head, concern softening her features. "Oh, Clara," she said. "Small towns have a way of twisting things."

Clara's jaw tightened. "They're saying my father *did something.*

That he snapped. That he was jealous. That he couldn't handle my mother being brilliant." She finally looked up at me, her eyes bright with hurt. "They're saying it like it's a fact."

"It isn't," I said firmly.

"But people believe it," Clara shot back. "I never would have pushed to find out the truth if I had known this would happen. I don't want my mother's memory tarnished, or my father's. This is just awful."

Dorothy reached over and took Clara's hand. "Sweetheart," she said softly, "no one is saying your father didn't love your mother."

LuLu's head snapped up. "That's not the same thing."

Dorothy's smile didn't falter. "Of course not, but love doesn't always protect us from fear." She squeezed Clara's hand gently. "Fear of losing the one you love can do strange things to people. Larry might have had an affair, desperate to make Maggie jealous. And when that didn't work, he might have lost control. That doesn't mean he still wouldn't love her."

"Dorothy," I said evenly, "that's a big leap."

Dorothy met my gaze calmly. "Is it?" she asked. "Maggie was my best friend. I saw the tension between them. And after she disappeared, Larry was beside himself with grief...or guilt." She sighed, shaking her head like the memory still weighed on her. "I tried to be there for him, but he wouldn't let me in. He wasn't a bad man, but he was broken." Her expression pinched. "And far too close to Connie if you ask me."

"That doesn't make him guilty of anything you're saying," LuLu pointed out logically like the journalist she was.

"No," Dorothy agreed easily. "But it does make people *wonder*."

Clara pulled her hand free. "I don't want people wondering. That's why we need to get to the truth."

"That's exactly what I want too," I said.

Dorothy nodded sympathetically. "I'm just saying that reopening the case brings all of this back for a lot of people in town, especially Clara and even me." She turned to me, blinking back tears. "Sometimes the kindest thing is to let the past stay buried."

"I understand this is hard," I said carefully, "but the truth is rarely easy."

The waitress appeared with impeccable timing and menus in hand. "Can I get anyone started with drinks?"

"Yes," Dorothy said warmly. "Tea for Clara. Chamomile. Water for me, dear."

Clara smiled her gratitude. I ordered coffee, and LuLu ordered a latte.

When the waitress left, Dorothy leaned in again. "Clara, whatever comes out of this...no matter what the town thinks happened...you'll always have me by your side. We're family."

"Thanks, Dorothy. I don't know what I would do without you."

"Of course. Connie took Larry's side. I have always been on your mother's. I just want you prepared for whatever might come to light and the consequences. Towns can be cruel."

"I know you have my best interest at heart, and I appreciate that as always." Clara pushed back from the table and stood. "I need some air," she added, her voice breaking.

Dorothy rose immediately, looking stricken. "I'm so sorry, dear. I never meant to upset you. I'll come with you."

Clara hesitated but didn't argue. As they moved toward the door, LuLu leaned close to me. "Dorothy is clearly drawing battle lines between her and Connie," she whispered.

"I know," I said. "And poor Clara is caught in the middle."

The bell jingled as they left.

LuLu whistled slowly. "That was not lunch."

"No," I said. "That was positioning. Now we just have to figure out which side is right." I stared at the door, at the street beyond it, and at a town that had decided rumors made a better story than truth.

It was time to set the record straight.

Eleven

THE AFTERNOON LIGHT slanted through the Whisperwoods at an angle that made everything look deceptively peaceful. Gold dust filtered through maple leaves, warming the air just enough to make you forget how easily this forest could swallow secrets whole.

I didn't forget.

Holden stood near the edge of the trail with his hands on his hips, listening while Park Ranger Tiana Ellison spoke in a low, practical voice, her box braids hanging down her back. She looked exactly like someone who belonged out here—boots scuffed, uniform crisp, eyes alert without being jumpy. The kind of person who noticed details because it was her job, not because she believed the woods were alive and listening.

Which, unfortunately, they were.

"Alden came in just after lunch," Tiana said. "He saw men moving crates near the old maple sugar shanty on the north ridge. Two trucks. One didn't have plates."

Holden's jaw tightened. "Armed?"

"Yes," she said without hesitation. "At least two posted outside. Rifles. They weren't hiding, exactly, but they weren't inviting company either."

My stomach knotted. "Did Alden get close?"

"No," Tiana said firmly. "He's not the kind to interfere. He knows our deal. I leave him alone, and he reports anything suspicious in the woods to me, then disappears. I don't know where he goes exactly, and I don't ask."

Holden nodded once. "Good. I don't want him going near them again."

Tiana glanced between us, her gaze lingering on me just a fraction longer than polite curiosity allowed. "I can put up trail advisories. Keep hikers away from that section, though no one really travels in that section of the woods. Probably why they chose it."

"That would help," Holden said. "Thanks, Ranger Ellison. I'll take it from here."

She hesitated, then added, "You want backup?"

"Not yet," Holden replied. "I need eyes first. Not noise."

Tiana accepted that without argument. She gave a short nod, then turned toward her vehicle. "I'll check back in before sunset." Her footsteps faded down the trail, and the woods closed in around us almost immediately, as if relieved to be left alone with people who knew better than to underestimate them.

I sighed. Vex padded at my side, his faint glow dialed down to a dull shimmer that looked like reflected sunlight if you didn't stare too hard. His tail flicked once, his irritation barely contained.

"She doesn't know," I murmured.

"No," Holden said. "And she doesn't need to." He glanced at me. "You good?"

I nodded. "Just recalibrating my definition of *normal afternoon*."

He smiled and gave me a wink, which never failed to make the butterflies dance in my stomach. We moved off the trail and into the woods, keeping low and quiet. The path Alden had mentioned wasn't official. It was just a worn line through brush and fallen leaves, the kind you only noticed if you spent time looking for what didn't belong.

The sugar shanty came into view slowly, like something the

forest had been trying to forget. It sat in a shallow hollow, half-hidden by young maples and creeping vines. The roof sagged. The boards were gray with age. It should have been empty.

It wasn't.

Holden dropped into a crouch behind a fallen log and held up a hand. I mirrored him, settling beside him while Vex pressed low near my boot. Through the branches, I counted movement.

Two men stood outside, rifles slung casually like they were guarding lawn equipment instead of something dangerous. Another man hauled a wooden crate from the back of a truck and disappeared inside. A moment later, the door opened again. Crate after crate made their way inside.

I whispered, "That's not camping gear."

"No," Holden agreed quietly. "That's storage."

My skin prickled, not from fear, exactly, but from the way the air felt stretched too tight, like the woods were bracing themselves. For what, I had no clue...yet.

"How many did you count?" Holden asked.

"Three outside. Two inside, at least."

"Any markings?"

I scanned carefully. "Nothing obvious. No logos. No symbols."

Holden's gaze tracked the scene with professional focus. "They're careful. Which means they've done this before."

Vex's ears twitched. His eyes lifted, tracking something above us.

I followed his gaze.

A hawk perched high in the branches, motionless except for the slow, deliberate turn of its head. It watched the shanty with unnerving attention, not hunting or resting, just observing with intelligent amber eyes, like a certain ginger feline I knew.

My lips pressed together into a flat line.

Holden noticed my reaction immediately and followed my gaze then quirked a brow. "What's so interesting about a hawk?"

"That's not a hawk," I said quietly. "And I didn't invite her."

Holden blinked and then frowned.

Vex let out a silent, deeply offended huff. *I can't believe she followed me here.*

We waited.

The hawk didn't move.

Minutes passed. Crates continued to disappear inside the shanty. One of the guards laughed at something someone inside said. The sound carried too far in the stillness, sharp and wrong.

I leaned closer to the shadows and whispered, "Fenrin."

The hawk's head snapped toward us.

"Well," Holden muttered. "That answers that."

The hawk launched from the branch and glided down, landing lightly on a mossy patch a few feet away. The shift was quick and controlled—feathers folding into fur, wings into limbs—until a sleek ginger cat stood where the bird had been, her tail flicking with unmistakable irritation.

Her gloating amber gaze locked on Vex immediately.

Vex bristled, his shimmering black fur standing on end.

"Oh no," I murmured. "We are not doing this now."

Fenrin stretched deliberately, then fixed me with a look that clearly said, *You left without me...again.*

"You were supposed to stay home, but you didn't," I whispered back. "You followed."

Her smug expression confirmed that, yes, she absolutely had.

Holden didn't react beyond a small sigh. "You two finished?"

Fenrin's ears flicked toward the shanty. Her posture shifted to professional and alert.

I followed her gaze, and something clicked. "They're not unloading," I murmured. "They're staging."

Holden nodded. "Which means they'll be moving later. Maybe tonight."

I glanced at Fenrin, then back at Holden. "She could stay."

Vex's glow flared faintly in protest. *You're putting her to work instead of me?*

Holden considered it for half a second. "She's quieter than we are. And if they spot her, they won't think anything of a wild animal."

Fenrin's tail flicked smugly.

I leaned toward her. "I'm thinking fox. Small. Stay hidden and watch the crates. If they move anything, or if more people arrive, you come get us. No heroics, understood?"

Her eyes gleamed. She didn't hesitate. The shift was smooth, once again controlled, and undeniably showy. A fox crouched where the cat had been, russet fur blending perfectly with fallen leaves, her amber eyes sharp and intelligent.

Vex made a sound that translated roughly to, *This is unfair.*

"Don't start," I whispered. "You're on comms."

He sulked but stayed close.

We watched a little longer, long enough to confirm patterns and to know we didn't have enough yet.

Holden touched my elbow lightly. "Let's pull back."

I nodded.

We retreated the way we came, slowly and carefully, the woods swallowing our presence as easily as it had accepted the intruders. Behind us, the shanty remained quiet. Guarded. Waiting. And somewhere in the brush, a fox kept watch—smug, silent, and very pleased with herself.

We left the Whisperwoods without a sound. But I knew one thing for certain as the trail opened back up into afternoon light. Whatever was in those crates wasn't meant to stay hidden.

And it was about time we found out what was inside.

The library smelled like dust and lemon oil, with a quiet that pressed in on your ears until you noticed your own breathing. *Maple Hollow* always felt steadier at night, as if the walls remembered every truth ever whispered between its shelves and were holding them until someone brave or foolish enough came back to ask again. The front desk lamp was the only light on, casting a warm circle across Clara's empty chair and the neat stack of returned books she'd left behind.

She'd gone home early. Headache, she'd said. I believed her. Some days grief didn't need a reason. She gave me the code to let myself in. I locked the door behind me and went straight to the back room, where Maggie Winslow's notebook sat in their archival box. Holden had agreed it was safest left with Clara.

It wasn't a dramatic notebook. No leather cover or scrawls, just an ordinary spiral-bound pad like the ones you buy in bulk because you don't want to waste good paper on half-finished thoughts. Maggie had filled it from edge to edge anyway.

I set the box on the long table and took the notebook out. The first few pages were familiar. Tunnel sketches, elevation notes, and cross-referenced dates with town permits. I'd already pored over this a few times, tracing routes and timelines until my eyes blurred.

Tonight, I wasn't looking for routes.

I was looking for *people*.

Vex appeared silently on the chair beside me, his tail flicking once before settling. He leaned over the page with exaggerated interest. *She wasn't afraid of the tunnels*, he said. *She was afraid of patterns.*

"I'm starting to see that," I murmured, but patterns of what?

I flipped deeper into the notebook, past the careful diagrams and into the margins where Maggie's handwriting grew slanted as if impatient. Her notes overlapped one another here, with arrows crossing arrows and words underlined so hard the pen nearly tore through the paper.

> *Sound carries differently after midnight.*
> *They pause before the bend.*
> *Always two ahead and one behind.*

I stopped. That wasn't about cargo. That was about people. I turned the page.

This one walks heavier than the others.
That one never carries anything—just watches.
They listen before moving.

My stomach tightened. Maggie hadn't been cataloging a historic discovery to put in the books. She'd been cataloging activity in the tunnels no one should know about. What was being moved and how it was being moved. Who waited. Who watched. Who guarded.

I flipped back to the dates they had occurred. Midweek nights. No festival events. No inspections scheduled. Quiet days when no one would question headlights on a back road or boots scuffing stone into the tunnels. No wonder she kept quiet when she noticed strange activity. She wanted proof before she went to the police.

I reached the page with the scratched symbol. The same one I'd seen in the tunnels. Maggie had drawn it hastily, almost angrily, then crossed it out and redrawn it again. Beside it, she'd written:

They think this means silence.

Below that, in smaller letters, as if she hadn't wanted even herself to see it:

It only works if everyone agrees.

I leaned back in my chair and stared at the ceiling. Who was 'everyone' and what were they being silent about? What was in those crates? Wishville agreed to silence the way it agreed to snow days and potluck sign-ups. Quietly and collectively, without anyone ever admitting they'd made a choice.

The mastermind could literally be anyone.

I flipped to a later page in the notebook. This section was

different. It was filled with fewer diagrams and more observations.

Someone is being protected.
Not the cargo. Not the routes. A person.

The room felt smaller suddenly, the stacks leaning in like they were listening, too.

Maggie had known. Maybe not everything, but enough to scare her. Enough to possibly get her killed or make her run away in fear.

I pressed my fingers flat against the page and forced myself to slow down. Panic wouldn't help. Maggie hadn't panicked. She'd observed and written and trusted that truth, documented the evidence properly, hoping it would protect her.

It hadn't.

The last few pages of the notebook were uneven, the handwriting rushed.

He told me to stop.
Said it wasn't safe.
Not like I think.

I knew without reading the next line who *he* was.

Larry is lying to me.
He's lying for someone else.

My chest tightened painfully. "Why didn't you tell anyone?" I whispered to the empty room.

Vex tilted his head. *Because telling the wrong person would have been worse.*

I closed the notebook and sat there for a long moment, the weight of it heavy in my hands. Maggie hadn't trusted the town, and she hadn't trusted the tunnels to stay buried either.

She'd trusted the library and history and facts.

A soft sound echoed somewhere in the building. A shift of wood, and a settling beam. I froze, listening. Nothing else followed. Still, I moved more carefully after that, sliding the notebook back into the archival box then locking it away again. This case had shown me that some truths needed to be protected at all costs.

Clearly, people would stop at nothing to keep them buried.

As I turned off the back-room light, my gaze snagged on the map pinned to the corkboard near the door. Clara must have hung it up, maybe to study it. Maggie's hand-drawn overlay still clung there, faded pencil tracing tunnels that shouldn't exist according to any official record. One route stopped abruptly just short of the mountain. She'd hesitated there, or had been interrupted, or had decided to come back later.

"You were so close," I murmured.

Outside, the night pressed against the windows, lantern light bobbing faintly in the distance as WishFest wound down. Laughter drifted up the hill, careless and bright, the sound of a town pretending everything was fine.

I turned off the last lamp and stepped into the darkened library, letting the door lock softly behind me. The mountain loomed against the stars, black and patient. Someone had been moving dangerous things through its bones, but Maggie hadn't been chasing the danger. She'd been chasing the lie. And whatever, or whoever, had decided she knew too much was still out there, confident enough to keep moving...

Still counting on Wishville's silence to hold.

I pulled my coat tighter around me and headed down the steps, the symbol from the tunnel wall and Maggie's notebook burned into my thoughts. They thought it meant silence. They were wrong. It meant someone was afraid of the truth coming out.

And fear, I was learning, always left a trail if you knew how to follow it.

CHAPTER
Twelve

BY THE TIME evening settled over Wishville, my house had officially crossed the line from *understocked* to *concerning*. I, too, had eaten cereal for dinner the night before and called it "freeing." I'd followed with toast and jam and pretended it counted as balance. Tonight, there was nothing left but a jar of pickles, three mismatched condiments, and something in the fridge that might once have been soup but had long since surrendered its identity.

So, I grabbed my backpack, pulled on a sweater, and headed out on my bike with its baskets toward *The General Store*. I didn't own a car. The one and only time I had tried to drive was when the automobile was first invented. It hadn't turned out well.

Maybe someday I would have Holden teach me.

The lights inside glowed warm and familiar against the early fall dusk. *The General Store* was small but dense, its shelves packed tight and handwritten signs taped wherever Maisie Flint felt like they belonged. A bell over the door announced every entrance like a town crier.

"Lyra!" Maisie called from behind the counter. "You're just in time. Apple cider donuts are fresh."

"Threatening me with kindness again?" I asked.

She grinned. "It's my brand."

I grabbed a shopping cart and turned toward the aisles, already building a mental list of things LuLu and I had forgotten to be responsible about. That was when I heard *their* voices. I stopped short at the end cap and peeked around the corner.

Professor Bernice Galloway stood ramrod straight with a sharp expression. She had one hand resting lightly on the handle of a mostly empty cart. Across from her was Randall Pike, former president of the Wishville Historical Society and current embodiment of everything that had gone wrong there. He'd been lying low ever since he got out on bail.

I eased my cart back down the aisle I was in and drifted closer to the center, pretending to study canned goods while very much listening in. I parted the cans just enough so I could see through the shelves.

"I'm just saying," Randall murmured, his voice low and tight, "if Maggie uncovered something, Bernice, it didn't disappear with her."

Bernice's lips pressed into a thin line. "You assume a great deal."

Randall scoffed softly. "I assume Maggie was nosy. Which she was."

My jaw tightened.

"She was thorough," Bernice corrected. "There's a difference."

Randall leaned closer, glancing down the aisle like he expected history itself to be eavesdropping. "You were on the board with her. You had access to the same records. If she found anything—anything at all—I need to know."

Need, I noted. Not *want*. Not *for the sake of the town*.

"For what purpose?" Bernice asked coolly.

Randall hesitated a beat too long. "Because if she was digging into old financials like the quarry agreements and the expansion permits—"

Bernice's eyes flashed. "Those were *your* projects, Randall."

"And approved," he snapped. "By the board."

"By *you*," Bernice shot back. "You controlled the purse strings.

Maggie raised concerns and you dismissed them. You made her sound crazy."

I leaned closer, my pulse quickening.

Randall lowered his voice further. "Maggie protested everything and was never clear on why she didn't want the expansion to go through. That doesn't mean she had proof I mismanaged anything."

"But it does mean she was asking the right questions," Bernice said. "Questions you didn't want answered."

Randall straightened, his irritation sharpening into something colder. "If Maggie kept records or documented anything that could be misinterpreted—"

"There it is," Bernice said flatly. "You're not worried about preserving history. You're worried about yourself."

Randall's jaw clenched. "I'm worried about my reputation, and the reputation of the Historical Society."

"You're worried about the consequences of being greedy," Bernice corrected. "And no, I don't know what Maggie found beneath the library. If I did, I wouldn't be sharing it with you."

For a moment, neither of them spoke. The hum of the refrigeration unit filled the space between them.

Then Randall said in an intimidating voice with an edge to it, "If you remember anything at all, you *will* come to me if you value your job. I have connections in the history department at the college."

Bernice met his gaze without flinching. "No, Randall. I won't. Your *connections* can't do anything more to me than they already have." She turned her cart and walked away, leaving him standing alone in the aisle with his jaw tight and eyes calculating.

I ducked back and slid the cans together just as Randall turned. Quickly making my way to the endcap, I pretended to examine the greeting cards until he stalked past me toward the register and out the door.

The bell jingled loudly behind him.

"Well," Maisie said mildly from the counter, "that man always smells like panic when he leaves."

I startled. "You heard that?"

She shrugged. "Hard not to. Randall never did master subtlety."

I wheeled my cart full of bread, eggs, actual soup, and...okay, fine, the donuts over to the counter. Bernice stalked past without buying anything, and I briefly wondered if she had heard Maisie and me.

Maisie rang me up, then paused, studying my face. "You're thinking about Maggie."

"Yes," I admitted. "You knew her?"

Maisie nodded slowly. "We were about the same age. She came in here a lot back when my father ran the store. He carried a lot of unique items for people just like Maggie. He even traded items with people and resold them like they did in the old days. She asked for things most people didn't think to ask."

"Like what?"

"Old maps. Handwritten ones. She wanted copies of things people brought in, like old family journals and letters not published in the history books. Everyone knew my father was a collector of oddities, so people brought him all sorts of things."

My fingers tightened on the shopping cart handle. "Did Maggie ever say why she wanted them?"

Maisie leaned on the counter. "She said history deserves to be recorded for future generations. All history. She was obsessed with making new discoveries."

I hesitated. "Did she have any enemies that you knew of?"

Maisie's expression shifted from thoughtful to wary. "A few, I'm afraid. Even her own husband."

My lips parted. "Larry?"

"He worked with Connie for the town back then," Maisie said. "He came in looking angry once, mad she still wasn't home. Maggie was here late again, sorting through things my father gave her."

"What were they arguing about?"

Maisie lowered her voice. "She told him she couldn't stop. That what she'd found was more than ancient, undiscovered history. It pointed to something still active. Something hidden."

"Did she say what?"

Maisie shook her head. "She told him the quarry expansion would interfere with something that was going on, and that certain people in town didn't want that."

"Did she have proof of what was going on?" I asked.

Maisie's mouth tightened. "She was real secretive. If he hadn't pushed her, she never would have said as much as she did, especially in public. Maggie liked to have all her I's dotted and T's crossed before she came forward with a story." The bell jingled as another customer entered, but Maisie didn't look away from me. "She wasn't scared, but she was careful. Like someone who knew the wrong proof could get her erased...permanently. I know the town is full of talk that either she ran away or Larry killed her." She shrugged. "I've always thought that maybe she found the *wrong proof* after all."

I paid, thanked Maisie, and stepped back into the cool evening air, my groceries heavy in my arms. Wishville looked peaceful under the rising stars. Too peaceful for a town layered with lies, tunnels, and secrets people had been paid to forget.

As I pedaled home, one truth settled hard in my chest. Randall Pike wasn't afraid of history. He was afraid Maggie Winslow had written it down. And whatever she'd uncovered was still close enough to make powerful people nervous.

The next morning, Wishville woke up to bright sunlight, air crisp enough to feel clean, and everyone acting as if the town wasn't vibrating with secrets. I didn't have the luxury of pretending. Not with crates in an abandoned sugar shanty, and Randall Pike circling Maggie's name like a vulture with a briefcase. Or poor

LuLu, asleep in my guest room with her phone on her chest like she'd been waiting for the next emergency to happen in her dreams.

But I had one small, stubborn reason to leave the house anyway. Holden's birthday was coming up. He hadn't told me the date like it mattered. He'd mentioned it once, flat and dismissive, like birthdays were for other people. Like celebrating meant admitting you were attached to something. Which, unfortunately for him, meant I had decided we were celebrating.

And there was only one place in Wishville I trusted to help me find the right gift without making it weird.

Once Upon a Time sat at the edge of Main Street where the sidewalk narrowed and the maple trees leaned closer, as if they, too, wanted to browse the bookstore. The windows were cluttered with book stacks and handwritten signs:

LOCAL AUTHOR SPOTLIGHT
MYSTERY BOOK CLUB TODAY
ASK ME ABOUT MY FAVORITE VILLAIN

And the door always opened with a soft creak that felt like stepping into a story. But the first thing you noticed wasn't the smell of old paper or the warm dust of well-loved shelves. It was the windchimes.

A cascade of jangling magic hung above the doorway in an impossible tangle of silver spoons, feathers, antique keys, and dried herbs. When I pushed inside, the chimes sang out in layered notes, bright and chaotic and oddly welcoming, like the shop itself recognized me and approved of my continued existence.

"Lyra Wells!" Fiona Fitzwhistle called before I'd even taken two steps.

Fiona owned the bookstore the way storms owned the sky, completely and unapologetically. She wore a swirl of plaid fabric that looked like it had once been several scarves and had decided to become an outfit through sheer force of personality. Her orange curls were caught up in a messy nest held together by pencils and feathers, and her tiny glasses—slightly cracked at one corner—balanced on the tip of her nose as she peered at me like I might be a plot twist.

"You're early," she said. "Or late. Hard to tell these days. Time's been weird."

"Time has always been weird in your shop," I told her.

She beamed. "Thank you."

The bookstore hummed with quiet life. A kettle whistled in the back. Pages turned. Somewhere, someone laughed softly at a line they hadn't expected. The shelves were crowded and cozy, the kind of place where you could vanish for hours and come out with ink on your fingers and a new worldview.

I took a breath that felt like stepping out of the world and into something softer. Then I heard the clink of teacups. In the front sitting nook, where Fiona had arranged mismatched chairs like she was casting a play rather than hosting a book club, Ruth and Dorothy sat with the Wellies. All of them were gathered around a low table set with a teapot, delicate cups, and a plate of scones that looked like they'd been baked with personal affection and possibly a blessing.

Monthly book club.

I'd forgotten it was today.

Tilly, Belle, and Dot were animated in the way only women who believed the universe was constantly sending them signs could be. They leaned in close, whispering furiously, scarves tangling, bangles clinking, knocking elbows like they were trying to fuse into a single, all-knowing entity.

Ruth spotted me first and lifted a hand in a cheerful wave. Dorothy's gaze followed, pausing on my face with polite curiosity.

"Lyra!" Ruth called. "Come join us!"

I forced a smile and lifted my basket like a shield. "I'm just here for—"

"A book," Dot said instantly, nodding with grave certainty as if she'd read it in the steam curling off her teacup.

Belle gasped, her hand flying to her chest. "For love? My pigeons whispered the gossip, so it has to be true."

Tilly narrowed her eyes at me. "My spleen journal says it's for justice."

"You're all wrong," I said quickly. "I'm buying a birthday gift."

Three sets of Wellie eyes widened in perfect synchronization.

Ruth's mouth curved into a delighted smile. "Oh?"

Dorothy's brows lifted. "Whose?"

From behind the counter, I could feel Fiona watching like a woman enjoying front-row seats to her favorite serial drama.

"A friend," I said carefully, heat flooding my cheeks.

Tilly sipped her tea. "Friends don't make you blush."

"Hot flash," I said.

Belle leaned in, whispering reverently. "You're not old enough for a hot flash."

If you only knew, I thought.

"Sit," Ruth said kindly, patting the chair beside her. "Just for a minute, dear. We're discussing *The Midnight Staircase Murders* and whether the butler's motive was believable."

I glanced at the book on the table: a dramatic silhouette, a looming staircase, and a shadow that looked suspiciously like it was holding a candlestick and bad intentions.

Dot tapped the cover. "The author broke the rules."

"Which rules?" I asked before I could stop myself.

Dot's face lit with pleasure. "The sacred ones."

Ruth leaned in conspiratorially. "Dot thinks every mystery should follow her personal code."

"Not personal," Dot corrected. "Cosmic."

Dorothy set her cup down with a precise clink. "The twist was cheap."

Belle inhaled like she'd been slapped. "It was shocking."

"It was convenient," Dorothy said calmly. "*Shocking* isn't the same as *earned.*"

Tilly nodded like Dorothy had just delivered a prophecy.

Ruth tilted her head at me. "What do you think, Lyra?"

I opened my mouth...then closed it again. What I *thought* was that I currently lived inside a mystery with too many suspects and not enough proof, and debating fictional twists felt like discussing umbrellas during a flood.

"I haven't read the book," I said.

Ruth's eyes were warm, inviting me into something normal for five seconds.

So I added, "I think if the clues weren't there, the twist doesn't count. But if the clues were there and you missed them, then that's on you."

Dot beamed. "Yes."

Dorothy's gaze sharpened. "Agreed."

Belle stared at us, betrayed. "You're all monsters."

Fiona glided out from behind the counter like a flamboyant bookstore spirit, her plaid skirt whispering around her ankles. "If you want monsters," she announced, "I have an entire shelf."

Ruth laughed. "We're safe, thank you."

Fiona's tiny, cracked glasses caught the light as she turned to me. "Now. What sort of birthday book are we hunting?"

I stood, grateful for the escape. "Something for Holden."

Dorothy's eyes flicked to Ruth. Ruth smothered a smile, and Dorothy winked.

Fiona clapped once. "Ah. A man with the personality of a closed door but the soul of a very sad poem."

"That's not wrong," I muttered.

"Come," Fiona said, sweeping toward the mystery section. "We have brooding detectives. Reluctant heroes. Men who solve crimes while refusing to admit they have feelings."

"That sounds like you're selling me his biography."

Fiona glanced over her shoulder. "Exactly."

She stopped at a shelf with a hand-lettered sign: **GRUMPY**

MEN WHO SECRETLY CARE (AND THE WOMEN WHO LOVE THEM).

"I cannot believe you wrote this," I said.

Fiona plucked out a hardcover with a dark blue jacket and silver lettering. "This one. Detective with a wounded soul. Small town. Buried secrets. Meets a mysterious woman."

"That's—"

"On the nose," Fiona finished brightly.

I skimmed the first page. Spare. Sharp. Quietly emotional. The kind Holden would claim not to like and then quote later when he thought no one was listening. "This might actually work," I admitted.

"Of course it will," Fiona said. "I am never wrong about books. Only about men."

The door creaked open and the windchimes exploded into fresh chaos. Howard Kline stepped inside, shaking snow from his jacket like he'd walked through a cloud of bad headlines. Tall, weathered, and suspicious of everything, including joy.

"You got it?" he demanded.

"Good morning to you too, Howard," Fiona said pleasantly.

"The new thriller," he said. "The hostage negotiator one. The library doesn't carry it."

The library doesn't carry it. I felt a flash of irritation on Clara's behalf. "They have budgets," I muttered.

Fiona leaned on the counter. "Which one?"

Howard slid over a crumpled note. "*Dead Man's Bargain.* Came out yesterday."

"Oh," Fiona said. "The one that makes people throw it."

"Perfect," Howard said.

From the nook, Dorothy called, "If you throw it, you admit it bested you."

"If I throw it," Howard said, "it cheated."

Ruth laughed. "He'll be fun at book club."

Howard recoiled. "I prefer to keep my thoughts private."

The Wellies immediately began arguing out loud about whose thoughts were correct.

Fiona produced the book like a magician. "I do, in fact, have it."

Howard grabbed it, paid, and turned to leave.

"And," Fiona added sweetly, "Lyra can tell Clara to request the next one."

Howard paused, startled to see me.

"I read," I said mildly. "And librarians are not mind readers."

He grunted and fled, windchimes screaming after him.

The book club resumed instantly.

Fiona turned back to me. "Birthday success?"

I lifted the book. "I think so."

Ruth raised her cup. "To thoughtful gifts and solving mysteries."

Dot smiled serenely. "To destinies."

Belle sighed dramatically. "To lovers who pretend they're not."

Dorothy watched me a moment longer than the rest, then returned to her tea without comment.

I paid Fiona, said my goodbyes, and stepped back into the cool sunshine with a book under my arm and a faint warmth in my chest. For five minutes, in a bookstore full of windchimes, scones, and women arguing about fictional murders, the world had almost felt normal.

Almost.

But as I walked back toward the street, I couldn't shake the memory of Randall's voice in *The General Store*, or the way Bernice had shut him down like she was guarding something more precious than pride.

Holden's birthday gift sat solid against my side.

And in my mind, Maggie Winslow's name flickered like a page that refused to stay closed.

CHAPTER
Thirteen

FENRIN DIDN'T KNOCK.

She never knocked.

One moment, the living room was quiet except for LuLu's muffled snore from the couch and the faint tick of the kitchen clock. The next, a ginger cat appeared on the windowsill like she'd been poured out of shadow with her tail flicking, eyes bright, and expression smug in that way that always made me want to argue even when she hadn't said a single word.

Vex, curled like a judgmental comma in the armchair, lifted his head. Fenrin's ears angled forward. Vex's glow pulsed once, offended on principle. And then he rose stiffly, affronted, and unmistakably alert. I didn't need translation magic to understand what that meant.

"What?" I asked, already sitting up and reaching for my phone.

Vex stared at me with those ancient eyes, then darted his gaze toward Fenrin like he was refusing to give her the satisfaction of speaking first.

Fenrin blinked slowly, the very picture of *I told you so.*

Vex let out a low, annoyed sound and trotted straight to me, placing one paw on my knee like he was filing an official report. *The men are on the move.* His tail flicked.

Fenrin hopped down from the sill and padded closer, her posture sharp, all smugness gone now that it mattered. She wasn't here to gloat. She was here to warn.

"On the move," I repeated, petting her head. "Good girl."

Vex glared.

"And good boy, of course."

Don't insult my intelligence. He gave a single, firm blink.

Fenrin's gaze swung toward the window, toward the dark line of trees beyond my yard, toward the mountains that loomed behind Wishville like a spine.

My stomach tightened. "They're heading for the mountains."

Vex rolled his eyes, offended that I'd needed to say it out loud. *On the move, just like I said.*

LuLu stirred on the couch, making a small sound and rolling over. Her phone slid off her chest and thumped onto the cushion. She didn't wake. For a second, I envied her. The ability to fall asleep anywhere, and then sleep through the town's secrets shifting under our feet like tectonic plates.

Then I stood. "Okay," I breathed, forcing my voice into something steady. "Holden needs to know." I didn't even bother calling. My fingers flew over the screen, sending a text: **Fenrin confirmed movement. Men from shanty headed toward mountains now.**

The reply came fast: **On my way. Don't move.**

I stared at it. "Don't move," I echoed aloud, incredulous.

Vex's ears flattened. *He has met you, hasn't he?*

Fenrin sat, wrapping her tail neatly around her paws like she was prepared to wait out the apocalypse if she had to.

I was not.

I shoved my feet into boots, grabbed my jacket, and tucked my hair into a messy knot that would hold for exactly twenty minutes. My hands shook only a little. I was halfway to the door when my phone buzzed again.

Stay home. I mean it.

I stared at the message until my eyes stung. Then I typed back: **I'm the Guardian of the Well. The tunnels are my problem, too. I'm coming.**

A pause. Then: **Fine. Back porch. Two minutes.**

I didn't give him the courtesy of waiting the full two. I slipped out into the cool evening air, my heart hammering and breath turning pale in the porch light. The sky had sunk into deep navy, the first stars sharp as pinpricks. Somewhere in town, someone's windchimes sang softly, oblivious.

Fenrin glided out after me, silent as mist. Vex followed, his glow dimmed down, but his posture radiated *importance* like he'd been promoted to command.

Holden's cruiser rolled up without its siren, lights off and tires whispering against the gravel. He climbed out and crossed the yard quickly, his gaze sweeping over me like he was checking for injuries before the danger even arrived.

"This is a bad idea," he said.

"You keep forgetting I'm only half-human," I replied.

His jaw flexed. "Lyra—"

"I appreciate your concern," I cut in, "but I'm more worried about you. Fenrin saw them. They're moving toward the mountains. That means the tunnels."

Holden's expression hardened at the word *tunnels*, like it carried weight he hadn't wanted to add to his badge. "Where is she?"

Fenrin flicked her tail as if answering.

Holden's gaze dropped to her, then to Vex. "You two sure?"

Vex's eyes narrowed.

Fenrin blinked, insulted.

"Great," Holden muttered. "I'll take that as a yes." He pulled out his phone and started typing with fast, practiced efficiency.

"Tiana," I realized.

Holden nodded. "If they're moving crates, they're using roads or trails. She'll have eyes on the forest edges. And Alden saw the initial activity. He might know which direction they favor. Check in with Weylan and Sparks. They might know something, too." He hit send, then looked up at me. "We need Calderis."

I nodded, texting Weylan and Sparks. I agreed Calderis meant extra power. "I'll call him."

I didn't use my cell phone for that. I used my crystal orb that Dwellers used to communicate and sent a quick video message. The night air sharpened. The shadows between my porch posts deepened. And then he was there, as if he'd stepped out of the space between heartbeats.

Calderis had materialized with the kind of stillness that made my skin prickle. He exchanged his dark Elarion cloak that normally hung heavy around his shoulders for a black leather jacket here in Wishville. His silver intense eyes turned pale blue in the human world as they swept the yard in a single, efficient scan.

"Lyra," he said, his voice low and controlled. Then his gaze landed on Holden. "Thorn."

Holden nodded once, not flinching or posturing. They weren't exactly friends yet, but they'd reached an uneasy rhythm lately. One of mutual respect layered over the tension of two men guarding the same woman from different directions.

"They're moving," Holden said without preamble. "Fenrin spotted it. Toward the mountains."

Calderis's expression sharpened. "The tunnels."

"Yes," I said. "If they've figured out how to use them, they could be moving anything. Quietly. Without anyone seeing. The question is, how long have they been moving things?"

Calderis's eyes flicked to Fenrin, who sat like a queen awaiting praise. "She watched?"

Fenrin's tail swished.

Calderis's mouth tightened faintly with amusement. "Good."

Vex looked personally wounded that the compliment hadn't been for him. *Good for nothing.*

Holden's phone buzzed. He checked it, then swore under his breath.

"Tiana?" I asked.

"Alden saw them cut toward the ridge trail that leads behind the quarry access road," Holden said. "He didn't follow, but he recognized the route. Tiana's moving to block hikers out and keep eyes on the tree line. I'll have Weylan and Sparks watch the town."

My stomach dropped. "We need to check out the quarry." Maggie's protests. The expansion. The whispers.

"Then we go now," Calderis said, already shifting his weight like the decision was made.

Holden hesitated only long enough to glance at me. "We shouldn't charge in blind."

"I'm not suggesting we charge anything," I said, though my heartbeat disagreed. "We should track and confirm before we decide on a course of action, but we do need to move before they get wind that we're onto them."

Calderis's gaze locked on mine. "Stay close."

Holden's eyes narrowed. "That's my line."

Calderis didn't look away. "Then we agree."

For a second, the night held its breath. Then Holden exhaled, short and sharp. "Fine. Move."

We didn't take the cruiser. It was too loud and visible. Holden parked it down the road near the end of the tree line, where it could be mistaken for an evening patrol. From there, we moved on foot, slipping into the Whisperwoods like we belonged to it.

Which, in my case, I did.

The forest felt different at night, more intimate and alive. Leaves whispered as we passed. The air tasted of damp earth and pine sap. Somewhere high above, an owl called, and the sound threaded through the trees like a warning.

Fenrin padded ahead in cat form, silent and focused. Vex stayed close to my ankle, glowing only faintly. Holden moved with practiced stealth, his boots landing softly despite their weight. Calderis moved like smoke, present, lethal, and somehow quieter than the darkness itself.

We followed the ridge trail Alden had described, cutting off the main path before it could funnel us into anything obvious. Holden kept checking the ground for scuffs, broken twigs, or disturbed leaf litter.

Calderis didn't need signs. He tilted his head once, his eyes narrowing. "They passed here," he murmured.

"How do you know?" Holden asked as if wanting to learn Dweller ways.

Calderis's gaze stayed on the woods. "The air remembers."

We reached the rock outcropping that marked one of the old tunnel mouths, half hidden behind brush. It was a place most hikers would mistake for a shallow cave. It didn't look like an entrance to anything. It looked like a dead end.

It wasn't.

I pressed my palm to the stone. The rock felt cool, but beneath it I sensed the faint pulse of old magic, tunnels carved by human hands and Dweller secrets intertwined. "This one," I whispered, certain this was the X Maggie had drawn on the map.

Holden's hand hovered near his weapon. "You sure they used this?"

Fenrin's ears flicked forward.

Vex stared at the darkness as if daring it to misbehave.

Calderis's expression tightened. "Yes."

We slipped inside.

The air changed immediately to something cooler and thicker, smelling of stone and damp, the sound of the forest cut off like a door closing behind us. The tunnel swallowed our footsteps, turning them into muffled echoes.

I hated how familiar it felt. Not because I'd been down here a thousand times. I hadn't. But because the tunnels were part of Wishville's bones. Part of the town's buried truth. And lately, everything buried kept trying to surface.

We moved deeper, guided by the faint slope downward. Holden used a small flashlight, angled low, careful not to send a beam ahead like an invitation. Calderis didn't need light. His eyes held their own pale shimmer, enough to catch the edges of stone.

A sound drifted from ahead. A scrape. A low murmur. The distinct thud of something heavy being dragged.

Holden froze, holding up a hand, and we all stopped.

The tunnel stretched forward, splitting into a narrower passage on the right and a wider one straight ahead. The sound came from the wider one.

Holden leaned close, his voice barely audible. "How many?"

I listened hard. "Two," I whispered. "Maybe three."

Calderis's gaze narrowed. "More, deeper."

Fenrin's body tensed.

Holden made a quick motion as if to say, *we follow, we don't engage unless we have to.*

We followed.

The passage widened into a chamber that looked like it had once been used for storage. It had old wooden supports, rusted hooks, and a cracked stone floor stained with decades of moisture. And there, half lit by Holden's low flashlight beam, we saw them. Men. Four of them, moving with practiced urgency. Two were hauling a crate. One held a rifle and kept scanning the tunnels like he expected an ambush. The fourth was ahead, checking the route.

They weren't random criminals. They moved like people trained not to panic.

Holden's jaw tightened. Calderis's hand flexed at his side. And my pulse turned to ice when I recognized the way they handled the crate. Careful and reverent, like it mattered. Like it wasn't just cargo.

One of the men muttered, "Hurry up. We're late."

Late for what?

Holden's eyes flicked to me, then to Calderis in question.

Calderis's gaze remained locked on the men. "They know this route." Which meant the tunnels had been used before. Which meant Maggie had been right back then and apparently still was now.

The men started forward again, dragging the crate toward the next passage.

Holden whispered, "Let's follow until we see an exit. We need to know where they're taking them."

But Fenrin's ears twitched sharply. She glanced back at me, her eyes bright with warning.

And then, as if the tunnels themselves betrayed us, a loose stone shifted under Holden's boot with a sharp click. It wasn't loud, but down here, sound carried.

The guard snapped his head toward us. "Who's there?"

Everything in my body tensed.

Holden lifted his flashlight out of instinct, then stopped himself...too late. The beam caught the guard's face, and in the split second of illumination, I saw his expression harden into recognition.

"Move!" he shouted.

The men grabbed the crate and bolted.

Holden surged forward. "Stop!"

They didn't.

The tunnels erupted into motion with boots pounding, breath sharp, stone scraping as the crate slammed against the floor.

We ran.

Holden took the lead, fast despite the confined space, his flashlight bobbing. Calderis moved beside him, his hair coming loose from its bun. I ran after them, my hands ready to summon power if needed. Vex was a small glowing streak near my feet, with Fenrin racing ahead with startling speed.

The men veered left at a fork without hesitation.

Holden cursed. "They know where they're going!"

Calderis lifted a hand, murmuring something in that old cadence of his, channeling Ember Pulse. The energy from the molten lava in the earth's core rose with pressure building like a storm gathering inside stone. A burst of energy slammed forward, aimed at the fleeing men. It should have knocked them off their feet. Instead, the lead man ducked, braced, and pulled something from his pocket, tossing it backward.

A small glass sphere shattered on the stone. Smoke exploded outward, thick, acrid, and choking. Holden swore, his hand flying to cover his mouth. I coughed, my eyes burning, then summoned Magma Ward with my hands to make a protective heat barrier over Holden. Channeling Skycall, I manipulated the air and swept the smoke aside. The cloud tore apart under the force of my magic, but it bought the men seconds.

Seconds mattered.

We burst through the thinning haze into another passage, and I saw the men ahead, closer now, but still moving fast. They dragged the crate with brutal urgency, scraping it along the stone. They reached another chamber, larger and darker.

The lead man shouted, "Burn it!"

My blood turned cold. "What—" I started.

Then the man with the rifle pulled out a canister and hurled it toward a stack of old wooden supports and discarded crates dry enough to catch in an instant. Flames bloomed. The fire spread fast, licking up the supports, filling the chamber with heat and smoke. They'd started it intentionally, an escape tactic. They knew the tunnels well enough to use them like a weapon.

Holden skidded to a stop, coughing. "They're trying to cut us off!"

Calderis lifted both hands, using Obsidian Crafting to conjure weapons from cooled magma. He threw spears at the men, the force slamming into them. One stumbled, screaming and clutching his leg. Another shouted and held his arm, but they were prepared.

The lead man yanked the crate hard, and the corner cracked against the stone. Then he shouted, "Leave it!" They abandoned it without hesitation and sprinted deeper into the tunnels, vanishing into the smoke-thick dark beyond the flames.

Holden started forward.

The fire surged, and the wooden supports groaned.

Calderis caught Holden by the shoulder, stopping him. "If the supports fall, the passage collapses."

Holden's eyes flashed. "We can't let them go."

"We can't die chasing them," I rasped, smoke clawing at my throat.

The fire was spreading faster than I could process. It wasn't just a barrier. It was a threat to the tunnels themselves which were old, fragile structures that could collapse and trap anyone inside.

Using Aqua Vein, my magic stirred instinctively. I didn't think. I acted. I threw my hands forward and reached for the moisture in the air, the damp in the stone, the condensation clinging to the tunnel walls, and the hidden veins of water that wove beneath Wishville like secrets.

The water answered. It surged out in a rush, cold and forceful, spilling across the stone in a wave that slammed into the flames. Steam exploded. The heat hissed and shrieked like an angry thing. The fire fought, flaring brighter for a second, hungry and stubborn. Then the water drowned it. The flames collapsed into smoking embers, leaving the air thick with steam and wet ash.

I stood there with my chest heaving and hands shaking.

Holden stared at the extinguished fire, then at me. "Nice."

"Thanks," I panted. "I'd prefer not to be roasted alive in a tunnel today."

Calderis's gaze stayed fixed on the darkness where the men had vanished. His expression was one of hard controlled fury. "They escaped too easily," he said. "Which makes me wonder if they had help."

Holden swore softly and turned his flashlight toward the abandoned crate. It sat half cracked at the corner, wood splintered, damp from my magic. The surface was scratched with marks, random at first glance, until my eyes caught one symbol that made my stomach drop.

A small, deliberate slash-and-hook like a sigil, like a warning. Like the mark Maggie had found.

The scratched symbol for silence.

My throat tightened. "Holden."

He followed my gaze. "What is that?"

"A symbol Maggie discovered," I said, my voice low. "For silence. For *don't speak about this.*"

Holden's face went still. "You're telling me these guys are connected to Maggie?"

"I don't think Maggie was a part of it back then, but I think she knew about it," I said. "And whoever's running this wanted silence at any cost back then and apparently now as well."

Calderis crouched, his fingers hovering over the scratch marks as if reading them with more than sight. "This is deliberate and possibly linked to the rebels."

Holden pulled out a knife and jammed it under the broken seam. "I think it's time we found out what's inside."

My heartbeat kicked harder. Part of me didn't want to know. But the larger part, the part that had been dragged into this by fate and blood and a well that never stopped whispering, needed answers as much as Clara did.

Holden pried. The lid gave with a sharp crack. He lifted it. For a second, the three of us just stared. Inside the crate were firearms neatly packed, wrapped in oilcloth, arranged with the kind of careful efficiency that screamed *operation*, not impulse. Not antique trinkets. Not rare artifacts. Weapons. Human weapons.

Not Dweller-made.

Holden's face drained of color. "Holy—" he started, then stopped himself, like he remembered I lived with a sarcastic magical cat and a shapeshifting Dweller Whispen, and somehow *that* wasn't the most shocking thing anymore. "They're smuggling guns," he said, his voice flat with disbelief.

My stomach rolled. "Through the tunnels."

Holden nodded slowly, his eyes locked on the crate like it might bite him. "This isn't just local."

"No," I whispered. "It's bigger. And well protected, if it's been going on for forty years. A small mountain town that looked the other way." And a guardian too preoccupied with finding her mother to notice.

Calderis's expression was lethal. "This is war-making."

Holden swallowed, then snapped into action. He took photos with his phone, careful angles, evidence. He shut the crate again, like closing it could contain what it represented. Then he straightened and looked at us both. "This has to go federal," he said.

The words hit like a gavel. I wasn't naïve. I knew crimes didn't stay small just because a town wanted them to. But Wishville was a place of festivals and gossip and cozy routines that tried to make everything feel manageable.

Federal meant something else.

Federal meant scope. Federal meant we weren't chasing one killer or one secret anymore, we were brushing up against a network. But mostly, Federal meant FBI in the tunnels that led to Elarion. And that was more dangerous than anything we'd discovered so far.

"Wait," I said. "What about Elarion?"

"We need more time to look into this and find a way to protect that realm," Calderis added.

"Look, I get what you're saying, but I don't have a choice. More than my job is on the line if I don't call it in and the Feds find out. We could all go to prison for obstructing justice." Holden pulled his phone out again and looked questioningly at us both.

Calderis nodded and Holden stepped a few feet away, his voice low as he spoke into his phone in the darkness. I couldn't hear the details, only the cadence and clipped seriousness, the way his posture changed into something more serious.

Calderis watched the tunnel behind us, protective and tense. Fenrin prowled near the charred embers, her ears flicking and eyes narrowed like she could still hear the men's footsteps fading into stone. Vex sat by my boot, his glow dimmed and expression pinched with the kind of frustration only a cat could make look like moral superiority.

When Holden returned, his face was set. "They're sending someone," he said. "But we're not going public."

My brows lifted, quickly followed by a wave of relief. "Thank goodness, but how did you pull that one off?"

"Because I told them if we go public," Holden said, his voice tight, "whoever's behind this knows we're onto them. They'll move faster. They'll vanish. And we still don't know the mastermind. They agreed to stay under the radar and I would keep them informed."

I felt a cold weight settle in my chest. "Quiet is good. We can control the tunnel access so there's less chance of Elarion being discovered."

Holden nodded. "We build the case and find the head, not just the hands."

Calderis's gaze sharpened. "And if the head is not human?"

Holden didn't flinch at the question anymore. "Then I'll let you take the lead, but make no mistake. We seek justice either way."

The tunnel air was damp and cold. The embers smoked faintly. The crate sat between us like a confession. I stared at it, at the scratched symbol that Maggie had discovered was being used for silence, secrecy, and warning. Maggie hadn't just found tunnels. She'd found a pipeline. And whoever had been using it back then hadn't wanted to expand the quarry for fear of discovery. They'd wanted to bury the questions and erase her work. And I feared they hadn't stopped.

They'd just gotten better at hiding.

Behind me, deeper in the tunnels, the men had escaped into the dark. And for the first time since I'd become Guardian of the Well, the threat didn't feel like a single crime to solve.

It felt like a system. A machine. Something bigger than Wishville, with roots in stone and money and power.

And possibly rebels.

Holden's gaze met mine. "We'll go back and regroup, but we need to keep eyes on every entrance."

"And Fenrin?" I asked, thinking of her stakeout, her silent watch.

Fenrin's tail flicked.

Holden nodded once. "She stays close. We need her."

Vex's ears flattened, clearly offended that he wasn't the only one needed. He sulked in silence.

Calderis stepped closer to me, his voice low. "You did well."

My throat tightened. "Yeah," I whispered. "But they did better."

He understood what I meant. They'd set a fire without hesitation. They'd vanished into the tunnels like ghosts. They'd abandoned a crate without fear. They knew the tunnels well enough to treat them as theirs. And the symbol Maggie found sat on that wood like a signature from the past.

Holden turned toward the exit path, his flashlight steady. "Let's move."

We started back the way we'd come, our footsteps muffled by damp stone, the tunnel walls pressing close as if they wanted to keep us from leaving with what we'd found.

But I knew we couldn't un-know it now. We'd seen the truth. And somewhere out there, the people behind the crates were already making their next move quietly, confidently, and protected by shadows and silence. Just the way Maggie had warned.

And now, it was our turn to break it.

CHAPTER

Fourteen

WISHFEST AT NIGHT always tried to convince you that nothing bad could ever happen in a town lit by lanterns.

The clearing by the well glowed the way it always did during festival hours, with warm strings of lights draped from branches, vendor tents lined up in cheerful rows, and the steady pulse of people moving between cider stands and craft tables like they were part of a carefully rehearsed dance. Laughter floated over the grass. Someone's guitar strummed softly near the stage. A kid in a handmade leaf crown ran past me with a sticky apple in one hand and a wooden wand in the other.

It should have felt safe.

But the well sat at the center of it all like a silent witness, and I couldn't stop seeing the tunnels beneath it. Stone corridors and hidden doors, damp air and old secrets. I couldn't stop thinking about the abandoned crate. The scratched symbol. The fact that someone had used the mark Maggie found for silence like a signature.

And I couldn't stop thinking about the men who had gotten away.

LuLu bumped my shoulder gently, snapping me out of it. "Lyra," she murmured, smiling brightly at a passing couple like she didn't have a care in the world. "Your face is doing that thing again."

"What thing?"

"The thing where you look like you're mentally rearranging someone's organs."

I blinked. "I do not—"

"You do," she said sweetly. "It's terrifying. Try 'Festival Chair' instead of 'Guardian of ancient power and cursed secrets.'"

I forced my mouth into something closer to a smile and turned toward the mayor. Doug Delaney stood near the information booth in a windbreaker that made him look like he'd dressed for practicality and then remembered he was supposed to be in charge of a celebration. Assistant Mayor turned acting mayor after Eliza Hemsworth's fall from grace, he had the tense posture of a man trying to keep a boat from sinking while smiling for the camera.

"Lyra! LuLu!" he called when he saw us, relief flashing across his face. "Thank you for coming so quickly. I know you have volunteers that normally keep the festivals running smoothly, but with Maggie's disappearance reopened, Fall WishFest is...well...falling apart. These festivals are the heart and soul of Wishville. I would hate to see one fail because of some cold case."

Connie stood with a clipboard in hand and headset on like she was the mayor herself, when in reality, she was a retired volunteer. She shot us a look that was half gratitude, half *don't you dare let anything explode on my watch.*

"We're doing our best," I said.

Doug's smile tightened. "Good. Great. Because the pumpkin carving contest is in twenty minutes, but we're short on pumpkins. The chili cook-off judge just texted that his truck won't start, and someone's complaining that the hayride line is 'emotionally oppressive.'"

LuLu leaned in. "That sounds like Belle."

Connie didn't even look up from her clipboard. "It *is* Belle."

Doug sighed. "And I've got reporters sniffing around again."

LuLu held up her hands. "It wasn't me this time."

"No, these ones are from out of town." Doug shook his head.

My stomach clenched. "Are they asking about the cold case?"

Doug's eyes shifted toward the well, then away. "About every-thing. The library renovation. The time capsule. Maggie Winslow. People love a tragedy when it's not theirs."

Connie's voice sharpened. "No one is saying anything on record. Everyone is enjoying WishFest. That is the official mood."

LuLu nodded solemnly. "The official mood is cider and denial."

Doug rubbed his forehead. "Holden's not here."

"He's working," I said carefully.

Doug's gaze sharpened. "Working...with whom? He's supposed to working for this town."

"He is. He's working with people who can help," I said lightly. "He'll be back when he can."

I didn't say *feds*.

I didn't say *tunnels*.

I didn't say *he's keeping them away from the wrong side of the mountain.*

Because in Wishville, the fastest way to create panic was to let people think they were entitled to the full truth.

Connie checked her clipboard. "Lyra, isn't the wish ribbon ceremony in fifteen minutes?"

I glanced at my watch in surprise. Usually, I was always on top of my schedule, but this cold case had even me distracted. "Yes," I said. "I'll be there."

Doug lowered his voice. "If anyone asks about the investiga-tion, I want them directed to me."

Connie's eyes narrowed. "No offense, Doug, but you're not intimidating."

Doug winced. "I'm working on it."

"I can be intimidating," LuLu offered. "I'm small but tough. It throws people off."

Doug looked unsure whether to thank her or retreat. "Just...

keep things running." He moved off, immediately intercepted by a vendor with strong feelings about extension cords.

We walked the vendor line, smoothing over small crises and making sure WishFest didn't collapse under the weight of its own charm. *The Twisted Loaf* booth sold out of pastries. *The General Store* booth had a table of knit scarves. *Once Upon a Time* had "mystery grab bags." *The Dapper Den* had fake handlebar mustaches. *Boar's Board and Brisket* passed out free samples of beef. *Blooms of Glory* had fall corsages on display. And Trip Danderly, with his handmade sparkly Wish Sheriff badge and wand flashlight, walked the festival, keeping people in line.

I saw Dorothy and Clara near the edge of the clearing. Clara's strawberry-blonde hair caught the lantern light. She looked exhausted but resolute. Dorothy stood beside her with perfect posture and a carefully neutral expression.

"Clara," I said softly. "Dorothy."

Clara's face brightened. "Lyra. LuLu. It's so good to see you both."

"How are you holding up?" I asked.

Clara shrugged. "Like I'm trying to renovate a building while someone keeps shaking the foundation."

"That tracks," LuLu said.

Dorothy's voice was smooth. "We're managing."

Clara glanced around the festival. "It feels wrong to celebrate while this is happening."

"It's Wishville," I said. "WishFest must go on. It's tradition and helps keep people from panicking."

Clara nodded. "Have you learned anything else?"

"Yes, anything at all?" Dorothy asked. "Poor Clara can't go on like this much longer. It's not good for her health."

"I'll be okay," she said with a reassuring smile.

"Not enough," I said truthfully. "But we're working on it."

LuLu added brightly, "Organizing things."

Dorothy blinked. "Organizing what?"

"People," LuLu said. "Emotions. Motives. Alibis."

"Good," Dorothy said, then looked past us. Her expression tightened.

Henry and Colin McAlister stood near the planning board booth, speaking with Evelyn Hart. Henry's silver hair was immaculate and teeth overly white. Colin, slightly younger, leaned in close and kept his voice low. Evelyn laughed, touching Colin's arm like they were old friends.

My eyes narrowed. "Let's talk to them."

LuLu's eyes gleamed. "Absolutely."

We headed over to the trio.

"Henry," I said. "Colin."

Henry turned smoothly. "Lyra! Enjoying WishFest?"

"Trying to," I said. "Evelyn."

Evelyn smiled brightly. "Lyra. LuLu. Clara."

Clara didn't smile.

"We're interested in old planning board records," I said calmly. "From 1984. Some files appear to be missing."

Henry's smile didn't falter, but something behind it cooled. "Missing?"

"Yes," Clara said. "Permits. Meeting minutes."

Evelyn laughed too quickly. "Archives lose things all the time, honey."

"Not like this," Clara said. "And I'm not your honey."

Colin crossed his arms. "Are you accusing the board of hiding records?"

"I'm asking where they went," I said, leveling my gaze on Evelyn, who began to squirm.

Henry stepped in front of her. "I only interned for the board back then. Now, I have my own development company. But I do recall Maggie Winslow was passionate about her projects, but passion can be misleading."

Dorothy's voice cut in, calm and sharp. "In my experience, money can mislead more than anything else. People will do just about anything to have it."

Henry's jaw tightened.

LuLu smiled sweetly. "I'm sure we can ask these questions officially down at the station, but we thought we'd give you a chance to come clean on your own."

Colin stiffened. "If we had something to tell you, we would."

"Would you?" I asked. "Or would you do anything to protect yourselves from your involvement. What were you covering up back then? Or are you still covering something up now?"

Henry stood straighter. "You can't prove anything. If you could, the authorities would already be involved. And neither of you are the authorities, so if that's all, I bid you adieu." He tilted his head.

As they turned away, it was clear we hadn't found proof, but we'd found a nerve.

That was when Ruth Bingham appeared beside us. At eighty, Ruth carried herself with the quiet authority of someone who had watched Wishville outlive its own secrets. Retired now, she was still the town's matriarch in all the ways that mattered. People listened when Ruth spoke, even when they didn't want to.

She held a cup of cider, the steam curling into the lantern light. "I heard that," she said calmly.

LuLu stiffened. "How much?"

"Enough," Ruth replied, her sharp eyes following the McAlisters. "And for what it's worth, I never trusted them back then or now."

Clara blinked. "You knew them back then?"

Ruth nodded once. "I sat on the planning board for a short time. Long enough to see who treated the town like a responsibility and who treated it like an opportunity."

Dorothy's gaze sharpened. "Wasn't George Fletcher on the board for a while back then, too?"

Ruth's mouth tightened. "He sure was. I trusted him the least."

My eyes widened. "Why?"

"He was in tight with the chief back then. He and Ron Maddox always left the room before hard questions started," Ruth said. "And when George retired, he left town fast. Too fast for someone who claimed Wishville was his life's work."

LuLu exhaled. "That's suspicious."

Ruth nodded. "It sure is."

The festival swelled around us with cheers, music, laughter, and lanterns glowing brighter as the night deepened. I looked at the well, the light shimmering on stone, and felt the weight of everything beneath it. Holden and Calderis were off keeping the federal attention pointed toward the quarry and woods, away from Elarion. And here I was, smiling through a festival while the past walked freely among us.

Ruth's voice softened. "Be careful, Lyra."

"I always am," I said.

She shook her head slightly. "No. Be careful the way Maggie tried to be. I fear she wasn't careful enough."

LuLu squeezed my hand. I lifted my chin and turned back toward the crowd, wearing the expression Connie wanted—festival-mystical instead of WishFest-Chair-wary. Because WishFest was still running. The town was still watching. And somewhere beneath the lantern light, the truth was tightening its grip—quiet, patient, and very much awake.

By the time we got back to my house, the festival noise had followed me home like glitter. Impossible to shake and clinging to my nerves in tiny, sparkling flecks. Not the happy kind of glitter, either. The kind that gets into your carpet and your lungs and makes you sneeze at the worst possible moment.

My porch light spilled a soft halo onto the steps. Inside, the living room was warm and lived-in, with blankets tossed over the couch, LuLu's shoes kicked off in a trail like she'd been shedding responsibility on the way in, and a faint smell of cinnamon lingering from the candle she kept lighting "for vibes."

Vex was already in the window, glowing faintly like a sulky

nightlight. Fenrin sat on the rug in full cat form, her tail wrapped neatly around her paws, and her posture so composed it felt like an apology. Vex's ears twitched toward her, and for once he didn't hiss or look personally offended by her existence.

Progress.

LuLu dropped onto the couch with the exhausted grace of someone who had spent four hours smiling at people who thought "hayride line oppression" was a serious civic issue. "If I have to hear one more person say, 'Well, Maggie wouldn't have wanted...' I'm going to start throwing scones," she muttered.

"You don't have scones," I said, toeing off my boots.

"I'll improvise."

The front door opened again, and Holden stepped in first, with his jacket unzipped, hair slightly damp from the night air, and tired eyes. We were at the don't-need-to-knock stage.

Calderis followed behind him like a shadow that had decided to take human form for the evening, his cloak traded for a dark coat, expression unreadable, and gaze scanning my house with that quiet, lethal awareness he carried everywhere.

Holden locked the door out of habit and leaned back against it for a second, as if he needed the wood to hold him upright.

"Well," LuLu said brightly, "if it isn't my two favorite stress responses."

Holden shot her a look that would've shut down a lesser person. "Funny."

LuLu smiled wider. "I thought so."

Calderis's mouth twitched faintly.

My gaze softened on them both. "How bad was it?"

Holden exhaled through his nose and crossed to the armchair, dropping into it like his body had finally remembered it was allowed to stop moving. "The Feds showed up faster than I wanted."

"Of course they did," LuLu murmured.

"They came in thinking it was simple," Holden continued. "Weapons trafficking, local tunnel network, small town that doesn't know what it's sitting on. They wanted access. Full sweep."

My stomach tightened. "And you said no."

"I said *limited*," he corrected. "I gave them the quarry-side entrances, the woods-side paths, and the sugar shanty route. I told them the rest of the tunnels are unstable and unsafe."

LuLu blinked. "You lied to federal agents."

Holden's stare remained flat. "I strategically curated the truth."

Calderis's eyes flicked toward him, something like approval tightening the air between them.

"They bought it?" I asked.

"When I made the tunnels shake, they bought it," Calderis said.

"A little, but not entirely," Holden clarified. "But they don't have reason to push yet. Not without a body count. And they want the same thing we do...the mastermind. They've got a task force contact they're looping in quietly. No press. No public statement. Not until we can make arrests that stick."

My ribs loosened a fraction. "So, they're not putting barricades around the well and digging up my backyard?"

"Not tonight," Holden said. "But they're going to want more eventually."

Calderis's gaze sharpened at the word eventually. "Then we must ensure they never learn where the other paths lead."

Holden glanced at him. "That's why you left."

Calderis stepped farther into the room, his presence shifting the energy like gravity had changed. "I spoke with my father." Calderis's eyes met mine. "He is concerned."

"That's his default setting," LuLu said, then winced. "Sorry. I know he's your father, but that Dweller clearly doesn't like me."

Calderis's voice softened. "I know, and I'm working on that." He looked back at me and his jaw tightened slightly. "The Veiled Vault remains sealed, and the well is intact, but Vaerion believes the tunnel activity on the human side may be stirring older currents."

My skin prickled. "Meaning?"

"Meaning the boundary between realms is stressed," Calderis said. "Not broken, but strained. And if humans continue to move contraband through the stone veins beneath this town, they will eventually brush against places they should not."

Holden's hand flexed on the armrest. "What does Vaerion want?"

Calderis's gaze went distant for a beat. "To place a full Dweller as Guardian."

Silence dropped like a stone.

My heart stumbled. "He can't. This is my legacy."

"He can," Calderis said quietly, looking away from me. "If he thinks the current Guardian is unfit, given you're a half-blood, he has the authority to place someone who is fully on Elarion's side."

"I'm on both sides," I said, the words sharper than I intended.

Calderis's eyes came back to mine with confidence. "I convinced him to give you a chance to prove yourself. You didn't allow the humans to open the sealed tunnels. Rebel Dwellers did. Which is why he did not act...yet."

LuLu sat up straighter. "So, what's the compromise?"

Calderis's expression remained controlled. "He will wait. For now. But he wants proof the human side is contained."

Holden let out a slow breath. "Then we will contain it."

I nodded, but the thought of Vaerion replacing me sat heavy in my chest. He didn't like me or even trust me that much. If he replaced me, he would most likely make me an outcast like Alden. And if I were an outcast, I would lose access to Elarion. The well wasn't just magic or my duty, it was access to my other half. To my home and lineage. To my mother.

Losing access to Elarion felt like losing air. I wasn't sure I could live without it.

LuLu turned toward me and nudged my knee. "Okay, enough

with this depressing conversation. Back to the cold case. It's our turn."

Holden's brows lifted. "Festival updates?"

LuLu moaned dramatically. "We managed hayride emotions. We kept Doug from combusting. Connie is still alive, which is basically a miracle."

"And," I added, "we talked to Dorothy and Clara. We updated them as much as we could, but we left out the part about the smuggling ring in the tunnels."

Holden nodded once, approval easing his posture.

LuLu continued, "Then we ran into Henry and Colin McAlister having a cozy little chat with Evelyn Hart."

Holden's face went still. "The McAlisters and Hart."

"They all played dumb," I said. "But they were *too* smooth about it. Like they'd practiced saying nothing. We pressed about the planning board activities and missing records from 1984. They didn't give anything away, but—"

"They're hiding something," Holden finished.

"Yes," I said. "And Ruth Bingham overheard."

At that, Holden's eyes flicked up. "Ruth Bingham? The matriarch Ruth?"

"The eighty-year-old legend herself," LuLu confirmed. "She said she briefly was on the planning board back then and never trusted the McAlisters then or now. She trusted George Fletcher even less."

Calderis's head tilted slightly. "George Fletcher. Do we know him?"

"Former board guy," I said. "Ruth thinks it's suspicious he left town fast right after retiring. Like he didn't want to be around when questions started. He was in tight with Chief Maddox back then."

Holden's jaw worked as he filed that away. "Good. That's a lead."

Vex hopped down from the window and padded toward Fenrin with cautious dignity. Fenrin lifted her head, her eyes bright but softer than earlier. Vex bumped his forehead against hers, quick and sharp like a truce made under protest, no words necessary. Fenrin's tail flicked, and she returned the gesture with a smug little purr.

LuLu made a small sound. "Aww. They're making up."

"They're negotiating," I corrected. "Like tiny furry diplomats with attitude."

Holden's mouth twitched. "I can relate."

The tension in the room eased like someone had loosened a too-tight knot.

I took a breath and glanced toward the kitchen. "Okay. Since we're all here, and since we're currently living inside a nightmare with lanterns..."

Holden narrowed his eyes. "Lyra..."

"Don't 'Lyra' me," I said, moving toward the counter. "Sit. Both of you."

LuLu's eyes widened with delight. "Oh my god, you're doing it."

Holden's suspicion deepened. "Doing what?"

"Happy Birthday to you," LuLu sang under her breath.

Holden froze. "LuLu."

"What?" she said innocently.

Holden's gaze snapped to me. "You didn't."

"I did," I admitted, pulling a small cake box from the fridge where I'd hidden it behind the pickle jar like a responsible adult. "And before you argue, this is not a big thing. It's a small thing."

"Lyra—"

"Holden," I countered, mirroring his tone. "If you can survive smugglers with firearms and federal agents sniffing around your town, then you can survive cake."

Calderis watched the exchange with an unreadable expression that said he didn't understand birthdays but found human stubbornness fascinating.

LuLu clapped once. "Yes! Cake is a Heaven-sent kiss."

Calderis arched a pale blond brow at her, looking as though he were pondering something.

I set the cake on the coffee table and pulled out four small glasses and a bottle of something amber that LuLu had bought "for emergencies," which apparently included emotional ones. Then I reached into my pack and pulled out the book—dark blue jacket, silver lettering—wrapped in brown paper, simple like Holden. He wasn't a shiny-wrapping-paper kind of guy.

I held the gift out to Holden. "This is for you," I said quietly. "Because you deserve something that isn't evidence, and well, it reminded me of us."

Holden stared at it like it might explode. Then he took it carefully, like accepting the gift meant accepting the sentiment. He was my boyfriend, and yes, I was falling in love with him, whether he could deal with it or not.

He unwrapped it slowly, his eyes scanning the cover. "A detective returns to a small town and a mysterious woman saves him," he read quietly.

LuLu made an ecstatic noise.

Holden shot her a look, but his grip on the book tightened just slightly, and I saw the faintest shift in his shoulders as if the weight of all that he carried had lifted. "Thank you," he said, his voice rougher than usual.

I swallowed. "You're welcome." I read the book first, of course, and it reminded me of our story. Maybe the ending would give him the courage to admit he was falling in love with me too, like the hero of the book did to his leading lady.

LuLu poured drinks with the seriousness of a priest performing a rite. Calderis accepted his glass with polite uncertainty, sniffed it once like it might be a potion, then took a careful sip. His eyes widened a fraction and he smiled a little.

LuLu grinned. "Right? Human joy in liquid form."

Holden set the book down beside him like it belonged there. He leaned back, his glass in hand, and for the first time all day, his face looked less like a wall and more like a man. Outside,

Wishville was still Wishville—lanterns still glowing in the distance, secrets still moving under stone, and tunnels still snaking beneath our feet. But for this one small moment, in my living room with cake and whiskey and a truce between cats, we let ourselves breathe.

Holden lifted his glass slightly. "To not going public."

LuLu clinked hers against his. "To catching the mastermind."

Calderis raised his with solemn precision. "To protecting both realms."

I lifted mine last, meeting Holden's gaze. "To small things like birthdays that keep us human." And when our glasses touched, our fingers brushed softly.

Almost like a promise.

CHAPTER
Fifteen

WISHVILLE WHEELS always smelled like metal, motor oil, and the particular kind of optimism it took to believe anything broken could be coaxed back to life. The sign outside was hand-painted and slightly crooked with **WISHVILLE WHEELS: Sparks Mechanic Shop** in bold letters, and beneath it, in smaller script that looked like it had been added after a long day and a longer argument, *"We fix what everyone else gives up on."*

I parked my bike by the fence and stepped inside, the bell above the door, giving a tired jingle, had probably heard more swearing than prayer. The shop was already humming with morning energy. A radio crackled softly in the corner. Tools clinked in steady rhythm. Sunlight spilled through the open bay door in pale stripes across the concrete floor.

Sparks stood under the hood of an old Subaru like he was performing surgery. He had grease on his forearms, fake tattoos because a Dweller's skin was flawless, a screwdriver tucked behind one ear, and his pale blond hair looked like it had been wrestled by a static storm.

Weylan perched on the shelf beside him with even paler hair, in his quiet, watchful way, almost too still to be real.

Sparks didn't look up when I walked in. "If you're here to tell me the world is on fire again, get in line," he called.

"I'm here because the world is on fire again," I said, and let the words land.

That got his attention.

He straightened slowly and wiped his hands on a rag, his eyes narrowing the way they did when something stopped being a rumor and started being a problem. "Lyra," he said. "You look like you didn't sleep."

"I slept," I replied. "Like how a person sleeps when their subconscious is doing paperwork."

Weylan's gaze slid over to me, and I got the distinct sense he approved of that comparison.

Sparks jerked his chin toward a stool near the workbench. "Sit. But I know you're not alone." His gaze wandered towards the door expectantly.

"Vex is at home supervising LuLu's breakfast choices."

Weylan snorted. "God help your roommate."

I didn't sit. My body didn't feel like it wanted to sit anymore. It wanted to move, to chase, to keep ahead of the next thing before it could leap out of the shadows. "So," I said, stepping closer and lowering my voice. "Holden told me you had an unmarked truck come through yesterday."

Sparks's expression sharpened, his blue eyes sizzling as the humor drained out of him like oil from a cracked pan. "Yeah."

Weylan shifted, and a gust of wind swept through the shop even though the trees outside were still. "Tell her."

Sparks leaned back against the workbench. "It rolled in right before close with its engine sputtering like it had swallowed a handful of nails. No plates. No company logo. Just...blank."

I frowned. "What about the driver?"

"Male. Mid-thirties. Ball cap pulled low. Didn't give a name," Sparks said. "Paid cash without blinking. Money people carry when they don't want receipts or questions asked, so I didn't."

I took a careful breath. "Did you check the back?"

Sparks's mouth twisted. "I didn't plan to. Then I smelled it."

"What?"

"Oil," he said immediately. "Old oil. Not engine. Like something stored and leaked. And underneath it..." His eyes hardened. "Gunpowder."

My pulse ticked faster. The image of the abandoned crate flashed in my mind. The firearms wrapped in oilcloth. The scratched symbol for silence. "Residue?" I asked.

Sparks nodded once. "In the bed. A film along the seams. I've been around enough hunters to know what gunpowder smells like. This wasn't one rifle that got cleaned badly. This was several."

"What did you do?"

Sparks glanced toward the open bay door as if he expected the truck to magically reappear. "I fixed it," he said simply.

My eyebrows shot up. "Sparks—"

"Not because I'm stupid," he cut in, his tone defensive and actual sparks snapping from his fingertips. "Because I wanted to see where it went. The moment it rolled in, my gut said it wasn't here by accident."

"And you used Charge Craft," I said softly.

His jaw flexed. "Yeah."

Charge Craft magic was Sparks's specialty, electrical coaxing, mechanical persuasion, talent that made dead batteries come to life again and engines purr like they'd never betrayed you. In a normal life, it would've been a quirky skill. In Wishville, it was another secret woven into the town's bones.

"I didn't do it flashy," Sparks continued. "Just enough. A nudge. A pulse. Like jump-starting a heart."

My chest tightened at the metaphor. "And then?"

"The guy waited by the counter the whole time," Sparks said. "Watching. Nervous. Impatient."

That detail chilled me more than the residue.

Sparks's gaze slid to the man beside him. "That's when I told Weylan. Watch him from the sky. Don't get close. Don't be seen."

I looked at Weylan. "You followed him?"

Weylan nodded. "I flew my balloon rides over the entire area until I spotted him, then I stayed on him."

Sparks continued, "The guy drove out like he'd done it a hundred times. He didn't hesitate or stop for coffee or head toward town."

"Toward the woods," I guessed.

Weylan nodded. "Straight for the quarry road."

My stomach clenched harder. The quarry again. The same place Maggie fought about. The same place wrapped in missing files and planning-board smiles.

"You watched it all?" I asked Weylan.

"I tracked him until he hit the quarry access road, then he peeled off. I kept high and stayed back until I lost him."

"Last night?" I asked.

"Yesterday evening," Sparks confirmed. "But that's not the part that matters."

I frowned. "Then what is?"

Sparks's gaze met mine. "He came back."

I blinked. "What do you mean he came back?"

"Before dawn," Weylan said. "I saw the same truck again with the same unmarked body. Same shape. Same route. The quarry road through the woods, heading toward the mountains."

"And then?" I asked, my voice tight.

Sparks blew out a long slow breath. "Then it disappeared."

I stared at him. "Disappeared how?"

"Not like it turned invisible," Sparks said, frowning. "Like it drove into something that swallowed it. It didn't come out the other side."

"I circled the area and watched the road. I even watched the treeline. There was no sign of it anywhere. It had to have gone inside the mountain."

Another access point. "There must be another tunnel entrance big enough to drive a truck through," I whispered.

Sparks nodded grimly. "That's what I'm thinking. The sugar shanty was for storing. The trucks and tunnels are for transfer."

Transfer. The smuggling ring wasn't improvising. They had infrastructure. They had routes. They had enough knowledge of the tunnels to make a federal case look like a local inconvenience. I had a feeling this was part of the same group we found and the same ones who smuggled forty years ago. They were a well-oiled machine if no one had discovered them in all this time. Still...there must be records of something somewhere.

"What about Alden?" I asked, already piecing together the next layer. "Is he watching?"

Sparks nodded. "Yeah. I reached out through Tiana."

Weylan lowered his voice, glancing toward the open bay door again. "Alden's keeping a lookout where he can, and Fenrin is still in hawk form at the shanty. Alden knows the trails. He knows what doesn't belong. If he sees that truck again, or any others, he'll tell Tiana. Tiana will tell Holden. I'm guessing Fenrin will tell you."

I nodded. "And if the truck disappears again?"

Sparks's gaze was hard. "Then we know exactly where to look."

I blew out a breath I hadn't realized I'd been holding. My hands felt cold. A smuggling ring through the woods, the quarry, and the tunnels under Wishville. And in those tunnels, we'd found guns marked with the symbol Maggie found. It wasn't just history anymore.

It was active.

"What did Holden say?" Weylan asked.

"He's trying to keep the Feds on the quarry side of the tunnels," I said. "He doesn't want them anywhere near Elarion."

Sparks nodded. "Good. Makes sense."

Weylan watched me for further instructions.

I lifted my chin. "We need to update Holden on anything new."

Sparks nodded. "Already sent the intel. Photos too. Of the bed residue, the tire tread, the VIN."

I blinked. "You got the VIN?"

Sparks's mouth quirked. "Mechanics notice things."

"Good," I said. "That's...very good." Because evidence mattered now. Because Holden was right. We couldn't go public until we had the head, not just the hands. But every new thread we found made the web feel even bigger than we thought. Crime syndicate big.

And life or death dangerous.

I looked past Sparks through the open bay door toward the line of trees in the distance, and the mountains beyond them like a dark promise. "Another access point near the quarry," I said softly.

Sparks's voice dropped to a warning. "Which means whoever's running this can move cargo without ever touching the well clearing. Without ever touching the library."

"And without anyone noticing," I finished.

Weylan gave a low, quiet sound of approval or agreement, I wasn't sure.

"Okay," I said. "We're officially ahead of them by one step."

Sparks's expression didn't soften. "Then don't let them take the next one."

"I don't plan to." And I knew just whom to go to for answers.

Connie Hale stood in the *Town Hall Records Office* at the records table, her palms flat against the scarred wood as if she needed the pressure to keep herself anchored. The fluorescent lights hummed overhead, too bright and unforgiving. This room wasn't built for confession. It was built for order. For things to stay exactly where they were put.

I took the chair she indicated, slow and deliberate, and set my hands in my lap. I had called her and told her my suspicions, but she surprised me when she asked me to meet her here. She might be retired, but she still had access to certain things and knew where to look.

Vex perched at my shoulder, a quiet, coiled presence. *She is deciding how much of herself to sacrifice,* he warned. *Humans do not do this lightly.*

She turned away from me and began pacing the narrow aisle between the shelves, her fingertips trailing along file spines like she was counting years instead of folders. "I've spent my entire career making sure Wishville didn't tear itself apart over things it couldn't control," she said. "Permits. Zoning fights. Historical arguments that never led anywhere except resentment." She stopped at a drawer labeled **ARCHIVED—PRE-DIGITIZATION** and rested her forehead briefly against the metal. "You think I don't recognize danger when I see it?"

"I think you recognize it," I said. "I think you learned how to manage it."

She laughed softly. "*Manage.* That's a polite word." She pulled the drawer open and slid out a thick folder. Not Maggie's. This one was marked with an innocuous code containing numbers and letters that meant nothing unless you knew how to read between them. Connie flipped it open and spread the contents across the table in front of me.

Shipping manifests.

Weight logs.

Delivery schedules.

All carefully worded. All legally vague.

"This is what Larry was afraid of," she said. "Not because he understood every piece of it, but because he understood enough."

My throat tightened. "The crates. You knew about them."

"Yes. But I didn't know what was in them or who ordered them. I just did my job. They came through the tunnels," Connie continued. "Not every night. Not even every month. People didn't notice, or they told themselves it wasn't their business."

"Maggie noticed," I said.

Connie's jaw clenched. "Maggie noticed everything." She turned the page and tapped a line with her finger. "This isn't a festival delivery schedule. And it's not quarry inventory. It's a transfer window."

I leaned closer. Dates lined up with what I'd seen in Maggie's notebooks—quiet nights, no events, foggy mornings that swallowed sound. "And you approved these," I said quietly.

Her gaze snapped to mine. "I *processed* them. That's different."

Vex snorted. *That is the difference humans use when they want to sleep well at night.*

"I didn't know exactly what was in those crates," Connie repeated sharply. "I didn't ask. And I didn't let anyone else ask either."

"Because Larry told you not to."

"Yes," she said, without hesitation. "And because I trusted him."

That trust sat heavy between us.

"You believed he was protecting you," I said gently.

She stiffened. "He was. He said it wasn't our business what town officials were involved in."

"He protected you from consequences," I pressed. "Not from guilt."

Connie turned away again, pacing. "You think I don't know what it looks like now? From the outside? A woman defending a married man. A town clerk covering paperwork. People whispering about affairs." She shook her head. "Let them whisper. I can live with that."

"Can you live with Maggie being erased?" I asked.

She stopped and slowly faced me. "That's not what I wanted," she said.

"But it's what happened," I replied.

Connie sank into the chair opposite me, the fight draining out of her shoulders all at once. For the first time since I'd known her, she looked...old. Not in years, but in weight. "Maggie wouldn't stop," she said quietly. "She kept writing things down. Names. Times. Patterns. I told Larry she was going to get herself hurt."

"And he agreed," I said.

"He said he'd handle it."

A chill slid down my spine. "Handle it how?"

Connie's hands clenched. "By keeping her distracted. By convincing her she was overreacting. By leaning on me to slow things down."

"You helped him," I said.

"Yes," she whispered. "I helped him *stall*. That's not murder," Connie said quickly, reading my face. "That's not what I'm saying."

"I know," I said.

She blew out a breath. "I thought if I could just buy time. If the movement stopped and things shifted elsewhere, then Maggie would lose interest."

"But it didn't stop," I said.

"No."

"And Maggie didn't lose interest."

Connie closed her eyes. "No."

Silence pressed in. The hum of the lights sounded louder now, like static before a storm.

"You said you and Larry were close," I said softly.

Her eyes opened. "We were."

"But he loved Maggie."

"Yes, and he loved me like a sister," she said fiercely. "And that's the part people never understand. Love isn't a ladder. It's a knot."

Vex hummed, thoughtful. *Knots tighten when pulled.*

Connie laughed weakly. "I thought—" She stopped herself, swallowing hard. "I thought that if things stayed quiet long enough, Maggie would back off. Or Larry would convince her to stop."

"And instead," I said.

"And instead," Connie echoed, her voice breaking, "she vanished."

I let that sit. Let her say it out loud. "You never believed Larry killed her," I said.

"No," Connie said immediately. "Never. He was terrified. Grieving. Lost."

"Then who did you think it was?"

Her mouth opened then closed. "I didn't," she admitted. "That's the truth I don't like. I didn't let myself think about who benefited from her silence."

"Because that question would lead somewhere you didn't want to go," I said.

"Yes," she whispered.

Vex's voice cut in, sharp. *She is at the edge now.*

I leaned forward. "Connie, who had access to those schedules besides you and Larry?"

Her gaze snapped up, startled.

"Who could see when transfers were happening," I pressed, "without lifting a single crate?"

Connie's breath hitched. "No," she said faintly. "That's—"

"You don't have to say it yet," I said quickly. "Just tell me this —did Maggie ever tell you she was afraid of a person?"

Connie stared at the table, her eyes unfocused. "She never told me, but Larry said she told him someone was always there," she murmured. "Watching. Never carrying anything. Just...present. She asked him once if he noticed it. He told her she was imagining things."

"He told her that?" I asked.

"Yes," Connie said, shame flooding her voice. "He told her she was letting her work get to her. I should have stepped in. I should have done more."

Vex's presence went cold and still. *The lie that killed her.*

Connie pressed her hands to her face. "I thought I was protecting everyone for all these years."

"You were protecting a story," I said. "And stories rot when they're sealed."

"There's another transfer tonight," she said quietly. "I looked the other way before, but Larry's gone now. I don't work there anymore, but I still have access. Maggie's case getting reopened made me see things differently, so I looked into things."

My breath caught. "You're sure about the transfer?"

She nodded. "They accelerated. Someone's nervous."

"Who?"

She shook her head. "I don't know. Or maybe I do, and I'm not ready to say it."

I stood slowly. "Then we don't wait."

Connie looked up at me, her eyes wet. "Lyra...if you pull this thread, everything unravels."

"It already has," I said. "We're just admitting it now."

She swallowed hard. "If Larry were alive—"

"He'd want Maggie remembered," I said firmly. "Not buried under paperwork."

That did it. Connie's shoulders slumped. She looked smaller somehow, folded inward by regret. "I'll show you everything," she said. "But I need time to gather it all without raising any red flags."

Vex's voice whispered through my thoughts, urgently. *Time is the one thing we do not have.*

I nodded anyway. "Tonight," I said. "After the transfer."

Connie hesitated, then nodded. "Tonight."

I turned toward the door, the weight of the room pressing against my spine.

As I stepped into the hallway, the fluorescent hum followed me like an accusation.

Behind me, Connie whispered, barely audible, "I never meant for anyone to die."

I paused, with my hand on the doorframe. "I know," I said. And that was what terrified me most of all. Because Maggie hadn't gone missing from malice alone. She'd vanished from good intentions, quiet choices, and people who thought silence was safer than truth. And somewhere beneath Wishville, something dangerous was still moving right on schedule.

Just like before.

CHAPTER
Sixteen

BY THE TIME I got home, Wishville was wearing dusk like a polite disguise. The last of the festival crowd drifted down Main Street in cozy clumps, their arms looped, cider cups in hand, and voices bright with laughter. Lanterns still glowed along the hill, and somewhere a fiddle kept playing like music could stitch a town back together.

I unlocked the front door of my little house, stepped inside, and the warmth hit me fast. Woodsmoke from the fireplace, cinnamon from a candle LuLu insisted made the place feel "less like a haunted cottage and more like a witchy Pinterest board," and the faint, ever-present sweetness of whatever Vex had decided my home smelled like when he wasn't sulking.

I kicked off my boots and hung my jacket, then paused. Because LuLu was talking.

Not out loud exactly—she wasn't on the phone—but I could hear her voice from the kitchen, quick and animated, like she was mid-thought and unwilling to let it die before it reached the air.

"...no, I'm telling you, it's not the movers. It's never the movers," she said, and then she noticed me in the doorway. "Oh! There you are. Good, because I'm about to make you mad on purpose."

"That's my favorite kind of evening," I muttered, stepping farther in.

LuLu stood at my kitchen counter with her hair piled into a messy bun and an oversized sweatshirt that definitely belonged to me. One of my soft, faded ones with a wishing well embroidered on the front. She'd somehow made it look like a deliberate fashion choice instead of a raccoon's stolen treasure.

On the counter sat my worn notebook, two mugs of tea, and a pile of paper she'd printed from somewhere. Vex lay sprawled on the windowsill, his black fur absorbing the lamplight. He looked like an accusation with whiskers, mad that Fenrin was on another mission without him.

"You broke into my office supplies again," I said.

LuLu lifted her chin. "I *liberated* your office supplies for justice."

Vex blinked slowly at me. *She also liberated your last packet of cocoa.*

I ignored him. Mostly. "Okay," I said, setting my bag down. "Tell me what you found."

LuLu didn't hesitate. She slid one mug toward me with the solemnity of a ritual offering. "Sit. Drink. Listen."

I sank into the chair, wrapping both hands around the mug even though it was too hot. The warmth was grounding. My brain had been racing since morning, chasing tunnels and trucks and Connie's confession.

LuLu leaned against the counter, her arms folded. "You know how everyone is focused on Larry and Connie? The whole 'who hated Maggie enough to kill her' thing?"

I didn't like where this was going. "Yes."

"Good," she said. "Now pretend you're not living inside Wishville's favorite soap opera and look at it like a system."

Vex's tail flicked in approval. *Finally. The human with the loud hair is useful.*

I lifted my eyebrows. "A system."

LuLu nodded. "Maggie wasn't killed because she got into a fight with one person."

My stomach tightened. "We don't know she was killed."

LuLu gave me a look so pointed it could've filed my taxes. "Lyra."

I sighed. "Fine."

"She wasn't *stopped* because of romance," LuLu continued. "She was stopped because she was disrupting logistics."

"Logistics," I repeated.

LuLu pushed off the counter and tapped the pile of paper. "Schedules. Timing. Who always knows when something is happening before the rest of the town does? Who has access without ever getting their hands dirty?"

My mind flashed to Maggie's note: *That one never carries anything—just watches.*

LuLu studied my face as it changed and nodded. "Exactly."

I set my mug down slowly. "Who?"

"Not *who* yet," she said quickly, holding up a hand. "I'm not naming anyone. I'm saying...we've been hunting the wrong kind of suspect."

"Explain," I said.

LuLu's eyes lit with that investigative excitement she tried to hide under sarcasm. "Okay. Today I spent three hours doing something you would never do because you have a heart and don't want to upset anyone."

"That's ominous."

"I chatted," she said. "With vendors. With volunteers. With the guy who sets up the portable stages. With the delivery drivers who keep getting rerouted because WishFest has turned the streets into a cinnamon-scented labyrinth."

My mouth tightened. "You interrogated people."

"I *sparkled* at people until they talked," LuLu corrected. "Huge difference."

Vex sighed dramatically. *Both are threats.*

LuLu continued, "And you know what I kept hearing, over and over?"

I waited.

"The same phrase," she said. "'Oh, don't worry, so-and-so already knows.' Or 'so-and-so already cleared it.' Or 'they already moved that.'"

My chest went tight. "So, someone is always ahead of the town."

"Yes," LuLu said. "Someone is always...informed. Don't jump to conclusions. Not yet."

"I'm not," I lied.

LuLu took a breath. "Here's what I *do* know: the people who physically move things? They're replaceable. Someone local has to coordinate."

"Someone with access," I said.

"Yes," LuLu agreed. "Access. Which means keys. Knowledge. Routes. Quiet little shortcuts." She flipped the top sheet around so I could see it. It was a printed map containing part of town, part of the mountain access roads, with hand-drawn circles and arrows in bright marker.

"You did arts and crafts," I said blankly.

LuLu beamed. "I did *crime* arts and crafts."

I stared at the map. "Where did you get this?"

"Town website," LuLu said. "Public works pages. Old PDFs. Nobody reads these things unless they're trying to plan a parade route or commit a felony."

My skin prickled.

She tapped a route line with her nail. "See this? Quarry access. These service roads. The 'maintenance' paths. People think they're for equipment and trail upkeep."

"And they are," I said, my voice cautious.

LuLu's gaze sharpened. "But they're also perfect for moving things without being seen. Especially if you have someone on the inside to tell you when hikers won't be there."

I swallowed. "Ranger Tiana Ellison?" She was too young to

have been involved the first time, but not too young to be involved now.

LuLu shrugged. "Or Finch. As the town maintenance man, he knows every locked gate in this town."

"Then there's Howard Kline," I said. "The groundskeeper. He's always been near the library, an avid hiker who knows every path, always claiming he was "just keeping things tidy." I tried not to let my face harden. "That doesn't mean he's the mastermind."

"No," LuLu agreed. "But it does mean he's useful."

I picked up my mug again, needing something to do with my hands. "What else?"

LuLu flipped to the next page. "Professor Bernice Galloway."

My eyebrows rose. "Bernice?"

LuLu made a face. "She is a walking migraine."

"She's also an academic," I said. "She likes to feel important."

"Exactly," LuLu said. "And Maggie embarrassed her."

I frowned. "I heard."

LuLu leaned forward, bracing her hands on the table. "Maggie's notes—some of them at least—were better than Bernice's published research. Not prettier or more official, but sharper and more accurate."

My throat tightened. "Maggie published a few things but not all of them."

"No," LuLu said, her eyes narrowing. "But she talked. Quietly and to the right people. Bernice hates being dismissed. Do you think she could've—"

"No. She wouldn't cross a line. I'm sure of it." I told her about Randall Pike pressuring her to spill anything she knew or lose her job. If that didn't make her cross a line, then nothing would.

"Agreed. I think Bernice would silence someone professionally, but not permanently. But I also think Bernice knows more than she admits that something was going on."

That felt true. Bernice had always treated Maggie's research like a theoretical curiosity, an academic footnote. But someone who knew the tunnels intimately could do a lot with that knowledge.

LuLu sat at the table across from me, her energy tightening into focus. "Here's the part that matters."

I met her gaze.

"I keep hearing the same names in the background," she said. "Not as suspects. As constants. People who are always nearby when things happen. The people everyone trusts."

My pulse began to thud.

LuLu's tone softened slightly. "Lyra...Maggie wasn't just tracking crates. She was tracking *control*."

Vex's voice slid through my mind, quiet and razor-sharp. *Control is the true contraband.*

I stared at LuLu. "So, what are you saying?"

LuLu held my gaze. "I'm saying the person we're looking for might not look like a criminal."

The words settled heavy. Because in Wishville, criminals looked like outsiders. Strangers. People who didn't belong. But Maggie had lived here. Disappeared here. And the town had swallowed her story like it was nothing more than a sad local legend.

I swallowed hard. "Okay," I said. "So, what do we do?"

LuLu's grin returned, bright, determined, and a little feral. "We go to the people you're avoiding and ask them questions they won't like."

I stared at her. "That's your plan?"

"That's always my plan," she said.

I exhaled slowly, then nodded. "Howard first," I said. "He's the easiest to rattle."

LuLu snapped her fingers. "Yes."

"And Bernice," I added. "Because she'll hate being questioned by someone she considers 'unqualified.'"

LuLu's eyes sparkled. "Double yes."

Vex hopped down from the windowsill and padded over,

rubbing against my leg like he was claiming me for battle. *And*, he added, *we watch the watchers.*

I looked down at him, then back at LuLu. My home felt smaller suddenly—not claustrophobic, just...full. Full of tension, full of leads, and full of people who didn't yet realize they were going to have to talk.

"Okay," she said, her voice steadier than her face. "Let's do this."

I nodded once, feeling the decision click into place inside me like a lock turning.

Wishville could keep pretending. But inside my little house, between a printed map, a cat who knew too much, and a woman who refused to let silence win, we were done waiting for the town to be ready.

Because Maggie Winslow hadn't waited.

And she'd paid the ultimate price.

Howard Kline's shed sat exactly where it always had, half swallowed by the trees at the edge of the library grounds, close enough to town to be ignored and far enough into the woods that no one ever lingered. It was the kind of place people walked past without really seeing, because it had always been there.

LuLu and I approached on foot, leaving my bike locked near the library fence. The sky had shifted into that bruised late-afternoon color that meant dusk was coming early, dragging long shadows behind it. The air smelled like leaves and damp earth...and underneath it, faint but unmistakable, oil.

LuLu caught it too. She shot me a look. "Please tell me that's lawn equipment," she murmured.

"I would," I said. "If I believed it."

Vex padded ahead of us, visible now, his black fur blending into shadow. His ears were flat, tail low and alert. *He is listening for footsteps*, he said. *Not machines.*

The shed door stood open. I stopped a few feet away and listened. Inside, something scraped softly against wood. A drawer sliding. A box being shifted. Careful sounds that weren't rushed.

"Howard?" I called.

The noise stopped instantly. A beat passed. Then Howard Kline stepped into view, wiping his hands on a rag that had once been white. He was thinner than I remembered, his shoulders hunched like the mountain itself had pressed down on him over the years. His eyes traveled from me to LuLu and back again, calculating.

"Lyra," he said, forcing a smile. "Didn't expect to see you out here."

"Funny," LuLu said lightly. "We didn't expect to find you either."

Howard's gaze snagged on her, his irritation flashing. "This area's closed to the public."

"I don't just live in this town," I said. "I'm the festival chair and aiding in the cold case investigation."

He grunted. "Still shouldn't be poking around maintenance areas."

"Then maybe don't leave them open," LuLu said, nodding at the door.

Howard's jaw tightened. "What do you want?" The directness startled me.

I stepped closer, keeping my voice calm. "We're asking the questions."

Howard laughed, a quick, hollow sound. "Everyone's asking questions these days."

"Yes," I said. "But you're one of the few people who actually knows the answers."

His eyes darkened. "Careful," he said. "That's how people get ideas about you."

Vex circled his legs, brushing against his boots. Howard didn't react, but his breathing changed, shallow and quick.

He senses watchers, Vex murmured. *He does not like being watched.*

"Howard," I said gently, "how long have you been maintaining the paths around the library?"

He shrugged. "Long time."

"Before Maggie disappeared?"

Another shrug. "Probably."

LuLu leaned against a nearby tree, as casual as could be. "You always seemed to know when inspectors were coming."

Howard snorted. "That's my job."

"And when they weren't," she added.

His smile vanished. "You accusing me of something?"

"I'm accusing you of being useful," LuLu said. "Which is much worse."

Howard took a step back, closer to the shed. I noticed then that the shadows inside were deeper than they should be. Too much space for a tool shed. Too organized.

"You don't know what you're talking about," he said, closing and locking the shed door.

I met his gaze. "Maggie Winslow knew someone was watching her."

The color drained from his face. "That's nonsense," he said too quickly.

"She said it wasn't one of the people carrying things," I continued. "She said it was someone who never lifted anything. Someone who always seemed to be there first."

Howard's hand tightened on the rag. "She was paranoid."

LuLu tilted her head. "Funny. That's exactly what people say when they don't want to admit someone saw them."

Howard's eyes darted toward the woods. That was all the answer I needed.

"You cleared paths for them," I said quietly. "Didn't you?"

His shoulders sagged just a fraction. "I kept trails passable," he muttered. "That's all."

"For whom?" I pressed.

He swallowed. "People who paid me."

LuLu raised her brows. "Paid you to mow?"

"Paid me to not ask questions," Howard snapped. "Paid me to make sure no hikers wandered where they shouldn't."

"And the tunnels?" I asked. "Don't pretend you didn't know about them."

Howard shook his head violently. "I didn't go down there."

"But you knew when people would," LuLu said.

Silence stretched between us. Finally, Howard exhaled hard. "I never touched anything," he said, basically admitting he had lied. "Never carried a crate. Never opened a box. I didn't want to know."

"But you knew it was dangerous," I said.

"Yes," he whispered. "Others knew, too, but no one cared so long as the money kept coming."

My chest tightened. "Did you see Maggie down there?"

Howard flinched.

"Did you see her in the tunnels?" I repeated.

He rubbed his face with both hands, his rag dropping to the dirt. "I saw her once," he said. "Late. Writing something down. I told her she shouldn't be there."

"What did she say?" I asked.

"She said," Howard swallowed, "'If I don't write it, no one will know about it, and my work will have been for nothing.'" The words hit like a bruise.

"And then?" LuLu asked.

"And then I left," he said. "I didn't want to be part of it."

"But you already were," LuLu said softly.

A truck engine rumbled somewhere in the distance—low, heavy, climbing. Howard's head snapped up, his eyes wide with panic. "They're moving early," he breathed.

My pulse spiked. "Who?"

Howard backed toward the woods. "I can't—" He broke, then turned and ran.

"Howard!" I shouted.

He bolted down the path toward the woods, spry for his age, his boots pounding and the branches snapping in his wake. LuLu swore and took off after him, but Vex streaked ahead faster than either of us, a black blur cutting him off at the fork where the path split.

Howard skidded to a stop, his chest heaving. "Don't," he begged, his hands raised. "Please. I didn't kill anyone."

I caught up to him, my breath burning. "I know." That seemed to confuse him. "I know you didn't kill Maggie, but you helped keep the truth buried."

Howard's shoulders collapsed. "I was scared."

"So was she," I said.

He looked at me then—really looked—and something in his eyes broke. "I wasn't the one watching her," he said hoarsely. "I swear."

"Who was?" LuLu demanded.

Howard shook his head, but couldn't quite meet our eyes. "I don't know. I just knew when to clear paths. When to look the other way."

"That's not *nothing*," LuLu said.

He wiped his face with trembling hands. "You don't understand. The people who run this...they don't get their hands dirty. They don't lift. They don't carry."

My pulse thudded. "They just control."

Howard nodded miserably. "They're always nearby. Always calm. Always telling everyone it'll be fine."

The air felt suddenly thinner.

LuLu and I exchanged a look.

"That's all?" I asked.

Howard nodded. "That's all I know. I swear."

Another truck growled in the distance, closer now.

Howard flinched. "I have to go."

"Where?" LuLu snapped.

"Anywhere but here," he said. He ran again, this time slower, broken, and vanishing into the trees like a man who knew he'd already lost. I let him go. Maybe he would turn up a new lead.

LuLu let out a shaky breath. "Well. That answers one question."

"That he's not the killer," I said.

"And that Maggie was right," LuLu added.

Vex padded back to my side, his tail flicking. *The watchers are still watching.*

I nodded, a cold certainty settling into my bones. Howard Kline was a piece of the puzzle, but not the hand that had moved it. And whoever that hand belonged to was closer to us than the woods. Much closer.

And still moving.

CROSSING into Elarion always felt like stepping into a held breath.

The portal beneath the well shimmered softly as I descended, the familiar cool of Dweller magic sliding over my skin like water that remembered my shape. Above me, Wishville buzzed with festival noise and rumor and the heavy grind of trucks climbing roads no one liked to look at too closely. Below, the air grew luminous and still, threaded with silver light and the low hum of a world that did not pretend to be simple.

I needed the quiet.

Or at least, a different kind of noise.

Calderis waited for me at the edge of the outer walkways, where the stone curved into graceful arches and bioluminescent moss painted the walls in shades of blue and green. He stood with his hands clasped behind his back, his posture rigid, and eyes fixed on the slow current of light drifting through the *Echo Basin* below.

"You came quickly," he said without turning.

"You sounded like it was urgent," I replied, stepping up beside him. "That's never a good sign."

The corner of his mouth twitched, but he didn't deny it.

Calderis rarely did. "Things are moving," he said. "On both sides of the mountain."

I leaned my elbows on the stone railing and looked out over Elarion. Dweller figures moved along the lower paths, their pale forms gliding with quiet purpose. Nothing looked wrong. Nothing ever did, right up until it was.

"That's what worries me," I said. "Everything looks...contained."

Calderis's gaze slid to mine. "Containment is not peace."

"No," I agreed. "It's just quieter."

We stood there for a moment, listening to the rhythm of the realm. Somewhere deeper, water fell in a steady cascade. Somewhere closer, voices murmured in a dialect that still felt like music I understood.

"I need to know if Maggie crossed into our world," I said finally.

Calderis stiffened. "She did not come to Elarion."

"That's not what I asked. We already know that."

His jaw tightened. "She did walk the ancient tunnels, but she did not enter any caverns."

I closed my eyes briefly. "Did she come close?"

Calderis hesitated just enough to matter. "She stood at even more thresholds than we realized," he confirmed. "She asked questions."

Of course she did. "What kind of questions?" I pressed.

"The kind that make the elders uncomfortable," he said flatly.

I huffed a quiet, humorless laugh. "She had a gift for that." And nearly cost me my job as Guardian. Still might, if I couldn't solve this case.

Calderis's gaze softened, just slightly. "She was persistent. Careful. She did not rush."

"She never did," I said. "She watched."

At that, Calderis's eyes sharpened. "How do you know this?"

"She wrote it down," I said. "About watchers. People who never carried anything."

Calderis went very still. "That is...interesting," he said slowly.

"Don't do that," I warned. "Don't switch into 'Dweller ominous' on me."

He inclined his head. "Very well. I will be direct."

Thank the stars.

"There are Dwellers," he continued, "who believe secrecy is stability. That if knowledge is controlled tightly enough, harm cannot spread."

My stomach sank. "Elders."

"Some," he said carefully. "Not all."

"Vaerion," I said.

Calderis did not look away this time. "My father believes order must be maintained at all costs."

"And you?" I asked.

"I believe silence rots," he replied without hesitation.

Footsteps approached from behind us—light, quick, and familiar. LuLu emerged from the path between the moss-lit columns, her hands shoved into the pockets of her jacket, and her dark hair loose around her shoulders flowing as if under water. She looked out of place and perfectly at ease at the same time, which was basically her brand.

"Okay," she said, glancing between us. "Either you two are about to tell me something important, or I walked in on another brooding contest."

"You aren't supposed to be here," I said, gaping at her. I would have known if she'd followed me because I had been extra careful since the last time nearly got her killed.

Calderis's mouth twitched again. "She's with me."

I gaped even harder at him, speechless. "How long has this been happening and what about your father?"

"Since he finally asked me out on a date." She winked up at him.

His lips formed a full smile...briefly...before he cleared his throat. "She has skills we can use."

"Oh, I'm well aware of my skills, honey, and if you play your cards right, you will be too."

He blinked. "Cards? I have no cards to play."

She just laughed and leaned on the railing beside him, her gaze sweeping over Elarion with open curiosity. "Still beautiful, and still unsettling."

I snorted. "Still not meant for humans."

"You're human."

"Half."

"Well, I'm not just human. I'm psychic." LuLu's expression shifted as she sobered. "I felt it," she said quietly. "The pressure."

Calderis turned toward her fully. "You should not have been able to."

LuLu shrugged. "Story of my life."

I studied her. "What did you feel?"

"Like someone closed a door very gently," she said. "Not to keep something out. To keep something *in.*"

That made the hair on my arms stand up.

Calderis's gaze snapped back to the basin. "Rebel movement has increased," he said. "Quietly. Routes are changing. Messages are being carried by those no one questions."

Watchers, I thought, realizing there were more than one kind. What exactly were the rebels up to? "Humans aren't the only ones who use the tunnels."

"No," Calderis agreed. "And humans are not the only ones who pretend ignorance is virtue."

LuLu frowned. "Okay, that sounds ominous in a 'someone's about to get hurt' way."

Calderis hesitated, then nodded once. "Yes."

I turned to LuLu. "Has Vaerion asked about you?"

Her eyebrows lifted. "I'll leave that question to my boyfriend."

Calderis didn't deny her declaration, and I was surprisingly okay with that. "He questioned Lourdes's continued involvement and suggested...precautionary measures."

My chest tightened. "What kind of measures, since memory

erasure isn't an option? Does Vaerion know it didn't work on her?"

Calderis's eyes met mine and then LuLu's. "He wasn't happy when he found out, and suggested a more permanent erasure."

LuLu laughed, short and incredulous. "Wow, I suspected your father didn't like me when you nearly died, but wanting to get rid of me permanently is a bit extreme even for him. Did you tell your parents we're dating?"

"Not exactly." Calderis looked uncomfortable.

"Why not?" LuLu crossed her arms. "Are you ashamed of me?"

"Never," he replied immediately, then cleared his throat. "It's a delicate matter. My father is more traditional when it comes to his children dating, but my mother is far more accepting. When things calm down, I will tell them. I promise."

"What *did* you say to him then?" I asked.

"That Lourdes was an ally the Covenant Three could use, and if anything happened to her, he would lose *me* permanently." His gaze was unwavering and firm.

I nodded once.

LuLu looked up at Calderis. "I can't believe your father wanted me dead."

"It's the Elarion way, but my mother is intuitive. She knows what you mean to me without me having to tell her. She would never have allowed it."

Her throat bobbed as she swallowed. "Still...you need to tell them soon. Also, that's a lot to drop on someone in a cave full of glowing rocks."

"I know," he said quietly, and took her hand.

I stepped closer to her. "Are you okay?"

LuLu shrugged. "Not really sure what *okay* looks like right now."

Calderis turned then, squaring his shoulders as footsteps echoed from *the Council Chamber* beyond the walkway. Dweller voices rose and fell, measured and concerned.

"Enforcers loyal to my father will try to kill you again," he said. "When I'm not around."

"But you're Chief Enforcer. Won't they listen to you?" I asked.

His eyes flashed. "Most will. A few won't." He looked at LuLu and squeezed her hand. "You are under my protection."

LuLu blinked. "I-I am?"

"You are," Calderis said. "I promise I won't let anything happen to you."

I stared at him. "You realize what that does to your standing with your father."

"Yes," he said simply.

LuLu's mouth curved into a small smile. "My hero."

"My troublemaker." Calderis grinned back.

I stared, dumbfounded over the change in him. Shaking off my brain fog, I focused. "This isn't just about LuLu or Maggie," I said quietly. "Or smuggling or rebels."

Calderis nodded. "It is about who decides what is allowed to be known."

LuLu looked between us. "And right now, a lot of people on both sides of this mountain are choosing silence."

"Silence is cracking," I said. "I can feel it."

Calderis's gaze shifted toward the mountain wall, toward the tunnels that joined both worlds together. "When silence breaks," he said, "it rarely does so gently."

LuLu straightened. "Then we should probably be ready."

I nodded, a hard certainty settling into place.

Above us, Wishville danced and whispered and told itself comforting stories. Below us, Elarion hummed with restrained power and unasked questions. Two worlds, bound by the same lie. And somewhere between them, Maggie Winslow's truth pressed outward—patient, relentless, and no longer content to stay buried. I turned back toward the portal, already bracing myself.

Because whatever came next would not wait for permission.

The knock on my door didn't sound like a knock. It sounded like a decision. Three sharp raps, controlled and urgent, followed by a silence that told me whoever stood on my porch already knew I was awake.

I sat up so fast my blanket slid to my waist. The house was dark except for the faint blue glow leaking from the living room window. I listened closely.

LuLu slept with her door closed, but I didn't hear any movement or snoring. Either she'd finally learned to sleep through the chaos, or she was about to wake up and throw something at me for existing.

I swung my feet to the floor and padded to the front door, my heart already climbing into my throat. I didn't bother with the porch light. When I opened the door, Holden stood there in the dim spill of moonlight, his jacket on, looking tired in a way that meant he'd been running on adrenaline and grim determination for hours.

"Get dressed," he said. No hello. No soft entry. Just the words I'd come to recognize as his version of, *I'm scared and I'm not going to say it.*

"What happened?" I asked, stepping back as he came inside.

He shut the door behind him without taking his eyes off me. "Alden."

My chest tightened. "Alden saw something?"

Holden nodded once. "He sent word to Tiana with the transfer location. Quarry side, happening now."

The word *transfer* turned my blood cold. It wasn't just a noun anymore. It was a machine movement. A scheduled handoff. Something that happened whether we were ready or not. I reached for my sweater draped over the chair. "How sure?"

"As sure as Alden gets," Holden said. "And Fenrin confirmed the rest."

That made me freeze mid-motion. "Fenrin?"

Holden's eyes flicked behind him. Vex appeared like he'd been summoned by the mention of his name, his glow dimmed but present, and ears forward. Fenrin slipped out of the shadows behind him in cat form, looking sleek, ginger, and far too awake for the middle of the night.

She didn't look smug tonight.

She looked focused.

Vex padded to my feet and stared up at me with that intense, unblinking expression that meant he was transmitting information through sheer annoyance. *The shanty.*

"It's empty," I whispered.

Holden nodded. "Fenrin told Vex. Vex told me and insisted I come back for you. The last of the crates are gone."

A slow, heavy dread settled in my ribs. "So, this is it."

"This is a move," Holden corrected. "Maybe not the final one, but it's a big one."

LuLu's door creaked open behind me. "Tell me we're not doing midnight field trips again," she muttered, her voice thick with sleep. It hadn't been that long since she'd gotten back from Elarion. I'd heard her come in after me.

Holden didn't flinch. "Go back to bed, LuLu."

LuLu blinked at him, then at my boots, then at the cats who were both watching her like she was an obstacle. Her eyes narrowed. "You're kidnapping Lyra."

"It's not kidnapping if she wants to go," Holden said.

LuLu stared at me.

I pulled on my boots. "I want to go."

LuLu sighed like she was accepting defeat from the universe. "Fine. But if you die, I'm commandeering your bookshelf and reorganizing it by vibes."

I paused. "That's horrifying."

"Exactly," she said, then shuffled back toward her room. "Bring me proof you didn't die." The door clicked shut.

Holden's mouth tightened, which was the closest he came to a smile. Then his expression hardened again. "You ready?"

I grabbed my coat, shoved my hair into a quick knot, and slid my hands into gloves. My phone was already in my pocket. I didn't call Calderis. Not because I didn't want him there. Because Holden had been communicating with the Feds, and they wanted to talk to a witness, aka me. And the less Dweller magic they saw at a quarry entrance in the middle of the night, the better our chances of keeping Elarion out of federal reports.

Fenrin brushed past my ankle, a silent promise that she wasn't staying behind this time. Vex trotted at my side, his glow dimmed low enough to pass as moonlight if you didn't stare too hard.

We slipped out into the cold night.

Wishville was quiet, like small towns got when everyone was asleep and the world belonged to streetlamps and shadows. The sky was ink-black and sharp with stars. The air tasted like damp stone and fallen leaves.

Holden's cruiser waited down the road, its lights off. As we drove, Holden kept both hands on the wheel like he was trying to squeeze control out of it.

"You talked to Tiana?" I asked.

"Briefly," he said. "She relayed Alden's message. He saw the trucks cut in near the quarry road, the same pattern as before. Weylan confirmed it from the air. Alden didn't get close, but he marked the approximate spot where they disappeared."

"Marked how?" I asked.

Holden glanced at me. "Tiana said he told her you would see it."

"Alden's a Dweller," I said, the knot in my chest easing. "He can mark a tree in a way only another Dweller will notice. He's careful and smart. He wouldn't get caught.

We turned off the main road and onto the rougher quarry access, the tires crunching over gravel. Trees crowded close, their branches skeletal in the moonlight. The quarry itself was a dark void beyond the treeline, heavy with the sense of something manmade that didn't belong in a place this old. Holden slowed as headlights appeared ahead. Two vehicles parked at an angle, with men standing near them.

Federal.

Even at night, you could feel the difference. The posture. The gear. The way they owned the space without ever raising their voices. Holden killed the lights and rolled forward slowly, then stopped. A man stepped away from the group and approached the driver's-side window. He wore a tactical jacket and a clipped expression that looked permanently irritated by small towns.

Holden lowered the window just enough. "Chief Thorn."

"Agent Hartley," the man replied. "You brought the witness."

I bristled at *witness*.

Holden's voice stayed even. "This is Lyra Wells. She's part of our local response."

Hartley's gaze settled on me, a quick assessment void of warmth. "Ma'am."

I gave him my best Festival Chair smile. Neutral, polite, and unreadable.

He nodded once and stepped back, signaling for us to park closer. When we got out, the cold hit harder. It smelled like crushed pine needles and exposed earth, with a faint metallic tang that made my skin prickle.

The quarry always smelled like something had been torn open and left that way.

The entrance they'd gathered around wasn't obvious to someone who didn't know what to look for. A rock face, a shadowed gap half blocked by brush, the kind of place hikers wouldn't choose but smugglers would love.

A portable floodlight bathed the area in harsh white glare.

Fenrin remained in the shadows, a low shape near my boot. Vex stayed close too, glow dampened to almost nothing.

Holden moved toward the agents, his voice low. "You have contact?"

Hartley's expression didn't change. "We had contact."

My stomach tightened. "You caught them?"

Another agent—a woman this time with blonde hair tucked tight under a cap—spoke from behind Hartley. "Two. The others slipped deeper before we sealed the access. We didn't pursue into unknown tunnels without a map."

Holden's jaw clenched. I felt a flicker of relief anyway. Two off the board was two fewer guns on the move.

"Where are they?" Holden asked.

Hartley jerked his chin toward a vehicle with dark windows. "Contained."

"And the cargo?" Holden pressed.

"In our possession," Hartley said. "We recovered weapons and ammunition."

I swallowed, my throat going dry. "Any markings?"

Hartley frowned. "Nothing obvious. Crates were plain."

Holden's eyes narrowed. "What did they say?"

Hartley's mouth tightened. "Nothing useful."

The blonde agent let out a short breath. "They're not talking. No names. No routes. No suppliers."

Holden's shoulders stiffened. "Not even to save themselves?"

Hartley's gaze was flat. "They're more afraid of whomever they work for than they are of prison."

The words hit the air like frost.

I glanced at the tunnel mouth, darkness yawning behind the floodlight glare. The idea of fear stronger than federal charges felt...ancient. Like an oath. Like a system built on consequences no court could deliver.

Holden stepped closer, his voice firm. "They gave you something."

Hartley hesitated, then nodded once with reluctance. "They said the same thing, both of them. Separately."

My skin prickled. "What thing?"

Hartley's eyes traveled briefly to the tunnel, then back. "That the mastermind is someone with great power. Someone you don't cross."

A chill crawled up my spine.

Power could mean money. Influence. Politics. It could also mean something else in this town. A power older than permits and board meetings. A power that lived in the bones of stone.

Holden's expression stayed controlled, but I saw the tension in his jaw. He didn't like vague warnings. He liked names he could handcuff.

"Did they describe the person?" Holden asked.

Hartley shrugged. "No. And we don't push in the field. We'll interrogate properly at station level."

Holden's gaze hardened. "And until then?"

Hartley straightened, slipping back into authority like it was armor. "Until then, no press. No public statement. We keep this quiet while we identify the network. Your cooperation is expected."

Holden's eyes flashed. "My cooperation is earned."

Hartley's mouth tightened, but he didn't challenge it. "We'll be in touch. Stay available."

He turned away, barking instructions to the other agents.

Holden stood still for a beat, staring at the tunnel entrance like he could force it to give up its secrets. Then he looked at me. "They caught two. It's something."

"It's not enough," I whispered.

"No," he agreed. "But it's proof this is real enough that federal resources are now in our backyard."

My stomach twisted. "And proof they're terrified of whoever's running it."

Holden nodded once. "Yeah."

Fenrin's tail flicked against my boot, a silent, restless signal. Vex's ears were forward, his eyes narrowed, as if he could hear the tunnels breathing.

I looked past the floodlights into the black gap of stone. Somewhere down there, the men we didn't catch were already moving again, deeper, faster, and smarter. And somewhere above us, someone with "great power" was watching this play out, confident enough to keep their name hidden.

Holden's voice dropped. "Let's go home and regroup in the morning. And we figure out who's powerful enough to scare armed smugglers into silence."

I swallowed, the weight of the night pressing close. "Holden," I murmured, "in Wishville...power doesn't always look like a person."

His eyes met mine, steady and grim. "I know."

The tunnels weren't just routes anymore. They were territory. And we were standing at the mouth of it, trying not to flinch.

Eighteen

THE FIRST THING I noticed was the quiet. Not the good kind, the library-after-hours kind, or the snow-about-to-fall kind. This was the wrong quiet. The kind that felt staged, like a room someone had just left and wanted to look untouched.

My phone buzzed on the nightstand, dragging me out of a shallow, restless half-sleep. The clock glowed **5:00 a.m.** in accusatory red numbers. **Connie Hale** *missed call.* My heart jumped hard enough to hurt. I was already sitting up when the second buzz came through. **Clara Winslow** *missed call.*

No voicemail.

No follow-up text.

Just silence.

Vex materialized at the foot of the bed, his black fur bristling and eyes bright in the dark.

Something is wrong, he said flatly.

"I know," I whispered, already reaching for my clothes again. First, Elarion at midnight, then smugglers at two, and now missing people at five. How much was a woman expected to take in one day?

The air outside bit sharp and clean, snapping my senses awake whether I wanted it to or not. The town was still asleep. Festival lanterns still glowed along Main Street, swaying slightly, their cheerfulness obscene at this hour.

Connie's house was dark. No porch light on, no glow through the curtains, just the shape of the place hunched back from the road like it was trying not to be noticed. My pulse roared in my ears as I climbed the steps and knocked.

Nothing.

I tried the handle.

Unlocked.

"Connie?" I called softly, stepping inside.

The house felt wrong. Like someone had tried to erase a day in a hurry. The living room lights were on. The coffee table was buried under folders, more than I'd seen at *Town Hall*. Boxes were open. Papers were stacked, sorted, and resorted. Connie's meticulous handwriting marked the margins in angry slashes.

She'd been close to finding the information for me.

"Clara?" I called on a hunch, louder now.

No answer.

Vex padded ahead of me, his tail low. *No struggle,* he said. *No flight.*

I moved through the house slowly, cataloging details the way Maggie would have wanted me to. Connie's purse sat on the hall table, her keys inside. Her coat hung on the back of the chair. Her phone lay face-down on the kitchen counter.

She hadn't planned to leave.

The back door stood ajar. Cold air spilled in, carrying the damp, loamy scent of the woods, and underneath it, faint and sharp, was oil. My stomach dropped. I was already moving, out the door and into the yard, a flashlight in hand. The grass was flattened in a narrow line leading toward the treeline, as if something heavy had been dragged rather than carried.

Two sets of footprints. One smaller. One heavier.

"They didn't go far," I murmured.

Vex sniffed the ground, his ears pinned back. *No roads. No cars. This way.*

The trees swallowed us whole within a dozen steps. The moonlight filtered through bare branches, painting everything in bone-pale silver. I followed the disturbed ground, my breath fogging, and nerves on edge. The trail didn't lead to the street. It led downhill toward the old service path.

Toward the tunnels.

"Of course," I muttered, my throat tight as I broke into a run.

By the time I reached the library grounds, my lungs were burning and my hands were shaking, not from the cold but from certainty. I didn't need to check Clara's house to know it would be empty too.

Someone hadn't panicked. They'd planned.

Realization dawned. The tunnel entrance was *inside* the old maintenance shed. How had I not seen that? It yawned open like a mouth that hadn't bothered pretending to stay shut. Inside the shed, I ventured to the dark shadows in the back, suddenly knowing what I would find. Maggie's spiral staircase. Fresh scrape marks scored the stone. A scarf lay tangled on the floor.

Clara's.

I swallowed a sob and forced myself to keep moving. Inside, the tunnel air hit me like a wall that was cold, damp, and metallic. My footsteps echoed too loudly, but I didn't slow. The path ahead was clear in a way that felt intentional, like someone had wanted me to follow.

"Don't," I whispered to myself. "Don't get sloppy."

Vex raced ahead, a black blur against the stone. *They want you to see this*, he warned. *They want you to come alone.*

I ignored him.

The tunnel angled sharply upward toward a passage I hadn't explored yet. One that was sealed off from the others with the only access being through the shed and Maggie's spiral stairs. One that led directly beneath the library. I slowed, my heart hammering as I scanned for signs. The upward path smelled cleaner as if recently cleared. I followed it.

The chamber at the end was small but deliberate, with lanterns set into wall niches, their light steady and warm. Too warm. Light meant to calm someone down. Clara sat on a low bench near the wall, her wrists bound in front of her and posture rigid with effort. Her eyes flew to me the second I stepped into the light.

"Lyra!" she whispered.

Relief crashed through me so hard I nearly staggered. "I'm here," I said softly. "Are you hurt?"

She shook her head quickly. "She hasn't—she said she wouldn't—"

"She?" I repeated.

Connie sat on the stone floor nearby, her hands bound behind her, with her back straight despite the strain. Her face was pale, her eyes blazing with fury and something like shame.

I looked at her in question. "You called me."

Her mouth twisted. "I tried."

"Why?"

Before she could answer, a figure stepped out of the shadows near the far wall. Calm, composed, and wrapped in a familiar cardigan like this was a late-night errand and not a crime scene.

Dorothy Rourke.

She held a lantern in one hand, its light steady and practiced. "I hoped you'd come," she said gently.

My blood went cold. "You," I said.

Dorothy inclined her head. "Lyra."

Behind me, the tunnel felt suddenly much narrower. "You took them," I said.

Dorothy's eyes softened. "I brought them somewhere safe."

"Safe?" Connie snapped. "You tied Clara up in a tunnel."

"I protected her," Dorothy said. "From what was coming."

"What was coming," I said slowly, "was the truth."

Dorothy sighed. "The truth destroys more than it saves."

I took a step forward. "Untie them. Now."

Dorothy didn't move. "I loved Maggie," she said instead. The name echoed painfully off the stone.

Connie laughed, raw and broken. "No. You loved control."

Dorothy's composure cracked, just slightly. "I loved her enough to know she wouldn't stop."

"And you killed her," Connie said.

Dorothy's eyes slid to Clara, then back to me. "I stopped her." The words landed like a blade.

I felt something settle inside me with cold, absolute certainty. "You thought you could have it all," Connie whispered. "Didn't you? Larry told me you were always jealous of Maggie. Of the life she had. A career, a husband, a child. That you were mad at her for taking that for granted and putting her research first."

Dorothy didn't answer. She didn't need to. The silence screamed.

"You thought if Maggie was gone," Connie continued, her voice shaking, "You could take her place."

"That's enough," Dorothy said sharply, the kindness gone.

I stepped between them, my heart pounding. "Where is Maggie?"

Dorothy's gaze traveled to the back of the chamber. "Right where she fell all those years ago," she said softly.

The lantern light didn't reach that far, but I saw it anyway. Pale curves against dark stone. Bones. The world tilted.

"No," I whispered, thinking of my own mother and my worst fears about her before I found out she was still alive.

Clara sobbed.

Connie made a sound that wasn't human.

Dorothy's voice softened again, almost tender. "She wouldn't stop writing it down. She wouldn't let it go. Even if it meant losing everything."

"And now you can't let it go either," I said, my voice shaking with rage. "You dragged two innocent people into the dark to keep a lie alive."

Dorothy straightened, her lantern lifting. "I finished what needed finishing."

Vex sprang forward, knocking the lantern from her hand. Glass shattered. Light died.

Footsteps pounded from the tunnel behind me. I had told Holden about the deep shadows in the back of the maintenance shed and my suspicions when I first saw it, but we hadn't checked it out yet. He didn't know I was down here. I could only hope it was him, but I didn't know how it could be.

Dorothy ran under the cover of darkness, and I couldn't risk revealing my powers to stop her. That didn't mean I wouldn't go after her as soon as I could.

I untied Connie and Clara then dropped to my knees beside the bones. "She's here," I whispered. "She never left."

Behind me, Connie sobbed. Clara clung to my arm, shaking. Somewhere deeper in the tunnels, Dorothy's footsteps faded into silence. But Maggie Winslow was no longer lost. And the lie that had kept her buried was finally breaking open.

The tunnel didn't rush back into noise after Dorothy ran. It didn't echo with dramatic footsteps or collapse in on itself like a warning. It just held. As if the mountain had seen this moment coming and decided to give us space to survive it.

I turned on my flashlight from my pack and stayed on my knees beside the bones, my hands hovering uselessly over pale curves and dark stone. I didn't touch them. I couldn't. Maggie Winslow had been reduced to fragments of what she once was, but she was still *herself*, still deserving of care, still more than evidence.

"She's here," I whispered again, because saying it once didn't seem enough. "She never left."

Connie's sob broke something open in my chest. It wasn't loud or theatrical. It was the sound of a woman who had spent decades holding a town together with paperwork and silence, and finally felt the weight of every decision crash down at once. She folded forward against her bindings, her shoulders shaking, and grief pouring out of her in raw, unstoppable waves.

"I told Maggie to wait. I told her she was imagining things. I told her to stop," Connie choked. "I supported Larry over her."

Clara made a sound like she was trying not to scream.

I turned toward her immediately, my heart lurching. She was shaking hard now, her eyes fixed on the remains like they might vanish if she blinked.

"She was right," Clara whispered. "She was right the whole time."

I crawled over to her and took her hands in mine, grounding myself in the warmth of her skin, the undeniable proof that she was alive. "She was right about everything," I said. "And she was brave. And none of this is your fault."

Clara's breath hitched. "She said if she didn't write it down, it would happen again."

I swallowed hard. "It won't. She stopped it with her proof."

Behind us, Holden's voice cut through the chamber, sharp with adrenaline and fury. "Lyra!"

"I'm here!" I called back. "They're alive!"

I sent word to Fenrin, who told Calderis, who told Holden. You're welcome. Vex licked his paw.

Holden's footsteps came fast then, his boots skidding on stone as he burst into the lanternless chamber with his flashlight raised. The beam swept over Connie and Clara, over the scattered papers, over the bones—and he froze.

"Oh God," he breathed.

Calderis arrived a heartbeat later, his presence shifting the air even without light. "Sorry I'm late. There was an altercation with a group of rebels at the border that detained me," he said for my ears only. When his gaze landed on Maggie's remains, something ancient and terrible crossed his face. "She was not allowed rest," he said to everyone.

"No," I replied. "But she will now."

Holden moved first, kneeling beside Connie and helping her to her feet. Connie didn't resist. She didn't even seem to notice until she slumped forward, clutching at nothing.

"I didn't mean for this," she said again, her voice wrecked. "I didn't mean—"

Holden placed a steady hand on her shoulder. "I know. But we need to get you both out of here."

Clara didn't move. She stared at her mother's bones like she was trying to memorize them, trying to anchor herself to something real after years of not knowing where to put her grief. "I won't leave her alone again," she whispered.

My throat tightened painfully. "Holden will bring her home."

Holden hesitated, then nodded. "Take a moment, then we need to move."

I helped Clara to her feet and guided her closer, staying with her as she knelt beside Maggie. She reached out with trembling fingers and rested her hand lightly on the stone near the remains, not touching bone, just close enough to feel connected.

"I'm sorry," she whispered. "I should have fought harder to find you."

I felt tears spill down my cheeks without my permission. "You were a child," I said softly. "She knew that. No one could have known where she was. These tunnels were sealed off."

Calderis turned away, scanning the tunnels, alert and tense. "She must have just missed us through the maintenance shed. She will not go far," he said. "But she will not return easily."

"You mean Dorothy," Holden said grimly.

Calderis nodded. "She believes what she did was necessary."

"And that makes her dangerous," Holden replied.

"Yes," Calderis agreed. "More dangerous than those who profit."

The words rang true.

Dorothy hadn't cared about crates or guns or money. She'd cared about control. About preserving a story where she was kind, indispensable, and necessary.

"She thought she was protecting us," Clara said suddenly, lifting her head. "She kept saying that."

I met her eyes. "She was protecting herself."

Clara closed her eyes, tears sliding down her cheeks. "She was like family. She raised me."

"I know," I said.

Connie made a broken sound behind us. "I trusted her."

"You trusted someone who knew how to be trusted," Holden said gently. "That's not a crime."

Connie shook her head violently. "I helped her. I helped keep Maggie quiet."

"You didn't kill her," I said firmly. "And you're done being quiet."

She looked at me then, her eyes red and hollow. "I'm done."

Vex padded over to Maggie's remains and sat, his tail curled neatly around his paws. He bowed his head—an oddly formal gesture for a creature who usually treated solemn moments like inconveniences. *She is no longer alone,* he said.

Something in my chest loosened just enough to breathe again.

Holden stood and spoke into his radio, his voice clipped and controlled. "I need backup at the old maintenance shed near the library. There's a spiral staircase that leads to an isolated tunnel. We have a suspect fleeing, and we've located the remains of Maggie Winslow." His jaw tightened on the last word.

As he listened to the response, Calderis crouched beside me. "You did not look away," he said quietly.

I wiped my face with the back of my hand. "Neither did she."

He inclined his head toward Maggie. "That is why she mattered."

"Yes, but she also mattered because she was a person. It didn't matter if she made a big breakthrough or went down in history. She was a wife, mother, daughter, friend...a human being whose life was cut unfairly short."

He nodded once. "You are right. Honor is about more than what you do. Who you are matters, too."

The sound of approaching voices echoed faintly through the tunnel—officers, search teams, the machinery of justice finally catching up to the truth.

I helped Clara to her feet, wrapping an arm around her shoulders as her knees wobbled. Connie stood as well, supported by Holden, her face set now with something harder than grief.

Resolve.

"She won't get away," Connie said hoarsely. "I'll tell you everything. The schedules. The names. All of it."

Holden nodded. "We'll talk."

Calderis's gaze flicked toward the deeper darkness where Dorothy had vanished. "The mountain remembers," he said. "She cannot outrun what she set in motion."

As we began the slow walk back toward the surface, I glanced over my shoulder one last time. The lantern shards glittered on the stone like fallen stars. Maggie's bones lay quiet now, no longer hidden, no longer erased. The truth had cost her everything.

But it hadn't died with her.

Above us, Wishville's lights would still be glowing. The festival would still be pretending. People would still argue over stories and blame and what they wished had happened instead. But tomorrow the town would wake up knowing Maggie Winslow hadn't vanished. She'd been silenced.

And silence, once broken, never went quietly again.

I squeezed Clara's shoulder as we climbed. "We'll take her home," I said. "All of her."

Clara nodded, tears streaking her face but her spine was straight. "She won't be buried alone."

"No," I agreed.

Behind us, the tunnel closed in gently as a promise kept far too late. And somewhere above or deeper still, Dorothy was running. But the mountain had already chosen what it would hold.

And what it would no longer protect.

CHAPTER
Nineteen

MORNING CAME ANYWAY.

It always did, no matter what had been uncovered beneath the mountain or how much blood and bone and truth had been dragged into the light. Wishville woke up wrapped in fog and denial. A soft gray that made everything look gentler than it had any right to be.

I stood at the edge of the library lawn with a paper cup of coffee cooling in my hands, and watched deputies string yellow tape across the maintenance shed like they were decorating for a funeral no one wanted to attend. The tunnel entrance yawned dark and final within, sealed now, at least temporarily, like the town could tape over what it had refused to see for decades.

Maggie Winslow was no longer missing.

That fact sat heavy and solid in my chest, equal parts relief and grief. Clara stood a few feet away with Connie, wrapped in a borrowed jacket that hung too loose on her shoulders. She looked older than she had two days ago, not wiser, just stripped down to what was real. Connie kept one hand at Clara's back, grounding and protective, like she was afraid if she let go even for a second the world might claim her, too.

Holden approached quietly, his boots damp with dew and his face drawn. "Medical examiner's on the way," he said. "For now, we've documented the site. Nothing's moving until they're done."

Clara nodded without looking at him. "Thank you." Her voice held steady, but I could feel the tremor beneath it.

Vex circled her ankles, his tail low. *Grief makes people blind to things they aren't ready to understand.*

"She'll be treated with respect," Holden added gently.

Connie's jaw tightened. "She better be."

He met her gaze without flinching. "She will."

A murmur rose near the sidewalk where a small knot of townspeople had gathered, curiosity winning out over tact. Phones were out. Whispers slid between coats and scarves like smoke.

"What happened?"

"They say they found something."

"I heard there was a tunnel beneath the library."

"I always knew that place wasn't right."

My shoulders tensed.

And then...the Wellies arrived.

Tilly came first, marching up the path with purpose, her scarf trailing behind her like a banner of intent. Belle followed, already halfway through a sharp inhale as if prepared to scold the entire scene into better behavior. Dot trailed just behind them, clutching her thermos with both hands and scanning the area like she was counting exits.

They stopped short the moment they saw Clara. The shift was immediate. No clanking bangles. No whispered commentary. No dramatic sighs. Tilly's hand flew to her mouth. Belle's shoulders dropped. Dot went very still.

"Oh," Tilly breathed, all bravado evaporating. "Oh, honey."

Belle recovered first, straightening and planting herself between Clara and the onlookers with the quiet authority of someone who had redirected many a town meeting. "That's far enough," she said, not raising her voice but somehow carrying anyway.

Dot turned slowly, fixing the crowd with a look so sharp it should've come with a warning label. "This is not a spectacle," she said. "Put the phones away."

A man hesitated.

Dot took one step closer.

The phone vanished.

Tilly reached Clara next, moving carefully now, every ounce of her dramatic energy folded into gentleness. She didn't touch, just stood close enough to be felt. "We're here," she said softly. "You're not alone."

Clara swallowed, nodded once.

Connie exhaled like she hadn't realized she'd been holding her breath.

Behind me, LuLu appeared at my side as if summoned, hair pulled back and eyes sharp despite the exhaustion dragging at her features. "I hate this part," she muttered. "The part where everyone pretends they didn't look away."

"Me too," I said.

She tipped her chin toward the crowd, now noticeably quieter and uncertain. "They're already building the story."

Across the clearing, Belle folded her arms and stared down a pair of whispering retirees until they found something very interesting in the gravel.

"Let them," I said quietly. "The facts will ruin it."

LuLu snorted. "You're a pessimist now?"

"No," I said. "I'm just tired."

Her expression softened. "Fair."

Tilly drifted back toward us, her eyes bright but steady now. "We've got the perimeter," she said, as if this were a military operation. "Dot's running interference, Belle's scaring off gawkers, and I'm...moral support."

Dot nodded once. "I brought tissues. And tea. Not the calming kind, the grounding kind."

Vex flicked his tail approvingly. *They are surprisingly competent when tragedy is involved.*

I watched the Wellies hold their positions with no jokes, no fuss, just presence, and felt something ease in my chest. Wishville had a way of turning everything into a story. But sometimes, just sometimes, it remembered how to be human first.

A county SUV rolled up, followed by another vehicle, plain, unmarked, not local. Holden stiffened.

"State?" I asked.

"ATF," he replied under his breath. "It's in their hands now."

Mayor Doug Delaney hurried across the lawn, his coat buttoned wrong and hair damp from a rushed shower. "Holden," he said, breathlessly. "What's going on? I'm getting calls from—" He faltered when he saw the tape, the uniforms, and the quiet devastation etched across Connie's face. "Oh."

"Yes," Holden said flatly. "Oh."

Doug swallowed. "Is it...is it true?"

Clara lifted her head. "They found my mother."

Doug's face drained of color. "I'm so sorry," he said, like people did when they didn't know what else to offer.

"Be sorry later," Connie snapped. "Right now, be useful."

Doug flinched, then nodded. "What do you need?"

"Transparency," Holden said. "Full cooperation. No spin."

Doug hesitated, just a heartbeat too long.

LuLu noticed, and so did I.

"You don't want this to be a WishFest headline," Doug said carefully.

"I don't care what it is," I said, my voice cutting through the morning fog. "As long as it's the truth."

Doug met my gaze, with something like fear flickering there. "We'll do this right."

"You'd better," Connie said. "Because I'm done protecting anyone." That landed harder than anything else spoken that morning.

Holden cleared his throat. "Dorothy is still at large. We have teams searching the deeper tunnels and the north ridge."

Clara's breath hitched. "She won't hurt anyone else," she said, as if trying to convince herself.

Holden didn't answer immediately. "We're not underestimating her."

Good, I thought grimly. Dorothy had never needed force to do damage. She wielded trust like a weapon.

Calderis stood a little apart from the group, his eyes fixed on the mountain line, where fog clung stubbornly to the trees. He looked carved out of stone—still, watchful, and utterly unyielding. "She believes the mountain will hide her," he said quietly when I joined him.

"Will it?" I asked.

He shook his head. "The mountain hides those who belong to it. Not those who betray it."

I glanced back at the taped-off entrance, the place where Maggie had waited in darkness for so long. "It hid her."

"It held her," Calderis corrected. "There is a difference."

I let that settle. Behind us, the medical examiner's van pulled in. Doors opened, gloves snapped, and procedure took over, brisk and merciful in its neutrality.

Clara reached for my hand.

I squeezed back, grounding both of us. "You don't have to stay."

"I know," she said. "But I want to."

Connie nodded. "We both do."

As the professionals moved toward the entrance, I felt the shift ripple through Wishville, something fragile finally giving way. The town could no longer pretend this was a story about old grief or private tragedy. This was about what it had allowed.

LuLu leaned in close. "You realize this isn't over, right?"

"I do," I said.

She followed my gaze to the mountain. "Dorothy. The guns. The people who knew and said nothing."

"And the people who thought silence was kindness," I added.

LuLu grimaced. "Those are always the hardest to convince."

I took a slow breath, steadying myself against the weight of it all. Maggie Winslow had been found. The truth was out. And now the town had to decide what it would do with it. The fog began to lift, inch by inch, revealing the familiar outlines of buildings and streets and faces that would never quite look the same again. Neither would I. Because once you saw what was buried beneath a place you loved, you couldn't unsee it.

It was my job to make sure they didn't see *more*.

By the time night settled back over Wishville, the town had stopped pretending this was a single story. It was many stories now, layered and contradictory and loud. I stood on my front porch with Vex pressed against my ankle, remembering the endless headlights that had swept past on Main Street earlier, one after another. Unmarked vehicles. County cruisers. A state SUV that had idled too long before moving on. The air had smelled like wet leaves and burnt coffee from a thermos someone had forgotten on a cruiser's hood.

The ATF agents had arrived quietly and taken over loudly.

Not with sirens or speeches, just with clipboards and measured questions and the kind of calm that came from knowing exactly how big a mess could get. Crates were being cataloged. Routes mapped. Names written down without ceremony. Like the town had been put under a magnifying glass.

LuLu joined me on the steps now, wrapping her cardigan tighter around herself. "I hate the part where everything gets organized," she said. "It always makes the damage feel permanent."

"It is," I replied. "Enjoy the quiet up here while you can."

She leaned her shoulder into mine. "They've got Howard."

I closed my eyes. "Already?"

"He didn't end up running," she said softly. "And he talked. He didn't say everything, but he said enough."

"Enough to corroborate our leads," I murmured.

"Enough to make some very uncomfortable phone calls," LuLu said. "Apparently, a few people who thought they were *adjacent* to this are discovering adjacency is not a defense."

A small, bitter smile tugged at my mouth. "Good."

We fell quiet, listening to the night. Somewhere up the hill, the festival lights flickered off one by one, like the town was finally admitting it needed rest.

"Any sign of Dorothy?" LuLu asked.

I shook my head. "She knows the mountain better than anyone. I have a feeling Maggie spotted her in the tunnels, and that's why Dorothy 'stopped' her from turning her in. We won't know for sure until we find Dorothy and get her to tell us what happened. At the very least, she owes Clara that much."

Vex's ears twitched. *Finding her might take a while. She knows the safe places. For now.*

That didn't comfort me. With nothing more to do on our end, LuLu, Vex, and I were about to head inside when a pair of headlights pulled into my driveway, crunching softly over gravel. Holden stepped out, his shoulders sagging and eyes rimmed with exhaustion. He carried a folder tucked under one arm and a paper bag under the other.

"I brought food," he said, holding up the bag. "It's not great."

"After today," I said, "I don't care."

He knew I wasn't much of a cook and forgot to eat half the time. We moved inside, the door clicking shut behind us. My living room felt smaller with all three of us in it, like the walls had crept in to listen. Holden set the bag on the table and spread the folder beside it.

"Preliminary," he said. "But it's enough."

I sat, my legs feeling weak. "Enough for what?"

"For charges," he said. "Multiple. Smuggling, conspiracy,

obstruction, and a few federal ones I'm still learning how to pronounce."

"Not to mention murder," I said flatly.

LuLu let out a low whistle. "Wishville's going to need a bigger bulletin board."

"They're tracing the pipeline now," Holden continued. "Where the guns came from. Where they were headed. This wasn't random."

I nodded. "It never is."

"They think Dorothy wasn't involved in the logistics," he added. "Not directly."

"No," I said quietly. "She didn't need to be."

Holden watched me closely. "You're sure about her."

"I am," I replied. "She didn't care about money or power. She cared about control. About choosing which truths survived."

LuLu grimaced. "That's almost worse."

"It *is* worse," Holden said. "Because it makes her unpredictable."

He flipped the folder open, revealing photographs of tunnels, crates, and paperwork that Connie had finally turned over without hesitation. "She gave them everything," he said. "Every schedule. Every signature. Every place she stalled."

I pictured Connie standing rigid beside Clara that morning, grief carved into her face like something permanent. "She's done protecting the story."

"She's protecting her friend's daughter now," Holden agreed. "And honestly? It might be the bravest thing she's ever done, given the trouble she might be in. Her cooperation will work in her favor."

A knock sounded at the door, soft and hesitant.

I stood, my pulse spiking, then relaxed when I saw Clara on the porch, wrapped in her coat, her eyes red but steady. Connie stood a step behind her, with her posture straighter than it had been all day, and resolve holding her up.

"We didn't want to intrude," Connie said.

"You're not," I replied, stepping aside. "Come in."

They did, the house rearranging itself around new grief. Clara sat carefully, like she wasn't sure the furniture would hold her. Connie remained standing for a moment, then lowered herself into the chair opposite Holden.

"I've been thinking," Clara said. "About what comes next. I want a burial. A real one. With her name. With her work recognized."

My throat tightened. "Of course."

"And I want the town to hear the truth," Clara continued. "Not the sanitized version. Not the one where everyone gets to feel kind."

Holden nodded. "That can be arranged."

Clara looked at me. "They're already saying things online."

I didn't ask what. I didn't need to. "They always will," I said. "Some will believe her, and others won't. You can't control that. But we'll know the truth, and that's all that matters."

Clara's mouth trembled. "She would've hated the attention."

"Yes," I agreed softly. "But she would've loved the accountability."

A silence settled, heavy, but not crushing. Then Vex hopped onto the table, his tail flicking dangerously close to the paperwork.

Connie startled, then blinked. "Where on earth did he come from?"

"He's sneaky," I said smoothly.

LuLu choked on a laugh. "That's one word for him."

Connie stared for a moment longer than most at Vex, then shook her head like she was too tired to question reality anymore.

Holden cleared his throat. "Search teams are expanding at dawn. The north ridge. The old switchbacks. Anywhere she might've staged a hideout."

"She won't leave the mountain yet," Calderis said from the doorway.

I turned, startled. I hadn't heard him arrive, then again, I never did. He stepped into the light, his eyes reflecting something older and colder than the night outside.

"She believes distance equals safety," he continued. "She is wrong. I know her *type*." The room went very still. "She will be found," he said. "The mountain does not shelter those who fracture it."

Holden studied him. "We'll hold you to that."

Calderis met his gaze without flinching. "See that you do."

After they left, after Clara hugged me with a fierceness that surprised us both, after Connie squeezed my hands and said, *Thank you for not letting her disappear too,* the house fell quiet. LuLu cleaned without being asked. Holden made a call he didn't want to make. Vex settled by the door, vigilant, with Fenrin by his side. I stood alone in the kitchen, staring at the place where Connie's papers had been spread hours earlier, thinking about how close Maggie had come to being erased completely. Outside, the mountain loomed dark and patient, holding secrets it no longer had permission to keep.

My phone buzzed.

An unknown number.

I answered without thinking.

"Lyra Wells," a woman's voice said calmly. "I know you're looking for me."

My blood went cold. "Dorothy," I said.

She paused a beat then took a breath. "I didn't mean for it to go this way," she said.

I closed my eyes. "You always say that when your control slips."

She laughed softly. "You're clever."

"No," I said. "I'm done being polite."

Another pause filled the space. Wind, faint and hollow, rushed across the line. "You won't find me where you're looking," Dorothy said. "And you won't stop what's already started."

"I already did," I replied. "You just don't know it yet."

Silence hovered again. "You think you did." Then the line went dead.

I stood there long after she'd hung up, my phone heavy in my hand, knowing the truth had one last reckoning left in it. The town had broken open. The mountain was watching. And Dorothy was still out there...

But no longer in control of the story.

CHAPTER

Twenty

DAWN IN WISHVILLE came pale and reluctant, like the sun didn't want to witness what it had helped illuminate. Fog clung low to the ground, snagging on fence posts and porch railings, softening every edge until the town looked almost gentle again. The festival banners still hung across Main Street, damp and drooping, their cheerful colors muted by moisture and regret. If you squinted, you could pretend nothing had changed.

If you listened, you couldn't.

I stood at the command post they'd set up in the library parking lot, two pop-up tents, a folding table covered in maps, coffee, and radios, and the unmistakable energy of people who hadn't slept but were running on purpose. Holden moved between officers and volunteers with the steady precision of someone who knew the difference between panic and urgency. His jaw was set, his eyes shadowed, and his voice clipped.

He looked up when he saw me and didn't bother with a greeting. "You're early."

"I usually am," I replied, wrapping my scarf tighter. The cold was sharp this morning. It slid under my sleeves and made my fingers stiff, but I barely felt it. My mind had been awake for hours, replaying Dorothy's voice on the phone, calm as a lullaby and twice as dangerous.

LuLu joined me at the edge of the tents, her hair tucked under a knit hat and cheeks flushed from the cold. "I have never hated morning people more," she muttered.

"You are morning people," I reminded her.

"I am a morning person when I'm voluntarily awake," she said. "This is grief caffeine."

Vex prowled near our boots, his tail low and ears sharp. He watched the volunteers arriving in clusters, some local, some from nearby towns, signing in, being handed gloves, and being warned not to go wandering off alone.

They do not understand the mountain, he said.

"No," I whispered. "They don't."

The medical examiner had removed Maggie's remains just before sunrise. I hadn't watched them carry her out. I'd stood outside the maintenance shed, staring up at the trees and forcing myself to breathe.

Clara and Connie hadn't left the site until it was done. Now Clara sat in a heated county SUV near the curb, a blanket around her shoulders, her eyes fixed on nothing. Connie stood beside the vehicle, her arms crossed, spine rigid, and face carved into a mask of restraint that didn't fool anyone who actually knew her.

Holden approached the map table and tapped a marked section with his finger. "We're running lines from the north ridge down to the quarry access and cutting across these switchbacks," he said to the group gathered. "We're looking for any sign of movement, shelter, recent fire, supplies—anything."

"Dorothy knows these trails," Connie said sharply from behind him.

The group turned, startled by her sudden presence. Connie didn't soften her voice for anyone anymore. She had nothing left to protect except Clara.

"She does," Holden agreed. "Which is why we're treating her like someone who knows how to survive."

That was why we had Alden and Tiana looking, along with Weylan and Sparks as well.

LuLu leaned toward me. "Translation: she's not hiding in a shed with a granola bar."

I nodded. "She's hiding where people don't go unless they're desperate or stupid."

Holden's gaze locked onto mine, reading the thought on my face. "Lyra, no tunnels today."

I opened my mouth.

"No," he repeated, firmer. "Not unless we have a confirmed sighting. That's not a search line. That's a trap."

I held his gaze. "You think she wants me down there."

"I *know* she does," he said quietly, stepping closer so no one else could hear. "You said she called you. She's playing to your instincts. She wants you isolated. I'm not really sure why."

My throat tightened. "I'm not either. She told me we won't find her where we're looking."

Holden's expression hardened. "She's right."

I stared at him. "You already know that."

"She's not on the ridge," he admitted. "Not anymore."

LuLu made a low sound. "Cool. Great. Love that."

"We're still searching it," Holden said, raising his voice for the group. "But I want teams checking the perimeters too, outbuildings, old hunting cabins, the abandoned ranger station."

The abandoned ranger station...

We had a new station that Tiana used. The old station sat farther up the mountain, beyond the popular hiking routes, half collapsed, rarely used, and exactly the kind of place Dorothy would choose if she wanted to disappear without leaving town.

I caught Calderis watching me from the edge of the parking lot. He stood with his arms folded, his posture still, and eyes bright against the dawn gloom. He didn't belong in this world of radios and thermoses and laminated maps, but somehow he made it feel less stable just by standing there, as if he was proof the ground beneath us was thinner than anyone wanted to admit.

He inclined his head slightly toward the map table. A subtle warning...or an invitation. Holden began dividing search groups. Names were called. Routes assigned. Walkie-talkies handed out.

"Lyra," Holden said finally, his voice low again. "You're with me."

I blinked. "What?"

"You're with me," he repeated. "I'm not letting you freelance. Not today."

A warmth flickered in my chest, annoyance and gratitude braided together. "Fine," I said. "But if I see something—"

"You tell me," he cut in.

LuLu snorted. "He means you tell him before you run directly into danger like a raccoon chasing a shiny object."

"I am not a raccoon," I muttered, adding, "and far stronger than he is."

"You absolutely are," LuLu said. "But you're also impulsive and occasionally reckless."

"Said the pot to the kettle." I laughed.

Holden didn't smile, but his eyes softened for a split second before hardening again. "LuLu," he said, "you're on perimeter checks with Deputy Reyes. Stay on radio."

"Yes, Dad," LuLu said cheerfully. Then she sobered. "Be careful."

I looked at her. "You too."

She squeezed my arm once, quickly and fiercely. "Don't let Dorothy turn you into Maggie." The words hit harder than I expected.

"Ditto," I whispered. But as I said it, I saw Maggie's handwriting in my mind. Heard her stubborn voice in Clara's memories. *If I don't write it, it disappears.* Dorothy had tried to make Maggie disappear. Now she was trying to make me chase her into the same darkness. I needed to find out why.

Holden and I started up the trail behind the library, heading toward the first switchback line. The fog was thinner up here, the air colder and sharper. Leaves crunched under our boots, damp enough to muffle sound. We walked in silence for several minutes, radios crackling intermittently with other teams checking in.

"Nothing on the ridge line."

"Found an old campfire, likely hikers."

"Tracks near the quarry road, unclear of age."

Holden stopped suddenly and crouched near a patch of mud beside the path. He angled his flashlight low, even though the sun had risen enough to see.

"What?" I asked.

He pointed.

A footprint.

Not a boot print like the searchers around us. It was smaller, cleaner, and beside it was a faint drag mark like a bag had been pulled.

My skin prickled. "She has supplies," I whispered.

Holden nodded grimly. "And she's moving carefully."

My pendant warmed, pulsing once against my skin. Not a warning. A calling. I stiffened. Why did my mother's pendant continue to call me? I still hadn't figured out what it kept trying to tell me.

Holden noticed. "What?"

"I—" I swallowed. "I can feel something."

His gaze sharpened. "Lyra."

"It's not like Elarion," I said quickly. "It's...it's the mountain. Like it's tugging at me."

Holden's expression tightened. "Toward where?"

I hesitated, then pointed slightly off-trail, toward a narrow deer path that vanished into thicker trees. "There."

Holden stared at it. "That's not on our map."

"No," I said softly. "But Dorothy would know it."

He exhaled hard, then spoke into his radio. "Unit Two, I've got fresh tracks off the main switchback trail. Moving to investigate. Stand by." Static crackled back in confirmation. Holden met my gaze. "We go slow," he warned. "Together."

I nodded, my heart hammering. We stepped off the trail and into the trees, the fog thickening again as if the woods didn't want to let us see too far ahead.

Vex slipped between us like a shadow. *She is close*, he murmured.

Fenrin flew overhead as a hawk.

And the mountain, patient and watchful, held its breath, waiting to see whether we would learn from the past or repeat it.

The deer path narrowed until it stopped pretending to be a path at all. Branches snagged my jacket. Wet leaves sucked at my boots. The fog thickened as we moved, swallowing sound and distance so thoroughly that the world felt reduced to ten feet of gray and the steady rhythm of our breathing. Somewhere ahead, the mountain rose in layered shelves and hollows, places that didn't show up on maps because they'd never needed names.

Holden moved just ahead of me, careful and deliberate, his shoulders set like he was bracing against a tide. I followed his footsteps exactly, because it felt safer to trust the shape of him in front of me than the instincts buzzing under my skin.

Vex ran ahead, then back, then ahead again, testing the air, tasting the fog. *She is circling*, he murmured. *Not fleeing.*

Fenrin circled above.

My pulse thudded. "She wants us here."

Holden glanced back, reading my face even before I spoke again. "You're feeling something."

"Yes," I said quietly. "Not danger. Direction."

We came to a low rock shelf where the ground flattened out briefly, the earth packed hard by years of runoff.

Holden crouched and swept his light along the edge. "There," he said.

Footprints again. Cleaner than the others, careful, and not

hurried. Whoever had made them knew how to move without leaving much behind...and didn't mind leaving just enough.

"Supplies," Holden muttered, spotting the faint imprint of a strap dragged across mud. "She's not improvising."

A shape loomed through the fog ahead, vertical lines cutting a darker block against the trees. The ranger station, or what was left of it. The building sat back from the trail like it was ashamed to be noticed, its roof caved in at one corner and windows boarded or broken. Moss crawled up the walls. A hand-painted **CLOSED** sign still clung to the door, optimism peeling away with the years.

My pendant warmed against my chest, stronger now and insistent. "That's where she's going," I whispered.

Holden raised a hand, halting me. He scanned the area, then keyed his radio. "Command, we've got fresh signs near the old ranger station. Possible suspect nearby. Advancing with caution."

Static answered, followed by a clipped acknowledgment.

"Slow," he said again, meeting my eyes. "If she's inside, she's listening."

We split slightly as we approached, Holden angling left and me right, keeping the building between us. The fog pooled around the station, hugging it like a secret. I smelled damp wood and rust, and beneath it, the faint tang of lamp oil.

She's been here recently, Vex said. *The quiet remembers her.*

I eased toward a broken window and peered inside. No one was in there, so I walked through the door. The room was stripped to bones with an overturned desk, a collapsed shelf, and old maps curling on the floor. A lantern sat on the table, unlit but warm to the touch. Beside it a thermos sat half full, with a folded blanket. Careful living instead of panic.

A floorboard creaked behind me.

I spun.

Dorothy stood in the doorway, framed by fog and rot and the patience of someone who had already decided how this would go. She raised her hands slowly. "Easy," she said, her voice calm and almost kind. "I don't want to startle you, dear."

"Too late," I replied, my breathing shallow.

Holden's voice cut in from the left. "Dorothy. Step away from the door."

She glanced toward him, then back to me, her eyes softening with something like regret. "You brought him."

"I wasn't coming alone," I said.

"That's a shame," she murmured. "I hoped we might talk without uniforms."

"There's nothing left to talk about," I said.

"Oh, but there is."

Holden stepped into view, his weapon lowered but ready. "Hands where I can see them."

Dorothy obeyed, her fingers laced loosely. "I know how this looks."

"You do," Holden said flatly.

She smiled faintly. "I always did."

I took a step forward despite Holden's warning glance. "You called me last night."

"Yes," she said. "I wanted you to understand."

"Understand what?" I asked. "That you murdered Maggie and tied up her daughter to keep your story intact?"

Her expression flickered with hurt then resolve. "I didn't murder her on purpose."

My stomach dropped. "You pushed her hard enough to hit her head, and then you left her there to die alone. Why?"

"She knew too much. Saw too much. I stopped her from ruining everything," Dorothy said, firmer now. "There's a difference from cold-blooded murder."

"There isn't," Holden snapped.

"There is," she insisted. "Sometimes sacrifices need to happen when someone is about to bring down a town and doesn't realize the weight of what they're carrying."

"She realized," I said. "That's why she wrote it down."

Dorothy's gaze locked on mine. "And look where that got her." The fog shifted, revealing more of the clearing.

Holden moved another step closer, careful not to rush. "Dorothy," he said, his voice steady. "This ends now."

She tilted her head, studying him. "Does it?"

"Yes," he said.

Her eyes slid back to me. "He thinks this is a line you cross and then it's over."

"And you don't?" I asked.

"I think lines move," she said. "And someone always gets crushed under them."

Vex's fur bristled. *She is buying time.*

I felt it too, the way Dorothy's gaze kept drifting, not to Holden, but to the trees behind him. Measuring. Counting. "You're not getting away," I said.

Dorothy sighed. "I don't need to get away forever. I just need to get away *now*."

Holden tensed. "Don't."

She moved anyway, not toward us, but sideways, slipping along the wall with a speed that surprised me. She reached for something just inside the doorway—

"Holden!" I shouted, lifting my hands to summon my magic.

He lunged too late.

The sound of breaking glass exploded as Dorothy hurled the lantern through the window. It shattered against the rock outside, flame bloomed and smoke poured in. The fog swallowed the light, turning the clearing into a blur of heat and gray.

I called on Lumen Wells to pull luminous energy from underground crystals to light the way. Vex darted past me, a black streak cutting toward the trees. *She's running!* I scrambled up and burst out the back of the station into the crystal lit fog, quickly dousing the fire using Aqua Vein. Dorothy was already ten yards ahead, moving fast but controlled, her coat flaring as she cut downhill toward a narrow ravine.

Holden followed, his boots pounding and radio crackling uselessly. "Stop!" he shouted.

She didn't.

I ran after them, my lungs burning and the world reduced to breath and branches and the echo of footsteps. My pendant burned hot now, not guiding but warning.

She knows this ground, Vex sent. *She's taking the long way around.*

The ravine split into two, one path slick with wet stone, the other choked with brambles. Dorothy veered left without hesitation. Holden slowed just enough to choose...and chose wrong.

"Holden, no!" I yelled, skidding to a stop. "She went left!"

He cursed and pivoted, but the moment was gone. Dorothy vanished, the fog too thick for even my magical light. We searched for another minute or two, circling and listening. I called on my Seismic Sense but there were no vibrations coming through the earth. The fog muffled everything, turning sound into guesswork. Even Fenrin had disappeared, the fog being too much for her to fly in.

Finally, Holden stopped, his shoulders sagging. "She's gone," he said hoarsely.

I stood there, shaking and furious. "She tried to burn down the forest with me in it. She planned that."

"Yes," he said. "She plans everything."

We made our way back to the station, where smoke still drifted lazily from the broken window. Holden spoke into his radio, relaying directions, frustration clipping into every word. I leaned against the wall, trying to slow my breathing.

Vex returned, his eyes bright and tail lashing. *She wanted you to follow. She wanted you to see how easily she can vanish.*

"She thinks this proves something," I said.

"That she's smarter," Holden replied.

"That she's in control," I said.

He met my gaze. "She's wrong."

I nodded, though the certainty wavered. Dorothy had escaped...again. But she hadn't erased the truth. She hadn't buried Maggie this time, and the town wasn't asleep anymore. As we headed back toward the trail, the fog began to thin, lifting just enough to show the path behind us trampled, scarred, and undeniable.

Evidence.

She could run. She couldn't undo what she'd broken. And as the mountain exhaled, releasing us back into the morning, I knew one thing with absolute clarity: Dorothy was no longer hiding.

She was being hunted.

And the story she'd controlled for decades was finally catching up to her, step by careful step.

CHAPTER
Twenty-One

WISHVILLE DIDN'T WAKE up gently the morning after Dorothy ran.

It woke up braced.

The fog had burned off early, leaving the sky a hard, polished blue that made every sound carry farther than it should. Church bells rang on the hour because someone had decided the town needed to mark time again, and remind itself that days still moved forward even when the ground underneath them had shifted.

I arrived at the library just after eight. The *Maple Hollow Library* had always been a place of refuge for me. The promise that answers could be found if you looked long enough. Today, it felt like a witness.

People arrived, hesitating at the threshold like they weren't sure if they were allowed inside anymore. By nine, the front tables were full with coffee cups, folded coats, and newspapers with half-truth headlines and too-large photographs of yellow tape.

FOUND AFTER 40 YEARS.
TUNNELS UNDER TOWN.

FORMER VOLUNTEER SOUGHT IN DEATH OF HISTORIAN.

They said Maggie Winslow's name now with reverence instead of condemnation. Clara sat at the long table near the back, her mother's notebooks spread carefully in front of her like sacred texts. She hadn't let anyone touch them except me. Connie hovered nearby, pretending to reorganize returned books while keeping Clara in her peripheral vision at all times.

"You don't have to be here," I'd told her earlier. "You have staff who will cover for you."

Clara had met my gaze, steady and unyielding. "I need this."

So I let the library become what it was always meant to be. A place where stories were an escape.

The Wellies arrived shortly after opening, not together for once. Dot slipped in first, scanning the room like she was counting breaths. Belle followed with a thermos tucked under one arm and a stack of clean napkins under the other. Tilly came last, her scarf already halfway off as she moved with purpose toward the coffee station.

Without a word, they divided the space.

Dot intercepted a whispering pair near the newspaper table with a gentle cough and a pointed look that sent them drifting toward the windows. Belle quietly replaced a loud mug with a padded coaster and murmured something that made the owner flush and lower his voice. Tilly refilled Clara's cup without asking, set it down within reach, and squeezed Connie's shoulder once, firm and grounding, with no nonsense.

Clara didn't look up, but her fingers tightened briefly around the mug.

LuLu arrived with a tray of muffins she hadn't baked—store-bought, practical, and very much on brand for the version of her who was still running on four hours of sleep and adrenaline.

"People are lining up outside *Town Hall*," she said under her breath as she set the tray down. "Press. ATF. A guy from Montpelier who smells like ambition."

"Let him," I said. "He won't find anything new."

She glanced at Clara. "You okay?"

Clara nodded once. "I will be."

That was enough.

By midmorning, the murmurs had turned into conversations. Not the defensive ones from days earlier. Not the brittle justifications or speculative cruelty. These were slower, quieter, and more careful.

"I always wondered why she stopped coming to book club."

"She asked me about the old maps once."

"I thought she was just...persistent."

Each sentence landed like a small stone placed on a grave.

Dot drifted past me and whispered, "They're choosing their words now."

"They should have earlier," I murmured.

"Yes," Belle said softly behind us. "But this is something."

Holden stopped by briefly, his jacket and jeans doing nothing to disguise the tension in his posture. He spoke quietly with Connie, exchanging updates, and nodded to Clara with a gentleness that made my chest ache.

"She didn't get far," he murmured to me when we had a moment. "Search teams are narrowing the area she could have gone."

"Dorothy?" I asked.

"Yes," he said. "And anyone else who thought silence was enough."

I followed his gaze to the windows, where the mountain loomed, deceptively calm.

"We're holding a vigil tonight at WishFest," I said. "For Maggie."

Holden nodded. "Good."

"It won't be small," I warned.

He gave a tired smile. "She deserves that."

The door opened again, and a hush rippled through the room. Mayor Doug Delaney stepped inside, removing his hat with visible discomfort. He looked older than he had a week ago, less buffered by titles and more exposed to consequences.

"I won't stay," he said quickly, addressing the room. "I just wanted to say that we failed her."

No one argued.

"As a town. As leadership. We should have listened."

The silence held, then Clara spoke. "She didn't need everyone to listen," she said quietly. "She just needed someone to believe her."

Doug nodded, his eyes shining. "We'll do better."

"Start by making the guilty tell the truth," LuLu said mildly.

Doug flushed. "We will."

He left not long after, his presence a reminder that apologies didn't close wounds...they just acknowledged them. A short time later, Calderis appeared at the edge of the stacks, a stillness moving through the library with him. A few people glanced his way, frowned, then looked away again.

"They're saying her name," he finally said. "The mountain listens when names are spoken without fear. And the mountain will reveal the truth. It always does. It also protects what belongs to it."

I thought of Dorothy running through fog and fire, clutching control like a lifeline. "Then she'll hear Maggie's name everywhere tonight."

The bell above the door chimed again as more people entered, some with flowers, some with questions, and some with the need to be present. The Wellies shifted automatically, making room, offering cups, redirecting conversations, anchoring the space without drawing attention to themselves. The library held them all. And as I moved among the shelves, offering quiet words, warm coffee, and the permission to remember, I felt the shift settle in.

Compassion instead of accusation.

By dusk, Wishville had stopped whispering.

The change was subtle at first, voices lifting just enough that you could hear what was being said without leaning in, faces no longer turning away when Maggie's name came up. By the time the sun slid behind the mountain and the air cooled into that clean, aching kind of autumn evening, the town had made a choice.

It gathered in support of Maggie Winslow.

Lanterns lined the path from the library all the way to the well, their light soft and steady. Holding the vigil during WishFest seemed appropriate. People arrived carrying candles, flowers, and folded notes they'd written.

The Wellies arrived early.

Dot was already there, fussing with the lantern spacing, moving one an inch to the left, then back again, muttering, "Symmetry matters in grief."

Belle followed with a basket of extra candles, handing them out with brisk efficiency and murmuring encouragement like a general deploying kindness.

Tilly hovered near the edge of the path, gently redirecting late arrivals so they didn't interrupt anyone already standing in silence. "Here," she whispered to one woman, pressing a candle into her hands. "Take a breath first."

I stood at the edge of the crowd with Clara and Connie, watching the last light fade from the sky. Clara wore a dark coat that had once been her mother's, the sleeves a touch too long. Connie stood close without crowding, her hands clasped tight in front of her like she was holding herself together by force of will.

"You don't have to speak," I murmured to Clara.

Clara shook her head. "I want to." Her voice was steady, but her fingers trembled where they curled around the folded page in her hand.

Vex wove between her ankles, his black fur catching lantern light.

Holden stood near the front, his jacket zipped against the chill and radio silent at his shoulder. He caught my eye and nodded once. LuLu hovered nearby with a crate of candles, her expression uncharacteristically serious. Calderis stood a little apart, the glow of lanterns reflecting in his eyes like stars caught under ice.

I stepped forward and the murmur quieted. "We're here," I said, and my voice carried farther than I expected, "to remember Maggie Winslow. She was a historian," I continued. "A teacher. A mother. A woman who believed that truth mattered even when it made people uncomfortable."

Heads nodded. Someone sniffed back tears. Belle passed a handkerchief without looking to see who needed it.

"She asked questions. She took notes. She trusted that if she wrote something down, it couldn't be erased." My throat tightened, and I let it. This wasn't the night for polished speeches.

"For a long time, this town told itself Maggie ran away. Tonight, we're telling a different story."

A ripple moved through the crowd in recognition.

"She was silenced," I said. "And that silence cost us all." I stepped back and gestured to Clara.

For a heartbeat, she didn't move. Then she did, one step in front of the other, until she stood in the pool of lantern light at the edge of the well. The stone rim glowed softly behind her, ancient and listening.

Clara unfolded her paper. "My mother," she said, her voice quiet but clear, "didn't think she was brave. She thought she was careful. She wrote things down because she was afraid people would forget, and she was right."

The Wellies bowed their heads as one.

Clara's hands steadied as she spoke, her words finding their footing. "She loved this town. Even when it didn't love her back. She believed that knowing the truth made us better." Clara looked up then, meeting faces one by one. "I don't want her remembered as a warning. I want her remembered as a witness."

The word landed like a bell.

Connie exhaled sharply beside me, one hand lifting to cover her mouth. I felt the tremor move through her, grief and guilt braided tight. She didn't step forward. This wasn't her moment. It would come later, when she could do something with her regret. When she could set the history books straight.

Clara folded the paper and held it to her chest. "Thank you for being here," she said simply.

Silence followed, with people nodding.

LuLu moved first, stepping forward to light the candle at the base of the well. One by one, others followed, flames blooming in the dusk. The lanterns seemed to lean closer, their glow deepening like they were paying attention too.

I caught snatches of voices as people leaned in to light the wicks.

"She helped me find my grandmother's letters."

"She asked me about the old quarry road."

"I thought she was just...intense."

Each confession felt like a knot being untangled.

Holden approached me quietly. "Search teams are holding position," he murmured. "No updates yet."

I nodded. "Tonight isn't about the hunt."

He glanced toward the mountain, dark against the stars. "It will be again."

"I know."

Calderis stepped closer, his gaze fixed on the well. He looked at Clara, then at Connie. "Truth leaves echoes."

As the last candle was lit, the crowd shifted, making space. Someone began to hum—a low, wordless tune that felt older than any hymn. Others joined, hesitant at first, then steadier.

I felt something in my chest loosen, just a little. This wasn't closure. It wasn't forgiveness.

It was acknowledgment.

When the hum faded, I stepped forward again. "If you want to leave something," I said, "you're welcome to."

People did. Notes tucked into the stone crevices. Flowers laid gently at the base. One man placed a dog-eared index card with a single sentence written in careful block letters: *You were right.* As the crowd thinned, Connie moved at last. She knelt by the well and set down a small, leather-bound book.

"Larry had a journal. Mostly full of his guilt and regrets. I kept it," Connie whispered, not looking at anyone. "I told myself it was safer." She closed her eyes. "I was wrong." She stood without waiting for absolution and stepped back to Clara's side.

Clara took her hand. She hadn't forgiven her yet, but this was the first sign there was a chance she would in time.

Nearby, Tilly wiped at her eyes and sniffed. "I hate when towns learn lessons the hard way."

"Yes," Belle said softly. "But at least they're learning"

LuLu slipped an arm around my shoulders. "This is lovely."

"Yes," I agreed, remembering the girl I knew so many years ago. "And she would've loved it."

The candles burned low. The lanterns swayed. The well held the light in silence. As the last people drifted away, I stayed behind with Clara, Connie, Holden, LuLu, and Calderis. The night felt steadier now, still sharp, still full of questions, but no longer suffocating.

A text flashed briefly across the screen before Holden silenced it. He met my eyes, a shadow crossing his face. "Nothing yet," he said quietly.

"She's still out there," I replied.

"Yes."

I looked up at the mountain, its outline stark against the stars. Somewhere in its folds, Dorothy was moving. Listening, planning, and telling herself a story where she was still in control.

But the control had shifted.

I turned back to the well and rested my hand on the cool stone. "We'll find her," I whispered. The lanterns flickered in agreement. As the night deepened, I felt it settle into my bones...

The certainty that whatever came next, silence would no longer be an option.

CHAPTER
Twenty-Two

DOROTHY DIDN'T RUN.

That was the first thing I noticed when Holden and I found her.

"She's not moving," Holden said quietly. "She wants to be found."

I felt it then. Not fear or triumph...finality.

Search teams were scattered everywhere around the mountain. Holden and I decided to check a tourist spot on a whim because no one had thought to look in a public place. The old quarry overlook, where the trail thinned and the drop-off fell away into fog and pine. It was a place tourists used to visit for the view, back when Wishville still saw the mountain as decorative instead of dangerous.

Dorothy stood near the edge, a lantern set carefully at her feet, and her hands folded in front of her like she was waiting for someone to arrive. She looked...tired. Not panicked or cornered, but tired in the way people got when they've carried something heavy for too long and finally decided to set it down.

"I wondered how long it would take you to find me," she said when she saw us. Her voice carried easily in the thin air.

Holden stepped forward, his posture professional and weapon

lowered but ready. "Dorothy Hale, you're under arrest for the murder of Margaret Winslow, kidnapping, obstruction, and—"

"Yes," Dorothy interrupted. "I know." She turned slowly, the lantern light catching the lines in her face I hadn't noticed before—fine cracks etched by years of careful kindness and swallowed resentment. "I suppose you'll want a confession," she added.

I took a step closer, trying not to let anger consume me. "I want the truth."

Her mouth curved into something like a smile. "Oh, sweetheart. Those are rarely the same thing."

Holden moved beside me, the cuffs visible now. "Turn around. Hands behind your back."

Dorothy obeyed without protest. The click of metal echoed too loudly in the open air.

When she spoke again, her voice was quieter. Stripped of performance.

"I loved Maggie," she said. The words landed heavier than any accusation. "We were best friends," Dorothy continued, staring out over the trees. "We were inseparable once. We did everything together back in high school. I was the maid of honor in her wedding. I babysat Clara when she was little, back when it was a gift and not a necessity. I sat on her kitchen floor while she cried over grant rejections and torn manuscripts."

My throat tightened.

"And I watched her build a life I never got," Dorothy said.

Holden's jaw clenched, but he stayed silent.

"She had everything," Dorothy went on, the bitterness finally bleeding through. "A husband who adored her. A child who worshipped her. A purpose she threw herself into like it was oxygen." Her voice sharpened. "And she never looked back to see whom she left behind."

"That's not true," I said.

Dorothy laughed softly. "Isn't it? She was obsessed, Lyra. With her research. With being right. With the tunnels, the maps, the patterns." She shook her head. "She didn't care who waited at home. She didn't care who loved her, as long as she had her work."

"That doesn't justify what you did," I said carefully.

"I know," Dorothy replied. "But it explains it." She finally looked at me then, her eyes bright with something raw and unfiltered. "I was jealous. Of her certainty. Of how easily she took love for granted." Her breath hitched. "Of how she could walk away from everything and trust it would still be there when she returned."

My chest ached.

"I told myself I was helping," Dorothy said. "That I was protecting her. Protecting Larry. Protecting Clara." She swallowed. "But what I wanted was for her to stop. To choose something else. To choose *us*."

"And when she didn't…" I said quietly.

Dorothy's shoulders sagged. "I thought…if she were gone…I could have everything she had."

The truth sat between us, ugly and naked. "But that wasn't your life, it was hers," I said.

"You're right," she whispered. "It wasn't my life. Larry mourned her for a year until it killed him." Her voice cracked for the first time. "So, I took what was left."

Clara.

"You raised her when you didn't have a right to," I said, my anger flaring hot and sudden. "Like she was yours to claim."

Dorothy flinched. "I loved her."

"You used her," I shot back. "You erased her mother and called it protection."

Dorothy's eyes filled with tears she didn't wipe away. "I gave her a life. Stability. Safety."

"You gave her a lie," I said. "And you almost killed her to keep it."

Holden stepped closer, his voice firm. "Dorothy, you need to stop. It's over."

She nodded slowly. "I know." For a moment, the wind stirred, carrying the scent of pine and damp stone. The mountain loomed behind us, vast and unmoved by human grief. "I thought if I could stop the pain," Dorothy said softly, "no one would get hurt again."

"But Maggie did," I said. "And so did Clara."

Dorothy closed her eyes. "Yes. I really didn't mean to kill her. We were arguing about how her obsession with the tunnels was ruining her marriage. I was so angry that she was willing to risk losing everything over activities in the tunnels that had nothing to do with her. I told her how I would give anything to have her life, but she wouldn't listen. I lost control and shoved her harder than I meant to, and she hit her head."

"But then you left her to die alone," I said.

"It's not what you think," Dorothy said. "I would never—"

Holden guided her forward, turning her gently away from the edge. "We're done here."

"I don't think so," came a voice from behind us.

We turned and saw Ruth Bingham holding a gun pointed directly at us.

"It's over, Ruth," Dorothy said. "I can't do your dirty work anymore."

I blinked. Ruth Bingham was the mastermind?

"You fool," she spat, sounding much younger suddenly. "You had to go and grow a conscience. If you had stayed hidden like I told you, this would have blown over. You could have taken your cut and moved anywhere."

"I had no choice. You saw what I did and made me leave Maggie there. This is my home, and now I've lost the last piece of my heart." Dorothy sighed. "I'm tired. It's over."

"Clara was never yours, you idiot," Ruth ground out. "Nothing is over until I say it is. I have people even more powerful than me counting on these shipments. You ruined that."

"You're trafficking weapons, aren't you," Holden said, putting the pieces together. He shifted his hand slightly.

Ruth shot the ground at Holden's feet. "I wouldn't try that,

Chief. I'm an expert shot, though I wouldn't trust the arthritis in my hands these days."

"Easy now," Holden said. "I'm just trying to understand."

"Understand this," Ruth sneered, "I never should have trusted such incompetent people."

"Like Henry and Collin McAlister?" I asked.

"They're small potatoes. I have powerful relatives in Canada who run a smuggling ring. Back in the day, I was quite the outdoor girl. When I discovered the quarry entrance to a tunnel system, I knew it would be a great new addition to my family's pipeline. So, I got a job serving on the planning board and then made my move. Chief Maddox and George Fletcher were simple-minded weak men, but all about making a buck. It didn't take long to convince them to look the other way for a cut. The McAlisters simply took over that role after George ran away in fear and Maddox died of a heart attack. Like I said, weak men. Evelyn Hart was sweet on them, so she would do whatever they asked her to. As for me, I could sit back and reap the rewards as the beloved town matriarch. It was the perfect setup."

"Except, you didn't count on Maggie Winslow finding access to the tunnels during the library renovations, did you," I said.

"Maggie was resourceful, and that made her dangerous. I would have left her alone. She was quiet about the tunnels at first and even stopped Pike from continuing with the quarry expansion project for fear they would discover the tunnels, which worked in our favor. But then she ventured too far and saw things she shouldn't. That was when she spoke up. Thank the Lord no one listened."

"So, you had Dorothy kill her," Holden said.

"No, that was all Dorothy's doing out of jealousy...but I saw the whole thing." An evil grin spread across Ruth's face. "Instead of killing Dorothy myself, I blackmailed her into working for me. Being my watcher. I was getting too old to do that myself."

"And she blackmailed Howard Kline into helping her build the maintenance shed over the entrance to the tunnel, seal it off so no one would find Maggie, and watch for hikers in the woods so they wouldn't interfere with the shipments," Holden said, nodding as if everything was starting to make sense.

"But again, another Winslow disrupted your plans when Clara decided to renovate the library once more, and found Maggie's box and the tunnels beneath the library," I said.

"She ordered me to kill Connie and Clara when Connie started digging through town records, ready to give the authorities everything she found," Dorothy said. "I couldn't do it, so I brought them to the tunnels. I never would have killed them. I planned to tell them everything and help them get away."

"Like I said, you're a fool," Ruth ground out. "They would have told the authorities the moment they could." Ruth cocked her gun.

"You won't get out of the mountains alive if you kill us," Holden said.

She laughed. "You honestly think anyone will expect little ole me as being the mastermind of a large smuggling ring?"

"I honestly think there's one more thing you didn't count on," I said.

"And what's that, my dear?"

"Me," I ground out as I lifted my hands, summoning Illusory Manipulation, and changed the landscape beneath our feet.

Ruth's eyes grew wide as she stumbled, but she managed to pull the trigger and get off a shot straight at my chest.

Having anticipated her move, I used my Skycall power and shifted the winds just in time into a gust that blew the bullet off target and over the cliff. Holden surged forward and knocked the gun out of Ruth's hands, tackling her to the ground and handcuffing her.

"What are you?" she screeched in horror.

"Something else that's not in the history books," I said.

Lifting my hands once more, I restored the landscape back to its original formation as Holden read her rights and called it in.

"Now it's over, and you'll never have power over anyone

again," I said, walking over to Ruth and placing my fingertips to her temple. Amber light seeped into her skin like an infusion, creating a memory seal and erasing what she saw from her memory.

She blinked, looking at me confused as the authorities showed up. "Wait, how did I...what happened?"

"You finally got what you deserve," Dorothy said, finally looking at peace.

As they led Ruth past me, Dorothy and I were alone for a minute. I just realized she hadn't looked surprised when she saw me use my powers.

"You know, don't you?" I asked.

"I met someone once, a lot like you. She never erased me because she knew one day this moment would come, and I would send you to her. Look deeper into the tunnels and you will find what you seek, but you might not like what you see."

I was about to speak, but Holden came back with his officers and helped Dorothy to her feet. He gave me a look, and I nodded slightly. While the officers were talking on their radios for a moment, I placed my fingertips to her temple and nodded my thanks. I let the memory seal seep into her and then stepped back as the officers proceeded to take her away. Behind me, the mountain stood unchanged. Ahead of me, something far worse waited.

And my mother was still out there.

Twenty~Three

I DIDN'T TELL Holden where I was going.

Not because I didn't trust him—because I did, with a certainty that had grown roots—but because I knew he would try to stop me. He would tell me this was reckless, that it was dangerous, that we needed backup and light and radios and names written down in neat columns that could be checked and rechecked. And he would be right.

That was the problem.

The mountain wasn't calling for procedure or authority or men with guns who still believed the world could be forced into order if you pressed hard enough. It wasn't asking for permission or warrants or a carefully staged approach. It was calling for blood and truth and memory.

And those things were mine.

The pull came just after Dorothy was taken away. Not gradual or subtle. It struck like a blade drawn along my spine, sharp and unmistakable, stealing the air from my lungs. My pendant flared hot against my chest. It wasn't the warning burn I'd learned to live with or the quiet hum that meant *pay attention*. This was a command.

A summons.

It vibrated through bone and breath alike, threading itself into muscle and marrow, tugging me uphill along paths no one used anymore. Paths that didn't exist on maps. I moved without questioning it, my feet finding stone and root as if they'd memorized the way long ago.

The farther I climbed, the more the world changed.

The air thinned, not just with altitude but with age. Pine and leaf and the soft rot of forest floor that gave way to mineral cold and the clean, unforgiving scent of stone. Trees loosened their grip on the earth, their roots clawing uselessly at rock before finally giving up altogether.

Under my boots, the ground smoothed in places where no modern trail should have been. Stone worn down by centuries of passage by feet like mine that had known exactly where they were going. Symbols appeared along the rock face. Shallow and nearly erased. Spirals fractured into lines, and lines broken into hooks. Marks so old they'd almost forgotten their own meaning, worn thin by time and silence and deliberate neglect.

Almost.

My pendant burned hotter. This wasn't a place people stumbled into. It was a place they were *allowed* to enter. The entrance revealed itself slowly, like the mountain itself was considering whether I still belonged. A seam in the stone widened as I approached, rock sliding back with a low, patient groan that resonated through my ribs. Cold air breathed out, heavy with damp stone and old torch smoke, and something deeper still. Resin. Iron. Oaths sworn and never released.

I stepped inside, and the cavern swallowed me whole.

It wasn't a tunnel. It wasn't even a chamber. It was a city, hollowed into the mountain's heart. Stone terraces rose in vast arcs, layered like an amphitheater built not for performance but for judgment. Wide steps spiraled upward toward elevated platforms draped in dark banners, their fabric heavy with sigils I half-recognized and half-wished I didn't. The ceiling vanished into shadow so high it felt as though night itself had been trapped underground, mineral veins catching torchlight and breaking it into thousands of dull, star-like points.

This wasn't hiding.

This was congregation.

Torches lined the walls in perfect intervals, flames steady and controlled with no flicker or smoke, fed by magic old enough to be disciplined. Dozens—no, *hundreds*—of figures moved through the space with practiced efficiency.

Dwellers. Some armored. Some robed. Some dressed like they'd stepped straight out of Wishville and simply never gone home. A secret society. A rebellion with structure, hierarchy, and ritual. They turned as one when I entered. Steel whispered free of sheaths. Magic stirred low and dangerous, humming against my skin like a threat.

Someone grabbed my arm hard enough to bruise.

I reacted without thought.

I twisted, my elbow snapping back, magic flaring white-hot as I tore free and sent my attacker staggering. Another figure lunged, his blade flashing in torchlight. I ducked, water magic surging up my spine as the stone beneath their boots slicked and betrayed them.

"Guardian!" The word hissed through the cavern like a curse.

Hands closed in, but I fought. Not gracefully or strategically. I fought like something cornered between grief and fury, magic bursting out of me in bright, uncontrolled waves. A shock of force sent bodies crashing into stone. Someone cried out. Another hit the ground hard enough that the sound echoed too long.

A rebel with pale gold hair and glowing gold eyes hurled a blade that cut the air inches from my face.

"Stop!" The word cracked through the cavern like thunder. "Stand down, Kael."

The air bent, and the rebel named Kael bowed his head and stepped aside.

Magic collapsed inward, freezing every movement mid-breath. Blades halted. Flames stilled. Even my own pulse seemed to pause, suspended between one heartbeat and the next. She stepped forward from the highest platform.

Serena...my mother.

The world tilted on its axis. She looked exactly like my memories, and nothing like them at all. It had been one hundred years since I had last seen her, yet it still felt like yesterday. Lavender threaded her long silver hair, braided tightly back from her face. Her clothing was simple but deliberate, a warrior's clothes, woven with enchantments so subtle they pressed against my senses rather than shining. Her eyes—those familiar, unyielding pale lavendar eyes—held conviction instead of warmth.

Power rolled off her in disciplined waves.

"You will not touch her," she said calmly, leveling a hard stare at Kael and the others. "Lower your weapons."

Every single one of them obeyed.

The silence that followed was deafening.

I stared at her with a lump in my throat and tears blurring the edges of the cavern. "You're alive."

She descended the steps slowly, the crowd parting without question. "I never stopped being."

Rage detonated in my chest. "You let me believe you were dead!" I shouted. My voice shattered against the stone. "You let me guard the well in your name. You let me *mourn* you."

She stopped a few feet away. For one fragile heartbeat, her composure cracked. "I let you survive," she said quietly. "You wouldn't have, otherwise."

"You don't get to decide that!" I screamed. "You don't get to choose silence again!"

Murmurs rippled through the cavern, uneasy and questioning.

Serena lifted a hand, and they fell silent instantly.

"The Elders are corrupt," she said, turning so her voice carried to every corner of the hollow. "The treaty protects power, not balance. We're bigger than the Rebel Five. We're the Rebel Revolution. These Dwellers..." she gestured around us "...were erased.

Silenced. Buried beneath rules written by those who never bled for them. And they're not the only ones. This affects both realms."

I laughed a sharp, broken sound that scraped my throat raw. "So, you built another secret. Another lie."

"I built resistance," Serena corrected. "Truth without permission."

"You built a mirror," I shot back. "And became the thing you swore to stop."

The cavern vibrated with tension, stone humming faintly underfoot.

She faced me fully. "You don't understand what's at stake."

"I understand perfectly," I said, tears spilling freely now, hot and unstoppable. "You traded one kind of silence for another. You buried truth and called it protection."

Her jaw tightened. "You think transparency saves lives?"

"I think control destroys them."

She reached out, stopping just short of touching me. "I did this to protect both worlds. To protect you."

"I don't want your protection," I said, my voice breaking. "I want my mother back."

That did it. Her breath hitched. For one devastating moment, she looked like the woman who had braided my hair and taught me the old songs. Her eyes filled. "I am here," she whispered.

"No," I said. "You're not."

Footsteps echoed behind her. Signals passed. Torches dimmed in a practiced sequence. The rebels shifted in a ready position.

Serena straightened. "This is not the end," she said softly. "It's the beginning of the truth. Join me."

"No," I replied, my grief crystallizing into resolve.

She held my gaze with love, regret, and iron certainty warring in her eyes. "I knew you'd choose this path. You'll see the truth one day, and then you'll understand."

"I'll finish it," I promised. "You can count on that."

She stepped back into a doorway, and the cavern breathed. Stone shifted, not collapsing or violent, but opening. Passages I hadn't seen split apart like seams in cloth. Rebels melted into the shadows with disciplined precision. She pressed her palm to the wall behind her.

"Lyra," she said one last time. "When the truth finally breaks everything...remember I tried to spare you."

And then she was gone.

The cavern emptied with terrifying speed. Torches died in waves. Banners vanished into darkness. Within seconds, I was alone in the vast hollow, the echo of their retreat ringing in my ears like a verdict.

I sank to my knees.

Grief roared through me, louder than the mountain itself. She wasn't lost or dead like Maggie. *My* mother had chosen to leave me.

Vex suddenly appeared, hissing over being too late. He padded to my side, solid and warm, anchoring me to the present. *She chose control over love,* he said gently. *That is always the easier road.*

I looked up at the dark ceiling, at the place where my mother had stood and commanded an army built on silence and fury.

"I'll find her," I whispered, then vowed, "And I'll stop her. Whatever it takes."

Epilogue

MY HOUSE SMELLED like cedar and tea and the faint scorch of something LuLu had sworn was "intentional caramelization."

It was quiet like after a storm, not empty or calm, just...settled. The windows were dark, the porch light low, and the mountain a patient silhouette beyond the glass. For the first time in days, there were no radios crackling, no search grids unfolding on tables, no lanterns swaying with borrowed hope.

Just us.

Holden sat on the arm of the couch, his jacket off and sleeves rolled up, with one boot hooked under the coffee table like he needed the floor to remind him he was still here. Calderis stood near the hearth, his hands clasped behind his back and eyes tracking the slow, simulated flames with a focus that felt more contemplative than watchful. LuLu had claimed the kitchen island, surrounded by mugs, folders, and exactly one notebook she'd labeled: **Things That Refuse to Stay Buried.**

Vex lay stretched along the back of the couch, his black fur absorbing the lamplight and eyes half-lidded but alert. Fenrin, equal parts menace and elegance, occupied the rug with regal disdain, her tail wrapped neatly around her paws like she was presiding over court.

They eyed each other without hostility.

A truce, then.

"Okay," LuLu said, tapping her pen against the notebook. "Let's do a final sweep. We wrap up the loose threads, and then..." she looked at me pointedly "...we eat the not-burned part of the brownies."

Holden huffed. "You burned brownies?"

"Emotionally," LuLu said. "They were under a lot of pressure."

I sank into the couch and let myself relax over another successful WishFest. "Who would have thought Clara's wish to find her missing mother would have been the wish that was chosen. Clara made her wish in the well on opening day, and that's the day she found her mother's box. The well was guiding us the entire time through my pendant. Finding Maggie just before the end of the festival completed the wish and kept the treaty intact."

It also brought you to your mother, Vex whispered through my mind.

I nodded, thinking, *That was true, though I wasn't sure how I felt about that yet.*

"I'm happy the well chose Clara," LuLu said, pulling me from my troubled thoughts. "She deserves the peace of finally knowing."

I sighed, thinking, *So did I.*

"The smuggling ring is dismantled once and for all," Holden said, businesslike but tired. "All parties involved have been charged accordingly."

"Dorothy?" LuLu asked.

"Her sentence will be lessened somewhat for her cooperation, but she'll spend the rest of her days in prison," Holden said quietly.

I closed my eyes for a second. "Such a senseless tragedy. At least she won't control the story anymore," I said.

"No," Holden agreed. "Neither will Ruth, but they won't be the last ones who try."

Calderis lifted his gaze from the hearth. "Control seeks new vessels."

"Great," LuLu muttered. "I love a cheery ending."

Calderis's mouth curved slightly. "I thought I was your cheery ending."

LuLu's face softened. "I predict you won't be able to handle the amount of cheer I'm bringing your way." She winked.

"And my mother?" I asked softly. I had told them about her leading the revolution, but I hadn't told them the part about the Elders being corrupt and the original treaty being based on a lie. I wasn't sure how Calderis would feel, because I wasn't sure how I even felt. I needed to know the full truth and what we were dealing with first.

The room stilled.

Calderis's smile faded as he looked my way. "She chose control of a different kind."

"Rebellion," LuLu said flatly.

"Revolution," Calderis corrected. "Organized. Ideological. And no longer secret."

Holden rubbed a hand over his face. "So, what does that mean for Wishville?"

"It means," I said quietly, "that silence is no longer our default."

Vex stretched, his claws kneading the couch fabric with delicate menace. *The lie has been evicted*, he said. *It will attempt to squat elsewhere.*

Fenrin flicked her tail, then transformed into a beautiful parrot, squawking, "Not here. Definitely, not here."

LuLu grinned. "Seconded...or rather thirded."

I reached for the stack of papers on the coffee table. Connie's final turnover. Permits, notes, letters Maggie had written and never sent. Clara had gone home earlier, exhausted but steadier than she'd been all week, carrying her mother's notebook and father's journal like something sacred and newly claimed.

"She's starting the archive," I said. "For Maggie's work."

Holden smiled softly. "That feels right."

"It does," I agreed.

LuLu leaned forward, her eyes wary. "And the Elders? How do they feel about me?"

Calderis blew out a long slow breath. "Divided. Vaerion cannot erase what you have seen. He will attempt to contain it, but he will fail."

"Bold," LuLu said approvingly.

Calderis met her gaze. "You remain anchored to me."

LuLu's pen paused. "Still weird."

"Still true," he replied with confidence.

"And you still haven't told your parents I'm more than useful. I'm your girlfriend." Fenrin flew down, transforming back into her ginger cat form on the way, then landed on LuLu's lap. She reached down automatically, her fingers sinking into her fur.

"I will, I promise. I was simply trying to get your presence in Elarion accepted first before...as you say...dropping the bomb."

She grinned. "Fine, I guess. Just know you're stuck with us."

Calderis inclined his head. "I have chosen my position and am happy to be stuck."

Holden raised an eyebrow. "You realize that puts a target on your back."

Calderis's eyes glanced at Holden's and then locked onto mine. "I've had a target on my back from the day I became an enforcer and sided with a half-blood."

Before I could respond, a knock sounded at the door.

Holden tensed, then relaxed as I stood. When I opened it, a courier stood on the porch, his breath fogging his glasses and hat pulled low.

"Lyra Wells?" he asked.

"Yes."

"Package for you," he said. "No return address."

That sent a ripple through the room.

I signed, closed the door, and set the small, weathered parcel on the table. The paper was old and bound with twine knotted in a way I recognized instantly. Vex sat up as I unwound it carefully. Inside there was a thin leather folio, cracked with age, and a single folded map.

Not Maggie's hand.

My mother's.

My chest tightened as I opened the folio. The pages were filled with precise annotations—routes, symbols, notes in the margin written in my mother's familiar, unforgiving script.

The tunnels were sealed for a different reason than you think.

When you're ready, the truth will be revealed.

Look deeper.

LuLu leaned over my shoulder. "She left you homework."

Calderis went still. "She has marked an *old* boundary."

Holden frowned. "Translation?"

"Next time," Calderis said quietly, "the fight will not be contained to tunnels."

I unfolded the map. A new mark glowed faintly at the edge of the ink. A symbol I'd seen before, scratched into stone and dismissed as decorative. The same one carved into the mountain cavern. The same one Maggie had circled and underlined twice.

They think this means silence.

Maybe she hadn't been talking about the smuggling ring. Maybe Maggie had met my mother just like Dorothy had. I felt something cold and steady settle into place. "Serena wants me to follow the clues to the truth," I said.

Holden stood and took my hands, grounding and real. "Not alone."

"I know," I said, and I meant it this time.

LuLu lifted her mug. "To not doing this the quiet way ever again."

Calderis nodded. "To choosing each other over control."

Vex hopped down and curled at my feet, solid and warm. *To stories that refuse to stay buried.*

Fenrin settled beside him, their tails touching, then entwining.

I closed the folio and placed it carefully on the table.

Outside, the mountain loomed, unchanged and honest in its patience. The well was quiet. The house was warm. The people I loved were alive and choosing truth. Whatever came next—rebels, Elders, secrets older than maps—I wouldn't face it alone. I wouldn't be silent.

And I wouldn't rest until I stopped my mother at any cost.

Powers

Dweller Powers Linked to Water, Lava, and the Core

Because Dwellers live beneath the well and near the Earth's hidden layers, their powers tie into subterranean elements—water tables, magma flows, and the planet's inner energy.

Water Affinity

1. **Aquifer Calling** – ability to summon fresh water from underground springs.
2. **Mists and Veils** – conjuring fog or vapor to obscure vision.
3. **Current Shaping** – manipulating underground rivers and directing them to flood or recede.
4. **Memory Pools** – reflections in water that reveal truths, memories, or wishes.

Lava and Magma Affinity

1. **Ember Pulse** – channeling molten heat into bursts of energy or fiery weaponry.

2. **Obsidian Crafting** – forming weapons, keys, or charms instantly from cooled lava.
3. **Seismic Heat** – creating pockets of intense heat to deter intruders or destroy evidence.
4. **Infernal Glow** – eyes or markings flare with inner magma-light when power is used.

Core/Earth Affinity

1. **Seismic Whisper** – sensing tremors or distant footsteps through the ground.
2. **Stone Weaving** – reshaping rock, tunnels, or caverns for defense or concealment.
3. **Core Binding** – drawing strength from geothermal energy, boosting speed or stamina.
4. **Gravity Veil** – slightly altering pull of gravity around them (leaping, pulling objects down).

Hybrid Powers (Water + Fire/Core)

1. **Steam Veil** – merging water and magma to create blinding, scalding mist.
2. **Healing Springs** – heated water with mineral-rich, magical properties for mending wounds.
3. **Crystalline Growth** – forming luminous crystal clusters where water meets lava under pressure.
4. **Pressure Command** – controlling deep-earth pressure, causing geysers or controlled quakes.

Lyra's Hybrid Powers

As the only half-human, half-Dweller, Lyra bridges above-ground elements (air, light, celestial forces) with subterranean ones (water, magma, core). Her uniqueness gives her some Dweller powers and other ones that no full Dweller can access.

Celestial Affinity

1. **Sunfire Touch** – channeling warmth and light to heal or inspire courage.
2. **Moonveil** – manipulating moonlight for illusions, cloaking, or calming emotions.
3. **Star Echo** – heightened intuition or visions tied to constellations and night sky patterns.
4. **Skycall** – Influence over breezes, gusts, or even guiding birds.

Core Affinity

1. **Seismic Sense** – feeling vibrations through earth, sensing danger or hidden chambers.
2. **Lumen Wells** – pulling luminous energy from underground crystals.
3. **Magma Ward** – summoning protective heat barriers or obsidian shards.
4. **Aqua Vein** – drawing water from beneath the ground in times of need.

Hybrid/Balance Powers

1. **Eclipse State** – when sun and moon energies align, she can blend surface light with core fire for immense bursts of power.
2. **Breath of Worlds** – exhaling mist that merges steam, air, and memory-infused water.
3. **Harmony Pulse** – ability to temporarily stabilize cracks between worlds.
4. **Dual Sight** – seeing both surface illusions and subterranean truths simultaneously.
5. **Illusory Manipulation** – The ability to shift their surroundings, making structures disappear or entire

landscapes transform.

Vex (half-cat, half-Whispen)

Whisper Magic
Abilities:

1. **Shadow Phase** – slip between shadows in both realms.
2. **Mist Purr** – calming veil of vapor.
3. **Mind Whisper** – can communicate with others through their mind.

Fenrin (Full Whispen)

Abilities:

4. **Shapeshifter** – take on the form of other animals.

Books By Kari Lee Townsend

A WISHVILLE MYSTERY

The Well-Kept Secret

The Well-Laid Trap

The Well-Hidden Clue

The Well-Placed Lie

KALLI BALLAS MYSTERY

Mind Over Murder

Two Cents of Doom

A Touch of Malice

An Inkling of Evil

Mayhem on the Mind

Trouble for Your Thoughts

CECE MONROE MYSTERY

Harmful Habits

SUNNY MEADOWS MYSTERY

Tempest in the Tea Leaves

Corpse in the Crystal Ball

Trouble in the Tarot

Shenanigans in the Shadows

Perish in the Palm

Hazard in the Horoscope

Chaos and Cold Feet

Murder in the Meditation

<u>SUNNY MEADOWS & KALLI BALLAS CROSSOVER</u>

Cruising into Danger

Road Trip to Ruin

Bachelors, Badeges & Bad Luck

My Big Fat Fatal Wedding

<u>DIGITAL DIVA</u>

Talk to the Hand

Rise of the Phenoteens

Books By Kari Lee Harmon

COLDWATER COVE

Dark Seas

Frozen Waters

Dangerous Thaw

Deadly Frost

STANDALONE NOVELS

Valley of Secrets

Until Tomorrow

Project Produce

Love Lessons

LAKEHOUSE TREASURES NOVELLAS

James

Amber

Meghan

Brook

MERRY SCROOG-MAS NOVELLAS

Naughty or Nice

Sleigh Bells Ring

Jingle all the Way

TRIPLE R RANCH

Destiny Wears Spurs

Spurred by Fate

PORTRAIT OF A WOMAN

Resilient

Resourceful

Rebellious

Reclusive

National Bestselling Author, Agatha, RT Reviewer's Choice & Golden Duck Award Nominee. Kari lives in Central New York with her husband & Samoyeds. She's a lover of wine & travel (especially cruising), obsessed with reality TV, and loves a good book with at least some mystery, romance & humor. She writes cozy mysteries & upper middle grade as Kari Lee Townsend, as well as suspense, romance, romantic comedy & women's fiction as Kari Lee Harmon. To keep up with all of Kari Lee's books, check out her website, join her newsletter, and follow her on Amazon, Goodreads, and Bookbub! All links are on her website.

https://www.karileetownsend.com

OLIVERHEBERBOOKS

A small press bound by the belief that every voice matters.

Sign up for our newsletter to learn about new releases and more.
https://oliver-heberbooks.com/subscribe/

Follow us on social media:

facebook.com/oliverheberbooks
instagram.com/oliverheberbooks
amazon.com/oliverheberbooks
youtube.com/@OliverHeberBooksPublisher